Before
She
WAKES

BOOKS BY ED JAMES

ED JAMES

Before She WAKES

Bookouture

Published by Bookouture in 2021

An imprint of Storyfire Ltd.
Carmelite House
50 Victoria Embankment
London EC4Y 0DZ

www.bookouture.com

ISBN: 978-1-83888-120-7
eBook ISBN: 978-1-83888-119-1

*To Paddy, thanks for keeping me as sane as the
Onion Man will let me be.*

PROLOGUE

Marissa

When Marissa woke up, it felt like her head had been turned inside out.

The vein in her temple was thudding like a disco tune, a constant drumbeat. She could barely open her eyes, the thick crystals surrounding her lids were breakfast cereal left in the bottom of the bowl.

It was still dark, and the house was silent.

She reached over to her nightstand—to where she thought it was, at least—and flicked the switch. The light was way too bright.

She rubbed the sleep away from her eyes and tried to sit up, pushing herself up. It really shouldn't be this hard.

Her cellphone sat on the charger. No missed calls or texts, just the time. Six thirty.

Way too early.

The digits seemed to swim in the air. How much had she drunk last night? Barely a glass. Well, that was all she could recall, but she couldn't remember anything more than the first disappointing mouthful. All day, she'd been looking forward to her treat, that half hour with something nice, something that gave her that warm, fuzzy feeling.

And she couldn't remember much of it.

Okay.

She needed to start the day.

An extra-hard session on the bike, then a hot shower, then breakfast, then she had to drive Liv to school. Breaking it down like that made it seem achievable, but right now, Marissa didn't feel like she could even put either foot down on the floorboards.

But she had to at least try.

There. Ice-cold against the sole, sending a tingle up her leg. And the other.

Done.

She winched herself up to standing and just about toppled over, but used a hand to brace herself against the wall.

All Marissa could do was stand there, breathing hard and slow. She was thirty-eight, could do two spin classes back-to-back, and then a whole day of teaching.

So why did she feel like she was eighty years old?

And not a healthy eighty either.

She caught a glimpse of herself in the full-length mirror. Gray shorts and pajama top. Blinking eyes set in puffed-up bags. Her hair flattened against the side of her head, the rest of it spiraling out to catch its natural curls.

With a deep breath, Marissa grabbed her robe from the door back and wrapped it around her shoulders. She was shivering, goosebumps puckering both arms, rising in waves.

What was wrong with her?

She had no idea, but the fear gnawed at her. If someone had done something to her, had they gotten to Liv?

A spike of something—adrenaline, fear, whatever—pushed her off and she was on autopilot, opening the bedroom door and padding through the hallway, out to the staircase.

Her room was down at street level and the front door was shut and locked, the alarm primed and blinking. At least it wasn't a home invasion.

Well, didn't seem to be one.

She set off up the stairs to the living area, the wood creaking under her feet.

The kitchen was empty, just the faint humming of the fridge. As much as she needed a glass of water, she didn't stop for one, instead charging on up to Liv's floor. She knocked on the door and waited. "Hey, you up?" Her voice sounded a hundred miles away.

She could barely focus on the sign stuck to the door:

LIV'S ROOM

PRIVATE

KEEP OUT

Seemed cute when they put it up last year, but now… Now, it felt different. Like a threat.

And it was silent in there.

Another knock. "Liv, it's Mom. You okay, honey?"

Still silent.

They had a rule—two knocks and it was okay to come in, so Marissa gave her the required second knock. "Liv, I'm coming in, okay?"

She gave it that little pause, waiting for a refusal from her daughter, but nothing came. The fridge downstairs did its little shiver thing, a beep followed by a wash of something. Otherwise, the only sound was Marissa's heavy breath.

"Honey, are you okay?" She grabbed the door handle and twisted it. "Liv?" Her voice sounded even more shaky, but it was louder now.

No response, so she opened the door. "Liv?"

Cold morning light spilled through the open curtains, and the room was sheer mayhem. Bedclothes strewn across the floor. The closet doors hung off their hinges, the contents spilled across the boards.

Marissa rushed in, but didn't know what the hell to do, where the hell to look, what the hell to think or feel, other than terrified.

Liv was gone. Her laptop sat sleeping on the desk next to her cellphone, her ever-present companion. But there was no sign of her.

Marissa turned around, ready to rush down to her room to grab her own cellphone. But she stopped dead.

Olivia's wall mirror was cracked, like someone had punched it, but only before they'd written a message in red Sharpie:

NEVER FORGET

CHAPTER ONE

Carter

FBI Special Agent Max Carter tied the poop scoop bag with a flourish. "Thank you for this gift." He set off again at a furious pace, pulling the leash behind him, his breath misting the air. The damp Seattle air, thick, just not rain. Not yet. The forecast was always for rain, but it hadn't arrived yet. He wasn't alone in the baseball diamond overlooked by houses on all sides, but he doubted many of the other dads out walking family dogs lived in those homes. Little League only needed one set of bleachers, and a woman sat up at the top talking on her cellphone.

Why he had let his daughter Kirsty call her dog Doggy was still a mystery to him. Carter called her Deogie though. D-O-G. He shouldn't have let her get the dog in the first place. How had she successfully worn down Carter and his wife Emma's continual refusals?

That he was the one who landed the morning walk while his father slept like a baby, despite promises that he would look after Deogie, well. That was something he should've seen coming a mile off.

Not that he *hated* his morning hikes with the strange hybrid of greyhound and… something else. Whatever it was, it still looked like a greyhound, just one with long fuzzy fur. And such soulful eyes.

No, he actually *liked* it. Getting up before six to do an hour of exercise with the dog, listening to podcasts and audiobooks while the rest of the world snoozed. And whatever the weather too. He had to *do* it. Time was, he would have gone into the field office and torn through some paperwork, but these days… Well, he definitely felt a lot calmer in his own head.

Carter led Deogie over to home base and, despite his age, he still did the same celebration he had as a kid, arms wide, like he was back in the early nineties competing in the Washington state championships, heading toward the minor leagues at least.

Kid had to dream, right?

Carter opened the gate and led Deogie through just as his cellphone blasted out through his earbuds, cutting off the podcast covering California's prison system.

This early in the day it could only mean one thing. Another parent waking up to find a missing kid or two, maybe three. Another call out, another case.

Carter quickened his pace as he headed home and answered it. "Carter."

"Max, it's Lori." Lori Alves, the duty agent on the roster for that night. She paused long enough for him to hear her breath through his earbuds, coming in short bursts in stereo.

"What's up? Another case?"

"Not that I know of." And there it was again, that pause. "Max, it's about your father."

Carter slowed his pace and swore he got a thank-you nod from Deogie. He didn't need to be reminded. It was a constant thorn in his side. There when he went to bed, still rattling around when he got up from a terrible sleep. A recurring thread all day. Yeah, all the endorphins he got from walking Deogie maybe didn't tell the full story.

Chewing himself up over whether he had made the right decision.

First, that London cop deciding not to prosecute his lousy father for his part in his mother's death, many years ago. Bill had protested to Carter that he had nothing to do with it, and Carter believed him.

Then, deciding to try to forgive his father for abducting him as a small child, for hauling him across the Atlantic and the States from London to Seattle, to a new life shut off from his old one, and from his mother.

Finally, the lost hours spent mulling over her death. A death that maybe, just maybe, wasn't an accident. Who was Carter kidding? His mother's accidental death was a direct result of Bill Carter trying to send her a message to let her son go.

Yeah, that was going to keep anyone up at night.

And he had asked them not to prosecute. Even Bill Carter didn't deserve a trial back in London. Or was it because Bill was dying? The Grim Reaper would catch him soon enough.

But maybe he really deserved it, and Carter had chosen to put his own daughter's short-term needs ahead of any justice?

Not that Carter had that much of a say in it, just a chance to sway a pending decision. He gripped Deogie's leash tight as he hauled her across the street, like the evil Superman in that movie where he turned a lump of coal into a diamond. "What about it, Lori?"

The Seattle rain started up, thick drops like baseballs falling to the ground.

"That London detective, Chris King, he's coming here, Max."

"To investigate?"

"I think so. He's landing at SeaTac at lunchtime."

Carter's turn to pause now. He hadn't heard from King in a while. Thousands of miles away, over the Atlantic Ocean, over most of England, DI Chris King had been investigating Bill—and a few others too. A real nest of vipers. "You've spoken to him?"

"A few times, Max. Look, I've thought long and hard about whether to discuss this with you. I decided not to, but it felt wrong, so here we go. Karen's ordered me to work with him."

"Why you? The FBI has a ton of agents."

"Apparently, he asked for me personally. That London cop I worked with in Miami? He's King's boss now."

Carter had to stop at the red man, waiting for the nonexistent traffic to flow past. "I thought King wasn't investigating Bill?"

"He tried to stop it, Max, but there are between five and twenty cases all linked together. All linked to your abduction as a child. King has no choice but to investigate Bill."

"Okay, well, thanks for letting me know."

"Max, don't be like that."

"Like what?"

"You know. You're going all cold again."

Carter tried to smile, tried to inject some humor or levity into his voice. "Lori, thanks for doing this. It's tough to hear, so I'm sorry I sound cold. But you do what you got to do, okay? Bill deserves what's coming to him."

"I know it's the right thing to happen for Bill, but I worry about you and about Kirsty."

"I can handle myself, Lori. And I'll look after her."

"Have you been doing that therapy?"

Carter nodded, even though she couldn't see it. Part of him was angry at the intrusion into his life, into his mental state, but a lot of him was relieved that someone took that level of interest in his mental wellbeing. So easy for an FBI agent to succumb to numbness. "I have been to a few sessions, Lori. I can sort of remember what happened. Fragments of memories. An airport, being on a plane, landing."

"Sounds promising, Max."

"It's been helpful, so thanks for the recommendation. Look, I better go. Thanks." Carter ended the call and stood there in the rain, feeling like he had been punched in the gut. He hit pause, because listening to a deep exploration of the California penal system felt a bit too close to home.

An investigation into Bill. It was serious.

This was the last thing Carter needed right now. Everything in his life felt so strained, like pizza dough stretching in a restaurant kitchen, but then snapping into a million pieces.

He didn't need anyone prosecuting his father.

And Kirsty sure as hell didn't. They'd grown so close; it'd be a wrench to her.

But there was nothing Carter could do about it.

He looked down at Deogie, shivering in the rain. He needed to get her home, dry her off, then get on with his day.

Should he speak to Bill about it? He hadn't so far, but maybe it was time. At least he could prepare something, prepare Bill for what was coming his way.

And maybe, just maybe, Bill would suffer that little bit more for what he had done to Carter's mother.

Carter powered down the lane toward their home. He could see their house, his SUV at the front, with Emma's plug-in charging under the carport. No lights on, so Bill was still asleep, still dreaming his sweet dreams without any regret or remorse for what he had done.

Carter's cell blasted out again. The rain was heavy now, so he answered it without checking the display. "Carter."

"Max, it's Karen." Special Agent in Charge Karen Nguyen. His boss. Her icy voice made his spine straighten.

"What's up?"

"Max, I just received a call in from Seattle PD. They've attended a suspicious child disappearance in Capitol Hill. Looks like an abduction."

CHAPTER TWO

Carter

In truth, the address was slightly too far south to be Capitol Hill.

Carter pulled off Madison, past the Trader Joe's entrance, then trundled along Fifteenth East, a tree-lined residential avenue, and counted the numbers down toward his target. Hard to see through the rain, but the joy of being an FBI agent was you never had to search for *the* house, just look for the one with a ton of police cruisers out front.

His and Emma's first apartment together was nearby, few blocks east, and even more north. Close to the heart of the action. Capitol Hill was hardly uptown living, but it had a charm and vibrancy that was hard to get elsewhere in the city. And boy had it changed over the years. Gentrification was creeping in, turning the old dive bars into craft beer breweries, pushing out the subcultures to other areas.

The number of police cruisers and FBI SUVs meant he was getting closer. And there it was, a row of apartment houses on the left. Some entrepreneur had wedged six thin slivers of apartments into a lot that would normally only allow three at most. Smart way of doubling your money.

Carter pulled up and got out into the rain, though his FBI windbreaker took the brunt of the downpour as he strode across the road. Up here, they needed *rain*breakers.

The small block was guarded by two SPD beat cops at the fifth door along, their navy jackets pulled up high. The older of the two took a look at Carter's shield. "You with the FBI, huh?"

Not the usual SPD displeasure at having their role usurped by federal law enforcement. "Max Carter. I head up the Child Abduction Rapid Deployment Unit." He put his shield away and gave them both a broad smile, the kind he knew earned trust. "Obviously not as quick off the mark as you guys, but here I am."

"Upstairs. Second floor." The cops separated and Carter got between them.

The door was held open, a trail of rain on the carpet inside. A high-end security system was beeping, but disarmed. At least it worked.

And the home was exactly as he expected. Three floors, with a staircase between them. Bedroom down here on the first, probably the master, and a living space up on second, then another bedroom or office on the third. Should be a roof garden up top too, with views to the downtown towers.

Two doors down on this floor though. One led to a master bath, with some cops working away, cataloguing, and inspecting. He got a nod from them as he passed. Definitely a master bedroom, for Mom and—

Carter didn't know if there was a Pop. Didn't know much, to be honest. Either way, it was a king bed, the covers splayed only on one side.

Curtained-off French doors that probably looked out onto a shared green space. One of those fancy sports bikes sat there in the window, the kind that cost a bomb to buy and you still had to pay a monthly subscription, all so you could do spin classes at home, broadcast over the internet. Probably meant just as many folks not exercising as if it was a gym, but still paying for the privilege. A super-expensive way to hang clean laundry.

Carter headed upstairs. No handrail, which always made him feel a little bit queasy.

Another SPD cop blocked the staircase up to the third floor, guarding it with a clipboard and a stack of Tyvek crime-scene suits.

Carter stopped and gave him a nod while he checked out the area.

A nice kitchen. Modern stainless-steel fridge, dark units and countertop. Through back was a spectacular view over rooftops to downtown, to the spreading skyscrapers. Couldn't even see the Space Needle these days.

The living area had an L-shaped couch looking at a wall-mounted flat-screen hanging over a small white soundbar. Some modern artwork hung on the walls, all greens and reds, but the place was ultra-minimal. Hardly homey.

A dark-haired woman sat at the glass dining table. Marissa Davis, presumably. She had a severe look. Her hair was pulled back in a tight ponytail, but a few curly spirals escaped. Glasses with designer frames but thick lenses. Fizzing with nervous energy, like she needed to *do* something right there and then, but all she could do was shake her head and stare into space.

The agent next to her caught Carter's gaze and returned it with a tight shake of the head, one that read "She's nowhere near able to talk."

One Carter had seen many, many times, and one he had a ton of strategies to counter.

And no matter how many times he saw it, it still cut him to his core. Seeing the mother or the father locked into a cycle of grief and panic. A missing child, every parent's worst nightmare, and they were living it. The physical sensations were almost overpowering—the colony of ants climbing his back, the acid burn in his gut, the thickness in his throat. Deep memories of his own past, his own abduction, mixed with the colossal fear of his own future, of losing Kirsty to similar circumstances.

Yeah, this is what drove him. Over and above it being his job, Max Carter was both a parent and a child. He knew what everyone was going through, and he needed to put it all right.

But to do that, he needed to get the lay of the land first, find out all the questions he needed to ask before he started, so he grabbed a crime-scene suit from the stack and tugged it on, lost to his winding thoughts. Before he knew it, he was dressed in puffy white. He pulled up the hood and snapped on the mask, then started climbing the steps, his mask puffing with each breath. When he'd started, he thought he would never get used to wearing one, and yet here he was, a total pro with them. He stepped out into the hallway, swarming with CSIs. Now the FBI were in, they were all his guys and gals.

He passed through carefully, taking stock of everything. Just a hallway, as far as he could tell, some arty black-and-white photos of eighties and nineties rock bands, but Carter could only name one of the seven and, even then, he was not sure if it was Sonic Youth or the Pixies.

Another bathroom at the end, with two CSIs working away inside.

The bedroom was another story.

The walls were a lot like so many others Carter had seen, all belonging to teenage girls, sadly all abducted. Over the years, the faces on the posters changed, but they were always the pop stars of the day. And today, K-pop was big to Olivia Davis.

But it wasn't just pop. She had women's soccer team photos. Carter recognized Megan Rapinoe, the purple-haired captain of the US women's soccer team.

Maybe some things did change, after all.

Through the throng of CSIs, the room was a mess. Splayed bedding on the floor. Tasteful, from a high-end store, not standard-issue teenager stuff. It was like they were living in a hotel or an Airbnb. The closet was chaos—clothes pulled out and dumped, the doors hauled off the hinges.

The wide window was being dusted for prints. As well as being thirty feet up in the air, it didn't look like it opened wide enough to get even a small child through. And certainly not a fifteen-year-old against her will. Meaning whoever had taken the girl, assuming she had been taken, had gone out the front door.

Past the alarm system. So they had the code to get in, and to get out. Or it had never been set. All the security in the world is perfect until somebody forgets to prime it.

A desk sat opposite the bed, with stacks of textbooks on either side of a sleeping laptop. Olivia was either academically minded, or at least pressured to be that way. Whoever had taken her was after *her* and not the laptop. Looked expensive too, though hard to tell if it was the latest model. It seemed Olivia's mom had invested in her education.

And the reason the Seattle Police Department had called in the FBI was obvious: the message on the cracked mirror. Red ink, probably from a Sharpie.

NEVER FORGET

Carter's cracked reflection appeared behind the writing, his face all twisted and distorted. He couldn't take his eyes off the message. It felt like it meant something to someone, some clear motive, but did it mean anything to Marissa or Olivia? That was the million-dollar question.

Someone was sending a message, but to who?

And why write on a mirror? A broken one, at that.

One of the suited figures looked over at Carter and made eye contact with him. A strand of blonde hair and manga-sized green eyes visible through the mask that wouldn't sit right on her ski-jump nose. Special Agent Lori Alves. "Hope you don't think I'm stepping on your toes, Max. Karen said you were taking this; just need to get people doing stuff."

"Lori, don't sweat it." Carter wanted to thank her for her earlier phone call, but it was neither the time nor the place. "Thanks for doing this. Where are we?"

"Not very far, I'm afraid." Lori's sigh puffed out her mask. "Mom isn't in a good place, so haven't spoken to her yet. And this…"

"Anything missing?"

"Not that we're aware of, yet. No clothes missing, according to the mom. Meaning that Olivia was taken in her pajamas."

Hard to disagree with that, though Carter wished there was more to go on. "Obvious signs of a struggle too."

Lori looked at the mirror. "Why leave that though?"

"That's what I hope we'll find out." Carter spotted a cellphone by the laptop, plugged in and charging. "Can you get Tyler Peterson to—"

"On it, sir." Another suited figure stepped between them, at least a foot taller than Lori. His dark eyes almost seared the mask's plastic. "Once they've finished cataloguing and photographing, sir, I'll run the laptop and the cellphone through our battery of tests. I should warn you now that we might run into some technical roadblocks getting in."

Carter fixed him with a hard stare. "Use any ways and means, Peterson. Do what you can to get into them."

"Sir." Tyler nodded. "I've requested the call records from the network. They're being hella slow with it."

"Good, but she probably doesn't call anyone. The missing girl is fifteen, right?"

Tyler looked at Lori. "We, uh, haven't spoken to—"

"She's fifteen, Tyler." Carter walked over to the cellphone. "Kids that age live their lives on their cellphones. And they are all about messaging. Text, voice, video calls, all will be done over the internet, not through the cellphone network. In fact, I'd be surprised if anyone under twenty-five actually *called* someone. Call records could be a good avenue to investigate, sure, but I don't have much hope for it giving us a result. And most cases like this, we never recover the cellphones. Could be anything on this, so please get in there."

Tyler swallowed. "Sir."

"But get hold of the mother's records in case she speaks to people the old-fashioned way."

"Sir."

"And look into her social media accounts."

"On it." Tyler charged off out of the room.

"Max…" Lori shook her head at Carter. "You shouldn't be so hard on him."

"What, because he's just a kid?"

Lori leaned in close to him. "No, just don't be a dick."

She was lucky she was a peer rather than a subordinate.

"Come on, he needs direction and leadership."

Lori rolled her eyes.

"That's all I'm giving him." Carter walked back over to the door. "Let's speak to the mom, shall we?"

It felt good to get the mask off and breathe in. Not fresh air, but the scent of the home. Baked vanilla cheesecake, probably from the candles sitting under the window. Carter had not spotted them earlier.

He wondered what else he hadn't spotted.

Marissa was still sitting there, but she seemed a bit brighter, a bit less frantic. Maybe they would be able to lure her out of the home. Her presence was ruining a lot of the forensic search, but Carter knew how strong the urge to stay behind was.

Agent Elisha Thompson looked over at Carter. A frown crossed her dark-brown eyes, then a smile of recognition spread to her sharp cheekbones. Black suit, lime blouse, flat heels. She got up with a quiet word, then came over to Carter. "Max. Hey."

"How's she been?"

Elisha wouldn't look Carter in the eye. "If you want to know if she's ready to answer questions from you, then I don't know. She's seriously not in a good way."

"She say much so far?"

"Afraid not."

"Okay, so abduction, suicide, runaway, fantasy, human trafficking, or parental interference?"

"Everything points to abduction, Max. Marissa was out of it from about ten until this morning, and the security system was primed."

"What about suicide?"

"I'm not sure. There's a psychologist she's been seeing, going through trauma from her parents' divorce. Marissa's signed a release. I've got an appointment; hopefully she can help build a profile or construct the victimology."

"Good work. What about that message in the mirror?"

"Never forget? She wouldn't look at me when I asked."

"Okay, thanks." Carter raised an eyebrow, showing he meant business. "You can take a break. Know how tough this kind of thing can be."

"Appreciate it." And with that, Elisha walked over to the stairs, then her heels clicked down to street level.

All the while, Carter focused on Marissa, trying to get a read on her. He would peg her for thirty-seven, give or take a couple of years. Staring into space, clutching a Kleenex. She looked right at him through glasses with a strong prescription. Nearsighted too, her red eyes swollen with tears.

Hard to tell if they were crocodile tears or not. The number of times Carter had seen it… No, he needed to get her story straight from her, no obfuscation or confusion, just the facts. What she thinks happened, what she knows, who she thinks might be behind it. Nothing more, nothing less.

"Let's do this. I'll see you in the Mobile Command Center."

CHAPTER THREE

Marissa

Marissa shivered in the morning rain. A massive truck had pulled up outside her home, like three Winnebagos end-to-end. Navy blue, with just the FBI eagle shield giving any indication as to what was inside.

This big guy stepped into Marissa's eye line. "Ms. Davis?" Tall, broad, like a movie star. "I'm Max Carter, Ms. Davis. I'm a special agent in the FBI, and I head up the Seattle Field Office's Child Abduction Rapid Deployment Unit. I will be leading the search for Olivia."

She looked up at him, blinking through her tears. "You've found nothing?"

"Ma'am, we need to do this inside."

"There we go, ma'am." Lori held the door. "On the right."

Marissa stepped into the room. It was like a police precinct on wheels. A bunch of agents sat around staring into laptops like that would find Liv.

No, she needed to think more positively. They were doing their job now.

"In here." Carter opened a door to a room with an L-shaped sofa and some armchairs. Very strange. Like being in IKEA, not an FBI office.

She sat on the couch and stared up at Lori. "Are you going to stop hiding things from me now?"

"We're not hiding anything, Marissa." Lori gave her a pinched sympathy smile. Marissa knew the exact type, gave it at every parents' evening when kids were doing badly. "We've been going door-to-door, and nobody's seen anything around the time Olivia went missing."

"Are you saying I'm *lying*?"

"No, Marissa, we're not. I need to ask you a few questions." Carter took the seat next to her. She had to crane her neck around to look at him. "You mind if I call you Marissa?"

"That's fine." But Marissa couldn't look at him. A thousand-yard stare over to the blank TV screen.

As much as she wanted to help these cops, these feds, she just felt so helpless, so trapped. Someone had taken her baby. And she had failed her. This all felt so pointless.

She should be out there, searching for Liv. But... Where the hell was her girl? Where to even start?

"Marissa, I need you to take us through what happened. Last night, then today when you found that your daughter was missing."

She took a deep breath, then let it out slowly, but it came out with the rattle of a train going over tracks. Unsteady. "Okay, so last night, my boyfriend, Gregg, was here for dinner." She paused, gnawing at her lips. "I haven't spoken to him today. I've called and left voicemails. I've sent texts, left messages with the front desk, but I haven't spoken to him yet."

Carter leaned forward, hands clasped together. "When was he last with you?"

"Um, last night, he was here from about four till about eight?"

"He doesn't live here?"

"No, he's got an apartment a few blocks away."

"So, he was just heading home for the night?"

"No, he had to go to work." This wasn't going to be easy. Every single item of her private life was going to be torn apart, scrutinized, analyzed, until there was nothing left uncovered. "He took a call about a break-in at school. Gregg's the sports coach at the neighborhood high school." She looked down at her fingers clutching a damp Kleenex. "He texted me to say he would be there until late. He must've headed back to his place."

"Are break-ins common?"

"Have been recently."

"Okay, Marissa. So when Gregg left, was Olivia still here?"

"Liv was in her room. I checked in on her just after he left. I spoke to her and…" Just thinking about it made her want to cry. "She seemed okay. Doing some homework. I came back down here and had a glass of wine." Marissa raised a finger. Whatever else Carter was going to unearth about her, she didn't want to get tarred as being a lush. "A small glass."

"Red or white?"

"Merlot. So, a red." Marissa swallowed hard. "But that's the last thing I remember."

"You had one glass, then you don't remember anything?"

"I woke up this morning with a thumping head, and Olivia was missing." Something hit her then, right in the pit of her stomach. Felt like grief, but it was different from the loss of her parents' deaths.

No, it was tangled with hope.

The hope that she or these cops would recover her daughter, but tinged again with the fear of what could happen to Liv.

And the constant drip, drip, drip of wanting to do something about it, *needing* to.

Carter got up and walked over to the door. A CSI handed him something in an evidence bag. Carter walked back over to her, holding a framed family photo. "Is this Olivia?"

Marissa stood with Liv, who looked very much like a smaller version of her. The same long dark curly hair as her mother, but let out to play. And no father in the picture.

Marissa remembered where it had been taken like it was yesterday. Remembered the man who took it, a happy old guy, eager to help out. She stared at it for a few seconds. "That's my baby."

"Olivia's fifteen years old, right?"

"Just turned."

"Any boys on the scene?"

Marissa shook her head. "No, Olivia's very academically minded."

"She get that from you, Marissa?"

"Both of us." Marissa ran a hand down her face. "I'm a single mom, okay?"

"Is there anything wrong with being a single mom?"

"I could give you a list a mile long." Marissa was still shaking her head. Acting like a crazy. Probably making Carter want to dig deeper into her life than he needed to. She popped the frame open and pulled out the photo. It had been folded back, and she showed it to Carter. "This is her father. My ex-husband, Deacon. Deacon Hill."

Deacon had been cut out of their lives. And Marissa herself had done that airbrushing, that photoshopping. In the photo, Deacon looked athletic, but maybe on the gaunt side, like he pushed himself to do one too many marathons.

"You still in touch with him?"

"Liv's father, he…" She was still shaking her head, but she didn't have anything else to say about Deacon Hill.

Carter nodded. "When was—?"

Marissa put the photo back. "Deacon is dead."

Carter stared hard at her, some calculation going on behind his eyes. "I'm sorry for your loss, Marissa."

"Don't be. He was an asshole." Marissa slumped in her chair. "We're not *sure* sure that he is dead."

"What do you mean by that?"

"We haven't heard from him in a long time. Almost two years. Our divorce was messy. Deacon would send me a check every month to cover his alimony and child support. Then, about a year ago, he stopped paying. Just dropped off the radar. Anyway, I had a cell number for him, but it wasn't like he stopped answering my calls, they just didn't get through. My lawyers couldn't track him down."

"He was sending checks?"

"He didn't try setting up a direct deposit. Not how he liked to roll. Didn't trust 'the man,' that kind of deal. It's a long way short of the seven years we need to legally assume he's dead, but I can't see him being alive, you know. Deacon bottomed out. Lived a reckless life, did some dumb things."

"Thinking he's dead seems like a bit of a stretch."

"There was a murder case. Seattle PD." Marissa tugged at her hair, hard enough to jerk a clump out. "Look, I think you're wasting your time. Our divorce settlement, as much as I didn't want it to, gave him access to Liv. If Deacon was still alive, he would have gotten in touch with me and arranged an afternoon with her, then driven to Canada or somewhere. And why take her at night?"

"I get all that." Carter smiled, briefly, then was back to his aggressive stare. "But I need to know if whoever has taken Olivia is connected to Deacon in some way."

"Right!" Marissa huffed out a deep sigh. "I can barely *think* about him, let alone talk about him."

"How was his relationship with Olivia?"

"Well." A thorn in Marissa's side that she could not easily remove. "Liv idolized him, which was the whole problem. Deacon just wasn't a good person. I trusted him and he let me down. Big time. Let us both down."

"You still in touch with his family?"

"His mom died when he was young. His dad's still around. Ray. Ray Hill. Lives down on Lake Washington."

"You still speak to Ray?"

"Not for a while, no."

She reached over for her cellphone and started searching through the contacts list. "There." She showed the page to Carter. "I don't know if that's his current number."

"Thanks." Carter got out his notebook and wrote it down. "These the last numbers you have for Deacon?"

"That's right."

Looked like Carter was following her logic, saw the sense in her words. Deacon was not the first man to just disappear rather than pay his dues. "These checks Deacon sent, did they have a return address?"

"Our old home." Marissa handed Carter another folder, marked with ASSHOLE in giant red letters. "I knew you'd ask about him." Nothing much they could do with them.

"Okay, Marissa, what about on your side of the family?"

"My parents are both… gone. Like Liv, I'm an only child."

"Liv. That's what you call her?"

"Short for Olivia, which seems too formal. Liv… Or Livvie sometimes, if I'm feeling affectionate, or when she was younger and tolerated it." Marissa ran a hand through her hair, spilling the curls everywhere. Carter deserved the truth here. "And the main reason was that her father called her Olivia. I decided to use the diminutive form after our divorce."

"How did she take to that?"

"Hard to say." Marissa shrugged. "Are you going to find her?"

"I hope to. What do you do for a living, Marissa?"

"I'm a teacher."

"Like Gregg, your boyfriend?"

"Right." For once, Marissa didn't feel herself flinch at the word "boyfriend." Maybe their relationship wasn't *that* serious after all. Strange how things tumbled out in adversity. She looked through the window. She knew the school wasn't in that direction, but still. "I teach math at Jimmy Carter High School. I met Gregg through work."

"Does your daughter attend there?"

"That's correct." Marissa locked her gaze on to him. "A lot of kids find it hard if their parents are teachers, but I'm not aware of Liv having any issues."

Carter sat back and looked at the FBI agent who'd turned up first. She seemed to want to ask some questions of her own, so Carter gave her the nod. "Go on, Lori."

Lori was sitting opposite Marissa. She leaned forward and splayed her hands on the table. "You have a nice place, Marissa."

"Thanks."

"Hard to imagine a schoolteacher being able to afford it."

Marissa sat back and folded her arms. "That's because I can't. This is a girlfriend's place. She's working in Europe for a few years, at least five. Might be seven. I'm basically paying her mortgage, no more, no less. Seattle's getting more and more expensive, so there's no way we can afford to live here long-term. By the time Kim's back, hopefully Olivia will be at college and…" She trailed off, her eyes moistening. "I'll find some sort of solution."

"And this Kim, can we speak to her?"

"Sure. But you don't… You don't think she could've taken Liv, do you?"

"Marissa, we need to explore all possibilities here. Okay?"

"Look, I changed the locks last November. Kim doesn't even have a key."

"What about the security system downstairs?"

"I installed it myself after our divorce. Only Liv and I know the code."

Carter leaned forward. "Gregg doesn't?'

"Okay, us and Gregg."

"You mind giving me his contact info?"

"Sure." Marissa was back to her phone. "Here."

Carter noted it down. "The message on the mirror in your daughter's room. Never forget. Did that mean anything to you?"

It was something Marissa had played through her mind since first thing that morning.

Never forget.

What was she supposed to remember? She knew it was aimed at her, but she had no clue what it meant. And who meant it?

"It means absolutely nothing to me. Sorry."

"Sure about that?"

"Look, I'm not hiding anything from you here. I have absolutely no idea who's taken Liv. Just promise me you'll find her."

Carter was standing again. "I promise we'll do our best, Marissa. We've got over a hundred cops and FBI agents out searching for her."

"And you still can't promise me?"

"I don't promise. It's policy. Company and personal. But I will promise to do my best to find your daughter."

"Okay." Marissa sat there, staring into her phone. All those names and numbers she had collected over the years. Whoever had taken Liv could be in there. And they might not be. She looked up at Carter and nodded. "I hear you."

Carter nodded back. "Marissa, one of us will be in touch at regular intervals and whenever we get a new breakthrough in the case. Now, I need to go."

"Okay." Marissa stared right through him. "And thank you."

"You're welcome, ma'am."

CHAPTER FOUR

Lori

Lori had to check the address Marissa gave was right. Sure enough, it matched the scribbled note.

Nice street, nice neighborhood, nicer house.

Two floors, big front yard, and not overlooked on any side. The hill leading back to Madison was lined with similar homes too, all with slight variations and personalizations added over the years.

This was where Olivia Davis had spent the first thirteen years of her life before her parents' divorce. Listening to Marissa talking earlier, it sounded like it had been a tough one.

Visiting the old family home was an outside bet, Lori knew that, but sometimes it paid off. And they would be able to gain some precious insight into the family life. As much as Marissa seemed to want to help, as much as she seemed to be telling the truth, sometimes a mother's personal truth didn't stack up against the reality.

Boy, did Lori know that.

"Well, ain't this fancy?" Agent Dane Rodgers joined her on the curb, a hulking brute of a man. Used to be a marine, and still wasn't anywhere near tired of telling everyone about it. Still had the attitude and the anger issues that lost him his posting, but the physique had softened from chiseled muscle to fat. And those mirrored aviators... Asshole. "Has to be worth, ooh, a million bucks?"

Lori had to agree with him. "Even in today's market."

Dane whistled. "Happy for me to lead here, boss?"

"Be my guest."

Dane opened the gate and powered up the path through the yard like a puppy chasing a ball. He might be a ball of anger, but he sure was capable of moments of childlike grace. With a series of loud thumps on the door, he shouted "FBI!"

Lori took her time approaching. The place seemed lived-in, but it was homey in that good old American way—some southern flourishes, maybe, or just Washington state's logging history still clinging on in the face of Seattle's hard modernity. Either way, it was hard to imagine Marissa Davis living here. She seemed more of an apartment kind of woman, whereas this was more a tech exec's home, somebody senior in Microsoft or Amazon or any of the countless other tech companies. Seattle's housing market was robust and pricey as hell now. Hard to live in the city or the 'burbs on anything below two hundred grand a year.

The door opened just as she caught up with Dane. A woman in her early forties peered out at them, her apron covered in flour, her wrists sticky with bread dough. "Can I help you?"

"FBI, ma'am." Dane held out his badge for her inspection.

But the woman just stood there. "I know you're FBI from the way you hammered on my door and shouted those three letters." A thin smile crossed her lips. "What's the matter?"

"Looking to speak to a Deacon Hill."

"Well, he's not here." Looked like she was going to shut the door in their faces.

"But he does live here?"

"No, sir. And I told the debt collectors that I never met the guy. You know it's impossible proving a negative, right? Debt collectors don't seem to think so. How the hell can I prove I never met the guy?"

"Debt collectors?"

"From the hospital. Unpaid hospital bills."

"You know what they related to?"

"No, and I didn't ask.

"Huh." Rodgers looked over at Lori, frowning, then back at the homeowner. "So you bought this place from him?"

"No, sir. The house was foreclosed, so we got a good deal with his lender."

"When was this?"

She exhaled slowly. "My wife and I have been here over a year."

And the modernity of Seattle butted against the old-time decor.

Dane wouldn't be knocked off his stride though. "You get a forwarding address?"

"Nope." The homeowner shook her head. "But we do still get a ton of his mail."

CHAPTER FIVE

Carter

Jimmy Carter High School wasn't too far from the house, just four blocks back and two over. Up here on Capitol Hill though, these blocks were long and leafy.

Despite the name, it looked like it was built during the George W. Bush presidency, in that wave of big expansion for the city. Schools built then took on new shapes and forms, all angled roofs and walls of glass instead of brick, a million miles away from the older designs—replicas of East Coast schools meant to look like old England's fancy universities, or at least the Ivy League colleges they aspired to send students to.

Carter splashed through the heavy rain up to the front door. He was hit by a wall of heat that the humming AC was struggling to fight. Problem with a building with that much glass was the interior was either boiling or freezing. There never seemed to be a sweet spot.

The reception office was out in the open, like they were selling tickets to a museum. A man and a woman either side of a path over to the main doors, both dressed in matching business suits and looking like they needed to get on with some pressing admin instead of dealing with Agent Elisha Thompson.

She stood at the desk on the left, drumming her pink fingernails off the wood.

The male receptionist was fussing over a paper file. Carter couldn't tell what they were trying to achieve. He focused on Elisha. "You getting anything?"

"That number for Ray Hill doesn't work. Ran it and it's out of service."

"Figures."

"Ma'am?" The first receptionist tilted her head to Elisha. "We've tracked him down. Coach Ingram is out on the sports field."

Gregg Ingram was sitting high up on the bleachers at the school baseball diamond as his students played out a lazy game. At least the rain had stopped, but puddles dotted the artificial turf.

Gregg was nothing like what Carter expected. Most high school sports coaches he had met, either as a student or in his professional life, had been big dudes. And big football dudes at that, built more like home appliances than people. Farm boys. But Gregg had a runner's frame, his toned arms poking out of a branded polo. His thick glasses made him look less at home with a whistle near a soaked end zone, and more at home in front of a laptop, crunching numbers. And his wiry red hair was a blaze that could be seen for miles.

Carter stood in front of him, trying to block his view, while Elisha stayed in the aisle. "I came here to see my daughter play once."

Gregg kept his focus on the game. "She a student here?"

"No, she's at Adams."

"Ballard, right?"

"You know your suburbs."

That got a coy grin from Gregg. And eye contact. "Did they beat us?"

"Don't recall. Kirsty scored at least one run, so she was pleased as punch." Carter wiped the rain from the seat next to him, then sat down. "Weirdest afternoon though. Three hours I was here, trying to follow the game, but all the time I was getting text updates from an ongoing case I didn't have primacy on, but which I might soon get hold of."

"Primacy?"

"Mr. Ingram, Agent Thompson and I are FBI agents, specializing in the recovery of victims of child abductions. Primacy is a big thing. See, if a parent finds their kid missing, that's a police matter. As soon as the cops establish that they have actually been abducted, then it's over to us." Carter sat next to Gregg just as the pitcher fired a howitzer at the batter. Another strike. The kid had promise; she would go far. "Strange as it sounds, I can remember cases I didn't even take up, but I can't remember scores at my daughter's baseball games."

"Doesn't sound strange to me." Gregg wasn't looking at him, instead keeping his focus on the ball game below. Another strike, but one to go. "I remember my kids, not the positions we finish in at the end of the school year."

"Anyway, that case… Seattle PD were running it. A fifteen-year-old girl had run away from home. They recovered her at King Street Station trying to catch a train to Portland."

"Huh." The way Gregg was focusing on the game, it was clear to Carter that nobody had told him Olivia was missing.

Which matched Marissa's story.

Carter leaned forward. "The reason we're here is because of a case we do have primacy on. Seattle PD called us in first thing this morning." He swept a hand across the baseball diamond sprawling in front of them just as the batter slugged the ball high over third base. So much for a strike. "I was walking my dog somewhere just like this when I got the call."

"Huh." Gregg was rocking forward in his seat, though Carter couldn't figure out if he was rooting for the batter hurtling around the diamond or the fielders hauling ass across to home plate. "Who's the kid?"

"Marissa's daughter."

Gregg shot around to look right at Carter. His green eyes were blown up by the glass lenses. His brow pulled in tight. "Liv?"

Using her familiar name. Interesting.

"I'm afraid so, sir." Carter held out a hand to stop Gregg charging off. "We need to ask you a few questions first."

"Why didn't she call me?"

"She's tried, sir. In situations like this, the parents rarely have any control. Marissa was smart though, did the right thing and called 9-1-1. She was lucky too, there happened to be a police cruiser parked on Madison, two cops getting coffee from that fancy new Starbucks. Their Monday-morning treat to themselves."

"How can I help?"

"When did you last see Olivia, Gregg?"

"Last night. I was at Marissa's for dinner."

"You're romantically involved?"

"Sure. We got together not long after her divorce. Me and Marissa had to arrange the school timetable. Everyone takes a turn. It's tough—you've got to arrange everything according to where kids are going to move to and from. Across all the grades. Marissa's brain was much more suited to it, but I saw it as a puzzle like a soccer team. How to negotiate space. And while we were doing this, things happened between us." He shrugged. "That's kind of it."

"Did Olivia eat supper with you last night?"

"She'd already eaten."

Carter held out his cellphone, showing the photo of the message on the mirror. "This mean anything to you?"

"Never forget?" Gregg screwed up his face. "No, sorry."

"Sure about that?"

"I mean, never forget what?"

"Which is what I'm asking you."

"Look, whatever. It's not something Liv ever mentioned to me. I'm not hiding anything from you."

Yeah, and people who said that never were.

Carter put the phone away. "There any hostility between you? Or maybe between mother and daughter?"

Gregg's leg was dancing, the nervous energy bursting out of him. The kind of guy who looked like he needed to be doing something at all times, to be focusing on something in the present. He stood, cupped his hands around his mouth, and shouted, "MOVE IN!" then collapsed back onto the bench. Took a few seconds for the leg to start sawing away again. "There is always some drama with Liv and Marissa."

"Anything I should be looking into?"

A curt shake of the head. "Nothing major. Typical stuff." He sat back and folded his arms across his chest. "Listen, it's not been easy for me. I'm not trying to replace the girl's father, but I just want to be there for her."

"You know her father?"

"Nope."

"What's that supposed to mean?"

"It means no. I don't know him."

"How was your relationship with Olivia?"

"Normal. Try to respect her need for distance."

"You know anything about her disappearance?"

That got a look, and not a nice one. "Are you saying I've taken her?"

"I'm not saying anything." Carter glanced over at Elisha, giving her that flash of eyebrow that teed her up as "good cop." More like FBI agent. Carter stared hard at Gregg. "But the very fact that you're denying the merest suggestion, rather than doing your damnedest to find her. Well, I find that interesting."

Gregg looked at him. "You honestly think I've got something to do with this?"

Carter held his gaze, just like he had done a hundred times before with a hundred suspects. Because that's what Gregg Ingram was becoming. A suspect. "I've worked a ton of these cases, sir. The most common reason is a separated parent taking the law into their own hands. But I've seen enough instances of single men in their forties moving in on divorcees so they can groom their teenage daughters."

Gregg laughed. "Fuck you!"

"You're still not denying it."

Gregg got up and rested his hands against the damp guardrail to look out across the wet baseball field.

Another strike, but the bases were loaded. Whatever was going to happen, it all came down to the next ball.

Elisha took Carter's old seat. "Sir, if we're going to stand any chance of finding Olivia, we need to build up a picture of her movements last night. You said she'd already eaten."

"That's right."

"Did you see her at all?"

"Very briefly when I got there. She was just finishing her food. Marissa was cooking. I brought a bottle of merlot to have with dinner."

Carter felt that sting of intrigue, but kept his attention on the next batter swinging and missing.

Someone shouted, "Strike two!"

That bottle of wine, the small glass Marissa had drunk on her own... if Gregg had brought it, then that looked good for his emerging theory. Drug the mom, take the girl.

Only problem was, why be so careless about it? Surely he would take the bottle and lose the evidence trail.

And it certainly didn't answer why he would take her.

"We never got a chance to drink the wine. I had to come here." Carter caught Gregg thumbing behind him. "Bunch of hoodlums broke into the football store again. Happening a lot recently."

"They take much?"

"Not that I could find. Place was a mess though. Took me hours to fix it back up."

"So they were just there for fun?"

"I don't know what they were doing in there. Jerking about with the gear. Helmets and pads everywhere."

"Anyone who can back this up?"

Gregg looked over at Carter, shaking his head. "You guys really don't believe me, do you?"

"Sir, it's not a matter of believing you." Elisha gave him a smile. "Put it this way, if this was someone else, would you want us to just take their word for it?"

Gregg's lips twisted up. "Guess not. Can I go help Marissa?"

"First, you need to help us. Right now, you're slap dab in the middle of this, and if you want to change that, you need to find someone who can back up your visit here last night."

CHAPTER SIX

Lori

Dane pulled down those aviators of his to get another look, then frowned. "Sure this is the place?"

"Sure I'm sure." Lori had a stack of mail in her lap, and this was the surest bet. A mailed-out check for labor from MoveU2New.

When she found it back at Deacon Hill's old home, she had no idea what it meant. Now that they were here, it didn't make much more sense.

The office was a low-slung brick building, one of the few that had not been bought up by hipsters and turned into a craft brewery and tap room. The place was tired, but not as tired as the woman leaning against the wall out front, sucking on a smoke—and a real cigarette too, not the latest vape stick the kids were huffing. Deep bags under her eyes and a fierce look that would stop bullets.

"Let's do this." Lori tossed the envelopes onto the back seat and got out into the Seattle rain. Soft and gentle now, more a mist than a drizzle. She walked over to the building, holding out her badge. "FBI, ma'am. You work here?"

"I'm the receptionist." Real southern twang to her voice too, but without the bright politeness you'd usually get.

Maybe those three initials upset her. Maybe she was like this with everyone.

Lori put her badge away. "We're looking for a Deacon Hill."

"That name don't ring a bell." The woman took a fresh drag and held it in.

"He worked here, I think." Lori handed over the envelope.

The receptionist inspected it. "Oh, Deac? Right, sure. Yeah, he worked here."

"Worked, past tense?"

"Hasn't been here for over a year."

"You fire him, or did he quit?"

"Hard to say." She exhaled a wall of smoke toward them. "Didn't get fired, just stopped showing up."

"You got an address on file?"

The receptionist tapped the check. "This one not good enough or something?"

"It's not current. Foreclosed a year back."

"In that case, ya'll should come inside." The receptionist stubbed out her smoke and walked into the building. "Let's just see here." She sat behind her desk, tapping and clicking at her computer. The machine looked as old as the building, that green-gray flavor of beige that died out at the turn of the millennium.

Lori looked around the place. "What is it you do here?"

"Moving company, ma'am." Now that she was behind the desk, she had recovered some of her native southern charm. Not that she looked over. Each press of her keyboard seemed to take a long time. "We rent out vans, like a U-Haul, but also do the moving for people."

"What did Mr. Hill do here?"

"The moving part. Carried stuff from the house to the van, loaded it up, then from the van to the new house. We've got storage units, so he took stuff to that too."

"Casual work?"

"To start with." She held up the envelope. "Came on the payroll after a few months. One of my many jobs around here was all that hassle."

"Was Deacon a hassle?"

"No. That ain't what I meant." She frowned at the keys, and Lori could see why any amount of typing might be a hassle to her. "But Deacon, that dude was *dark*."

"Dark how?"

"His sense of humor, to start with. Right? When he started. Good for a joke. Never anything R-rated. Not racist or sexist or homophobic, nothing like that. He was sharp, had a wit about him. And then…" She exhaled and gave them a taste of smoker's breath. "It just stopped. He'd just nod when he showed up, which was always late. And he'd disappear before shift end. No words."

"He stopped speaking to you?"

"Just like that."

"What about anyone else?"

"Same. Deac was a motormouth. Then, all of a sudden, he wasn't. He was a ghost at his job. Turned up, did the work, then went home."

"You any idea what happened?"

"Wish I did, but like I say, he stopped talking."

"When he was here, he ever mention his kid?"

She frowned at Lori. "His *kid*?"

"That's why we're here, ma'am. His daughter, Olivia, has been abducted."

She blew air up her face. "Man alive."

"He talk about his divorce?"

"Nope. He didn't wear a ring." There was a fragment of hope in there, like she had hoped to move in on Deacon, a single man. And the regret of not doing so. "Damn." She squinted at the screen, then at the payslip. "Well, this is the address we've got on file for Deac. Sorry."

So, a dead end.

"You ever get any debt collectors here?"

"Oh, yeah." She sucked in a deep breath. "I mean, what could we do? Some hospital clerk lets him out of the ER without paying? That's not our concern."

"You know why he was in there?"

"I got an idea." A dark look passed over her face. "We found him sprawled over the bathroom floor."

"What happened?"

"Turns out he was a junkie. Smack, heroin, whatever you want to call it. He'd overdosed. A real Kurt Cobain shot, the EMT said. Like he was trying to kill himself."

CHAPTER SEVEN

Carter

"Just a second." Iona Harrison didn't look up from her computer. Her fingers danced across the keyboard with the grace of a concert pianist, not the dull plod of Carter hammering out yet another report. Her office was filled with flashes of color, but she just wore gray, including her hair, streaks of white and black in among the tight curls.

"No problem." Carter waited for Elisha to sit, then took the chair in front of the desk.

Iona locked her computer then devoted her attention to them, her intense gaze sweeping them up and down. Probably seen more lies in her time as school principal than Carter had in his career, hell, probably more than the whole FBI had. "This is about Olivia Davis, right?"

"That's correct, ma'am."

"Please, call me Iona."

"Okay. I understand Olivia's a student here?"

"Not easy for her, with her mom being one of my teachers."

"Math, right?"

"Marissa's one of the best. Been here five years. Before that, our math grades were ten points below average. Now, they're fifteen points above."

"And that's all because of one teacher?"

"She's a passionate woman. Gets involved in many of our community engagement programs here. She came in with fresh ideas. Not many people can implement them, but she's got the chops. And let me tell you, it helps me out a lot having someone like that I can trust."

"So you're close?"

"Not particularly. I mean, I know what she's been through. And it's a lot."

"What do you mean by that?"

Iona's cool exterior slipped for a brief moment, the debonair grace of school principal revealing a flash of unbridled anger. "That jackass husband of hers. How could anyone put a woman and their own kid through that? A horrible divorce, and I mean *toxic*. Marissa lost her home, had to take some sick leave because of the sheer stress. It was *brutal*."

"Anything we should know about?"

"Psychological torture, Mr. Carter. I've been through a divorce like that myself. Some people sail through them, just two people agreeing to go their separate ways. But some men want to stick the knife in and twist it. A few women too. I hear her husband died, and I can't say I feel bad about it." And just like that, Iona's calm resolve reappeared. "I gather you were here to speak to Gregg Ingram?"

"We understand that he's romantically involved with Ms. Davis."

"As much as I hate it when that happens between my staff, there's precious little I can do to stop it. But other than the usual, I had no specific concerns."

"Was it serious?"

"You should be taking this up with Mr. Ingram and Ms. Davis."

"I'm asking what you know."

Iona sighed. "It seemed fairly serious, but if you're asking me what I know, I think Marissa's divorce scarred her, so she was taking it slow. Keeping a distance."

Which made sense to Carter. And seemed to be exactly what Marissa was doing.

"We're trying to build a picture here of what happened last night. It seems like Mr. Ingram was over for dinner, then had to come in here."

"Right." Another flash of anger twisted Iona's lips into a snarl. "Kids keep breaking in here. They never take anything, and it just seems to be some kids fooling around, but it's a pain in the ass."

"And it's happened a few times?"

"Sure did. Last month, they broke into the pool and goofed around in there. We got video of that, but haven't managed to identify anyone. Last night it was the sports store they were messing up."

"You got the police report numbers?"

She bit her lip. "I'd have to check."

"You know if a report was filed?"

"That is up to Mr. Ingram. His portfolio as head of department extends to all matters of safety and security in that part of the school. My name's on the dotted line, sure, but it's all formally delegated to him."

Carter took out his cellphone and held out the photo of the cracked mirror. "Does that mean anything to you?"

"Never forget?" Iona frowned. "No… I mean, my students go through some freaky fads and memes spread like wildfire here. If it's not on Instagram or TikTok, they don't care. But that…? Nope. Never heard of it. Never heard anything vaguely like it."

"Okay. You know anyone here who Olivia was close to?"

"Olivia was a good student, one of the best in her year. But she wasn't a sociable kid—like her mom. As far as I'm aware, she didn't have many close friends." Iona frowned, brief but deep. "But that whole thing with her parents' divorce, I know she spoke to my guidance counselor a lot about it."

Carter knocked on the school counselor's office door, labeled DEANNA QUIMPER, and waited. It sounded like Deanna Quimper was on the phone with someone, and judging by the volume and tone, it wasn't someone she particularly liked.

For a brief moment, Carter felt like that troubled child again, back at school and dealing with all the noise in his head. Struggling. Failing. But he remembered his own guidance counselor, the kindly woman who had helped him through it, helped him process the grief at losing his mother, the day-to-day absence of his busy father and, worse, the presence of his father, whenever it suited him.

He didn't know where he would be now if it hadn't been for Mrs. Ferguson's timely intervention.

The phone slammed down and an almighty sigh erupted. "Come in!"

Carter opened the door and tried to walk in like an FBI agent, not a lost boy. "Ms. Quimper?"

"Mrs." She gave him a kind smile, puffing up her cheeks. Her dark hair was gathered up on top of her head and looked like it weighed as much as she did. Which wasn't much. "Please, have a seat."

Carter sat down and felt just like that small child years ago. Alone. He struggled to clear his throat. "Okay, Mrs. Quimper. I take it you've heard about Olivia Davis?"

"The most *awful* business." She shook her head and it looked like she was going to dislodge the bird's nest of hair. "Will you find her?"

"We hope to. It'd help if we could build a picture of her life here. I gather from your principal that you spent a lot of time with her recently?"

"Sure have. Olivia's grade ten. Good kid, very academic, but had issues. A lot of the kids I speak to struggle with that middle school to high school transition, among other things. School becomes very difficult at that point for a lot of students. The pressure to get a good-enough GPA for college."

"And what did Olivia talk about?"

"I mean, normally I'd be refusing to even see you. These are supposed to be confidential sessions. But given she's missing... Aside from the usual issues, Olivia was struggling with her parents' divorce."

"Struggling how?"

"Well, I gather it was fairly hostile. Her father was a central part of her life, then all of a sudden he wasn't."

"Did she blame her mother?"

Deanna looked at the window, then dipped her head. "Marissa's a colleague. I shouldn't discuss it."

"Do you want me to stress the pressures I'm under here? I need to find Olivia. If her father has—"

"But Deacon's dead."

"Presumed dead."

Quimper huffed out a sigh. "I don't think he's alive. And I don't think he could take her."

"I'd still like to understand."

"Listen, I've been through what Olivia's going through. My folks split when I was younger than her. I hated my dad. Worshipped my mom. It's how I coped. Then, as an adult, I reconnected with him and I understood that it wasn't so black and white. Everything is shades of gray. In time, I've seen flaws in my mom's behavior, and seen the good in my father's. Raising a kid in a toxic environment isn't good for anyone."

And boy did Carter know.

"Do you know any close friends?"

"Olivia didn't have many."

"But there were some?"

Shania Anderson had a constant pout, her lips like that Instagram duck pout even though she was barely fifteen. Natural blonde hair and she was skin and bone, the living embodiment of all that was wrong with kids living on social media 24/7. She sat cross-legged on the desk, perfect poise and balance, but didn't want to even look at Carter.

Quimper stood next to her. "Shania, Mr. Carter is an FBI agent. He's looking to find Olivia."

Shania shrugged, and it seemed like her duck lips puckered that little bit more.

Carter crouched next to her. "Shania, we think she was abducted from her home."

Her eyes widened. It looked like she had eyelash extensions. "Gawd." Hard to tell if it was genuine or sarcastic.

"We're looking for any clues as to her whereabouts."

"Well, don't look at me."

Mrs. Quimper smiled at her. "You're her friend, right?"

"Hardly. I mean, she sits next to me in Spanish and math, but Olivia… She's, like, nobody's friend?"

Carter had seen it so often. The lonely kid at a high school, the one who didn't play the game like Shania here did, who marched to her own beat, but who suffered for it. "So you never spoke to Olivia at all?"

"Dude, she wasn't a cheerleader, wasn't on the soccer team, so why would I?"

"She liked soccer, right?"

"But she was no good at it."

"Shania, are you telling me that all those times in Spanish class and math class, that Olivia just sat there? She never mentioned anything? Never spoke to you?"

"No. I mean, of course she did, but it was all work, work, work with her. One time, she tried to get me to meet up and go to the library."

"And did you?"

"*No.*" Shania seemed the type to not want to even be seen dead with someone like Olivia.

And Carter had a dead end here.

Well, it closed off some possible leads. While her school life yielded no further clues, it didn't open up a whole avenue he would need to wade down.

Olivia Davis was a loner. Definitely struggling with her parents' divorce, her changing body, and the pressures of high school. Probably bullied, possibly even by Shania here.

But none of that would likely lead to an abduction.

Quimper patted her arm. "Okay, Shania, thanks for your time."

"Just one last thing." Carter reached into his pocket for his cellphone. "Does this mean anything to you?" He held out the mirror message to Shania.

She took one look at it and the pout slipped away, replaced by open-mouthed shock. And not the practiced kind. Genuine.

"Shania, you recognize this, don't you?"

"Not really."

"So why the surprise then?"

"No reason."

"Sure? 'Never forget' doesn't mean anything to you?"

"Wait, there was… Wait a sec." She frowned. "Here's the thing. Olivia used to doodle on her schoolbooks, and it was mostly just stuff for her. But I started looking at it, seeing what she was doing. And it was 'Never Forget.' In all kinds of different letters, like graffiti or like a billboard or like in a book. I mean, she had talent."

"Any idea what it meant to her?"

"Could be lots of things."

"You asked her?"

"Yeah, sure. Most times she wouldn't answer my questions, thought I was bullying her. But she said some boy had told her it. Told her to never forget how good she was. It's the best motivation, keep the anger fresh."

"What anger?"

"Didn't say."

Carter could picture it. A slip of the tongue, letting someone like Shania know something personal and private, and she would be abused about it for months. Back in the day, it would be bullying, but now it was memes and so on. The anger could be about school, her ordeal every day, or it could be about her parents' divorce. Maybe she knew something about her father's death, something she hadn't shared with her mother or Deanna Quimper. "Did she say who this boy was?"

"Josh."

"Definitely?"

"Definitely. I mean, she wrote *his* name too. She seemed to be in love with him."

CHAPTER EIGHT

Carter

No sign of news crews yet, but it was only a matter of time.

Carter looked up at Marissa's tall, thin townhouse. Still caught flashes of light from CSI cameras, but really, what use were they? They needed boots on the ground and people who told the truth, the whole truth, and nothing but the truth, not people who kept things back. Who were looking out for themselves first and foremost.

Problem was, in a world of sharing more with strangers online than in homelife, when privacy has become a rare commodity, people still felt reluctant to share the truth face-to-face.

Maybe Marissa or Olivia were like that; maybe the people in the orbit of their lives were. Maybe. But maybe not.

Carter entered the mobile command center. The family room seemed to drown Marissa. A big space, enough for a family to sit in while their home was searched. She shot to her feet. "You've found her?"

"No. Sorry."

Marissa collapsed onto the couch, elbows digging into her thighs, the heels of her hands attacking her eye sockets. At least she still had hope, even if Carter had just crushed some of it. He could leave her with that lingering worry, or he could distract her, get her to assist the case. The active use of energy helped some parents.

"I do need to ask you a few questions." Carter took the free armchair and sat down. "Marissa, I've just been to Olivia's school. Does the name Josh mean anything to you?"

Marissa frowned like it did, then shook her head. "Should it?"

"It appears Olivia had a boyfriend."

Marissa sat back, shaking her head. "No. No way."

"We're trying to back this up from other classmates at school, but—"

"No!" Marissa jumped up to standing, towering over Carter. "She would've told me!"

Carter had to join her standing. He locked eyes with her and saw confusion in her eyes, mixed with the bitter taste of anger. Most of the time, secrets were normal. Natural. Coping mechanisms, especially for adolescents. But Olivia's were unexploded ordnance. "Marissa, Olivia wouldn't be the first teenager to hide anything from her parents."

"But we were so close…"

"Look, it's possible that Josh could be involved here. That message on the mirror—"

"I don't know anything about him." And she didn't. Her quivering mouth, her pulsing cheeks betrayed the emotions Carter had seen a thousand times before. The emerging fear at the secrets hidden from a parent. The realization that those secrets could be the reason why their child is missing. She collapsed back on the couch, arms wrapped around her torso. "I don't know anything about him."

And Carter knew another thing about Marissa. That level of shock was going to keep her quiet and block any further answers. "Marissa, we'll give you some space, okay? But I'll be back."

Carter found Lori in the mobile command center's other room, checking her watch. "You okay?"

"I need to dash, Max." Lori did not have to say where she was going, or why.

Carter knew. To investigate his own lousy father. On today of all days. It never rained but it poured in Seattle. "Let me guess, your search for Deacon Hill has proved fruitless?"

"So far." Lori shook her head. "Can't find the ex. I've been to his workplace, and he just cut and run. But it was a year ago, Max."

Carter sensed something else though. "What is it?"

"Well, it's something nagging at me. All we've got on the divorce is from Marissa. I hate it when we've only got one side of the story. Could be that he really was the problem, and that's the end of it. Marissa shut him out of their life. But what if it was Marissa's fault and she's blaming him?"

"Get her to sign a release and talk with her divorce lawyer. Come on, this is basic stuff."

"Sure."

"We know any buddies of his?"

"Not that I know of. He seemed to be a ghost at his job. Turned up, did the work, then went home. Nobody went for a beer with him; he never joined in."

"You visited the old home, right?"

"Sure, but no neighbors were home."

"Might be worth heading back there and asking around."

Lori patted Carter on the arm. "Max, I've got to go, but it's possible he took his own life."

"Why do you think that?"

"A history of overdoses."

"Overdoses?"

"Heroin. Hospitalizations. Checked it out on the way back here. Three separate hospitals."

And that unexploded bomb blew up in Carter's face, giving him a lot more sympathy for Marissa's plight. An AWOL father, addicted to opiates, probably dead. And it gave him more insight into the trauma Olivia was living through. He pinched his nose. "Okay, can you get Dane to hand over to Elisha. If you can find her."

"Will do."

Footsteps clattered from the street. Carter had to step aside to let a male agent into the mobile command center. "Thanks, Lori."

Elisha was sitting behind a laptop, headphones over one ear so she could type and, Carter knew, listen to the chatter in the room. She looked around at him. "Hey."

"Hey." Carter sat next to her. "That what I think it is?"

"Sure is. Just checking it."

The screen showed a transcript of the interview an Agent O'Neill had done with Marissa. Olivia's online habits, social media, groups, clubs, access to money, introvert/extrovert, streetwise, tolerance for risk, sociability, any mental illness or medication (prescribed or recreational). All textbook stuff, but whether it gave any real insight into what was happening here, well...

"Anything?"

"A big fat zero." Elisha hit pause on the recorder. "Going through her previous addresses now, but Lori's on that. No childhood friends that the mother could name. The family, well, it's a bit of a mess. Nobody talking to each other. But we've got warrants for the ISP to see what sites she's visited. That could rule out suicide, as you know."

"Can you get Tyler on it?"

"Sure."

Speak of the devil and he shall come racing through the door of the mobile command center.

"Sir." Tyler Peterson still had the look of a kid fresh out of college, even though he had spent four years in dusty hellholes on the other side of the world. Losing half an ear to an IED hadn't affected him, probably made him appreciate not losing the rest of his body. "Need to speak to you." He had an evidence bag containing Olivia's cellphone and laptop. "First thing, the cell is smashed into pieces."

"Recoverable pieces?"

"Drilled and fried. You name it, we're getting nothing from it."

"And the laptop?"

"Well, it was locked with a passcode, but I got in. Trouble is, it's clean. Too clean."

"How can it be too clean?"

"I could impress you with my detective work, but basically there's a missing drive that stored all her personal stuff."

"Like a pen drive?"

"I think so. Either way, it's not in the machine. So we need to find it."

"Okay, keep me updated."

"I finished the social media search. Olivia does have accounts, but there are no posts, certainly not public ones. I've been through her friends lists and she doesn't follow anyone shady. I'm processing the posts she has liked and shared, but we'll need to subpoena for the private information."

"I'll get on to that." Carter took the bag from him. "These are high-end, right? Expensive."

Tyler nodded. "You're wondering where Marissa got the money?"

"Right."

"Well, you're wrong. This cellphone is two and a half years old, and the laptop... I'm surprised it still works."

"Does that help us any?"

"It's why I'm trying to brute force it. It just depends if she's kept them up to date or not."

"Try your best."

"Sure." Tyler took the bag back but didn't move off.

Carter looked up at the apartment above them. "Before you get any further, are you aware of any school notebooks?"

"I've told you about the laptop."

"No, I mean paper. A journal. A legal notepad. Might've been covered with doodles."

"Okay. Well, there might be something." Tyler went over to the huddle of officers near the front of the command center. "Beverley?"

A woman swung around and did a double take at Tyler. "What now?"

"That stack of journals from her room?" Tyler reached around her to the pile of evidence bags.

She slapped his wrist. "I haven't started these yet!"

Tyler raised both hands. "I need to show him something."

She took a long look at Carter then stepped aside. "Don't mess with anything."

"Okay, okay, okay."

Carter almost found it amusing to see uber-cool Tyler ruffled by a CSI, but then they were up against an ultra-tight clock.

"Got it." Tyler held a bag out to Carter.

Showing precisely what he would call a notebook. Recycled brown card cover, letter sized. And covered in doodles. All seemed to say, "Never forget," mostly in a graffiti style—hard to read, but it was there.

And so was "Josh," surrounded by love hearts.

Carter handed it back to Tyler. "Nobody connected this to the message on the mirror?"

He closed his eyes. "Sorry, sir."

"This isn't good enough."

"Sorry." Tyler was all alone, no sign of Beverley.

Carter could stay there for hours, hauling him over the coals for it, but that didn't feel right. He stepped aside to let Elisha out of the mobile command center, then focused on Tyler. "Process it, okay? Find out if anyone else knows about that phrase."

"Sir."

Carter dashed off and caught Elisha in the middle of the road. "Can you take over the hunt for Deacon Hill, please?"

"I thought Dane Rodgers was—"

Carter just had to raise an eyebrow.

"Sure." Elisha nodded slowly. "But you'll want to hear this first. Just been down at the precinct house. Deacon Hill's murder is still a live case."

"They haven't caught who did it?"

"Nope."

"But they've got a body?"

"No idea. I've asked the detective to call me, but he's out at court."

Carter frowned. "Got a name for them?"

"Think this is a mistake, but I've written down Nesh Warburton."

Carter's frown deepened into a wince. "Him."

"You know him?"

"He's a basic dick." And the sort of basic dick that Carter had on his cellphone. He bashed out a quick text.

Nesh, need some of your expertise. Call me. Max.

He pocketed his cell and looked back at Elisha. "What else did you get?"

"You'll love this, Max. Like we expect, there was no police report about the break-in last night. Cool, groovy, fine. But nobody I spoke to at the school can place Gregg Ingram at the school last night. Two janitors there."

"And they should've been the ones to call him, right?"

"But neither would go on record to say they did." Elisha narrowed her eyes. "And there are no surveillance cameras in that part of the school. There's an afterhours monitoring service, but it didn't get triggered."

"Suspicious?"

"Well, it's a private changing area, so it figures."

Carter looked at it another way. A man who did want to leave a trail as he got up to no good. Sure. But was that no good abducting his girlfriend's kid? Still seemed like a stretch. Down the street, he spotted Gregg talking on his cellphone. "So, his alibi is sketchy as hell?"

"If not sketchier."

"Sir!" Tyler was charging toward them, followed by Beverley. "We've found some hairs in the bedroom. Hard to visually separate Olivia and Marissa's, but she's going to try. But there are another two."

Beverley took over. "One is bright red."

"A match for Gregg." Carter felt that singing in his gut, but he tried to ignore it. "Could be innocent though. He was involved with Olivia's mother."

Tyler looked like he thought he had solved the JFK mystery. "But it could be guilty, sir."

"We got his DNA on file?"

"Nope, and he's refused to give it."

"Figures. But it won't prove anything. He was here regularly, spent a lot of time there. Big deal. This is only useful for a stranger who has never officially been in there."

"Well, about that. There's another hair. White but dark at both ends."

So, it was somebody else. "Take it you're running the DNA?"

"All over it." Beverley was nodding. "One of my guys is doing it right now in our mobile lab. He's just finished with the wine bottle. There are traces of Rohypnol in it."

It hit Carter like a truck. "Rohypnol. You're sure?"

"Adamant." Beverley didn't seem like the type to mess around, or to mess up. "Marissa's blood has tested positive too. But we found some in the wine itself."

"How big a dose?"

"Hard to say. Enough to knock her out after one glass. I mean, it's a good thing she's not an FBI CSI—I would've chugged that whole bottle and be dead." She paused for a reaction, but didn't get one, so frowned instead. "And the strangest thing. There's a tiny hole in the cork."

"In the *cork?*"

"I'd say it's a syringe mark. Looks like someone injected into it."

And that gave Carter a straight line to a suspect.

CHAPTER NINE

Carter

Marissa was next door in the mobile command center's family room, treated with dignity and respect, but Gregg Ingram sat in the interrogation room, looking frayed and rattled. Looking guilty as hell. His glasses were smudged with thumb prints, so he took them off, blew on the lenses, rubbed them, then put them back on, but they didn't seem much clearer. He picked up the glass of water and sipped it with a frown. "You're sure?"

"Positive." Carter sat back in the chair and stretched out. Typical alpha-male bro bullshit, but sometimes it was the only language men like Gregg understood. Or complied with, some deep-seated instinct taking over. "Strangest thing, huh?"

"I mean, I was there. Me and Chad. We... He was wearing a green shirt, I had a navy T-shirt on. We were in the main hallway, we should be there."

Carter scratched at the stubble on his neck, starting to itch real bad. What he'd give for a shave right then. "I mean, if you'd reported it to the police, we'd have a police report and that would back up your story."

"It's not a *story*."

"So make it reality for me, Gregg. A witness, a police report, a notification from the alarm company, a glimpse of your car in the lot or video of you walking through the front door. Let's see your alarm code resetting the intrusion code when you left. Sorry Gregg, it's a story."

"Look, I was there, at school. These assholes had broken in, trashed the place, then left. And I'm the schmuck who has to clean up after them."

"That what you were doing?"

"What?"

"Cleaning up after them?"

"Uh, yeah."

Carter leaned forward over the table until he was looking right into Gregg's eyes. Most people would blanch in that situation, but Gregg stood his ground, owning his own territory. "Mr. Ingram, I'm not quite sure you're taking in the magnitude of the situation I'm dealing with here. Marissa's daughter has been abducted, and I need to find her."

Gregg pointed out the door. "You don't think I wish I was *here* when she was taken?"

"You stay over regularly?"

Gregg frowned. "Few times a week, why?"

"And Marissa's room is down on street level."

"Well, that's right."

"She ever stay at your place?"

Gregg broke eye contact. "Marissa has trust issues."

"I totally get why. From Deacon, right?"

"Not just that." Gregg looked back at him. "That whole divorce was real tough on Marissa. Hard on Liv too."

Carter clocked something in that, something not quite right. Most people had pet names for their partners, even after weeks. Sure, some didn't have them, totally down to the individual. Gregg didn't have one for Marissa, say Riss or Mar or whatever, but he did for Olivia, even if it was Marissa's own one. "You know how many agents I've got working this case?"

Gregg sat back and folded his arms. "You trying to impress me?"

"No. Take a guess."

Gregg let his breath go in a long puff. "Twenty?"

"Forty-three. And over sixty cops."

"That supposed to mean something to me?"

"Those numbers add up. We call it the burn rate. Every hour we work on a case, we burn money. Over a hundred people means we are burning a lot of cash. A big pile of it, every hour. Kind of like Scrooge McDuck swimming in his bank vault. But it's all on fire."

None of that got anything from Gregg. Nothing.

"You know, the worst part is that somebody knows what happened to Olivia. I've got agents and cops out looking in all the places I can think of. Could be I've missed something though, or it could be someone hasn't told me something, or we haven't found the right person to tell us yet. But it all comes down to the fact that I've got all these people on this case, but I've got nobody looking in that one place I really should be."

Gregg still didn't say anything, just looked hard at Carter.

"Mr. Ingram, if there's something you're not telling me about Olivia—Liv as you call her—then now is the time. I don't want to sound like I'm obsessed with money here, but I'd hate to be wasting all that time, annoying all those folks with our questions, spending all that money, when I'm looking at the wrong angle because someone hasn't told me the truth."

"What do you want from me?"

"Just the truth, Gregg. The whole, unvarnished truth."

"You've had nothing *but* the truth from me."

"Okay, but if you have left something out, changed a word of the truth or thrown something extra in, my team will find it, they are that good. Now's the time for you to come clean." Carter placed a hand on his shoulder. "Gregg, right now there is no doubt in my mind that you haven't been completely honest. So let's start with where you really were last night."

Those micro-gestures gave the whole thing away. The down-turned mouth that kept snapping back into a smile or a neutral expression. The narrowing of his brow, pushing his eyebrows up, then straightening out. The flickering twitches around his nostrils. They all gave the game away.

And just like that, Gregg folded. "I wasn't at the school last night."

Carter locked on to Gregg, keeping up the eye contact. "Tell me where you were."

"I can't…"

"You will. This is serious, Mr. Ingram. Gregg. You've given us a false alibi. You are wasting FBI and Seattle PD time. We're looking for Olivia in the wrong place. And you've been very evasive with me. Everything about you screams that you are not telling the truth. I know that and you know that, so let's move forward. It's just you and me here. Now. Where were you last night?"

"I wasn't at the school."

"Go on."

"We've had a ton of break-ins, sure, so I thought I could use them as a cover."

"Keep going."

"To get away." Gregg ran a hand down his face. "You asked earlier if I've been staying here at Marissa's? Well, yeah. It's most nights. Practically moved in, but I've still got my own apartment. Costs a bomb. But that's fine, because Marissa's got trust issues and I don't want to push her into anything. But I'm stuck in this weird limbo where I'm not at my own place and she expects me to be at hers, but doesn't want me to move in."

"Tell me what really happened, Gregg."

"It's not that."

"So what is it?"

"I didn't expect Olivia to be taken like that when I was away." He held up his hands. "I didn't expect her to be taken at all!"

These guys usually had their own twisted, circuitous logic, and Carter had to walk the path with them if he wanted to get anywhere near the kernel of truth. "You need to tell me, Gregg. You'll feel better once you do." He made a viewfinder with his thumbs and forefingers, the shot trained right on Gregg's face. "It's written all over your face, Gregg. Time to let it out."

Gregg scraped his chair back and stood up. Guy was fizzing with nervous energy. The kind of energy you got from storing up something eating away at your soul. He walked over to the locked door, but just stood there, leaning against it with his eyes shut.

"You look like you need to talk, Gregg."

Gregg didn't look back over. He collapsed against the wall. Seemed like he was doing everything he could not to fall over.

"It'll help if you tell me the truth. If I can recover Olivia, then this'll feel—"

"I didn't take her!"

"Sure looks a lot like you did."

"I didn't." Gregg shook his head. Eyes still shut, so whatever was burning away in there was bad. "I *couldn't* do that. I love Liv like she's my own daughter."

"So who did you get to do it?"

"What?"

"You weren't here, sure. Couldn't take her yourself. Fine. So you got someone else to do your dirty work, didn't you?"

"No!" Gregg lurched across the room toward Carter, fists clenched. But he wasn't a fighting man. His anger could only come out in his words, not his punches. "No way, man."

"Help me understand."

"It was all very innocent."

"Tell me about that."

"You honestly think I could take Liv? Really?"

"Gregg, all I care about is reuniting Olivia with her mother. Everything else is gravy. On a case like this, we put all that prosecution stuff into the long grass, and prioritize recovering the child. Right now, I *need* to find Olivia. And it feels like you know a lot about what happened here."

"You want to know where I was?"

Carter pointed at the empty chair. "Please."

Gregg stared at it for a few seconds, weighing up the biggest decision of his life. Then he just sat down, rested his elbows on the wood, and started unburdening himself. "I was speaking to Marissa's father-in-law."

That was straight out of left field.

"Raymond Hill." Gregg rubbed his eyes.

"We've tried getting in touch with him, but that number Marissa gave us doesn't work anymore."

Gregg shook his head. "Well... Marissa hasn't told you this, but he's been visiting the house a few times, trying to speak to Marissa. Thing is, she doesn't want anything to do with him. Reminds her of her marriage, all that nasty stuff. Ray always picked a time when I was out. I play squash and racquetball a few nights a week, so he came over during those times. It's like he had been staking the place out."

"But there must be a reason you contacted him?"

"Marissa told me he'd been here a few times and I saw the pattern, so I drove off like I was heading to my club. But I parked around the block and walked back here. Bingo. Ray gets out of his Mercedes and strolls right up to the door. This time, I got him and told him to back off."

Even with Gregg's whole "lover not a fighter" image, he was tall and athletic enough that he at least looked like he could kick someone's ass if he needed to.

"Did you threaten him?"

"I didn't have to. Ray crumpled like a paper bag, then started crying. I took him to this bar a few blocks away and got him straightened out. Took a few whiskeys. Then he started talking."

Gregg looked right into Carter's eyes with blinding clarity. "Ray's got a young daughter—Frankie. Deacon's half-sister from his second marriage. And she's real sick. Leukemia. And he needs a bone marrow transplant from Olivia."

Carter felt his earlier talk about looking in the right place biting at his throat. They'd missed this entirely. And Gregg had held it back. Why? "Go on."

"About eight weeks ago, it was Liv's annual check-up. Way I hear it, he paid the lab tech to draw an extra vial. He got a friendly doctor to run it, and the doctor said Olivia had enough HLAs to be a match for Frankie. Can't remember what an HLA is, but it's what stops the blood cancer. Anyway, Liv could be a donor for a bone marrow transplant. If it worked, Frankie would be in the clear."

"But?"

"Ray got in touch with Marissa. But Marissa wanted nothing to do with it. He already knew Liv was a match. He didn't ask, just took."

"You know why?"

"Everything relating to her ex-husband triggers her rage. She's seeing a counselor, but it's still real early. What Deacon did, cutting them off like that, it was real tough on her."

"And Marissa is happy to let Frankie die?"

"God no. As far as Marissa was aware, Ray had other options."

"But?"

"In this bar, Ray told me that Liv is the only match they've found. She was their only hope."

"Did Olivia know?"

"I didn't tell her. Marissa didn't, that I know of."

"Gregg, when I talked earlier about burning money and looking in the wrong place... Why didn't you mention it? At any point?"

"This is Marissa's business, not mine."

"You said she feels like a daughter to you."

"That's still only 'like,' though. She's not my kid. It's Marissa's thing."

"So why did you meet Ray?"

"I want to help in any way I can. I can only imagine what Ray's going through right now. So I met him last night to try and grease the wheels, talk through how to influence Marissa into letting Liv donate."

"How much did he pay you?"

"A thousand bucks upfront. Three if she went through with the procedure."

"You expect me to believe that?"

"What? It's the truth!"

And it actually looked like it, but Carter wasn't going to give him it that quickly.

"This whole school robbery thing was to—"

"Look, Marissa knows people at the squash club. I couldn't just not show up. We needed to get a big chunk of time together and plan out how to influence her."

Any way he cut it, Carter had a new prime suspect now, with a crystal-clear motive. "Okay, Gregg, I need you to give me Ray's number and home address."

CHAPTER TEN

Lori

Lori scanned the faces coming through from immigration and baggage claim. Mostly businessmen with laptop bags over their shoulders, all trying to bust through the crowd and steal precious seconds on the way to their cabs to whichever tech business they were visiting. And there were so many.

But none matched the photo she had. Still, Lori held up the sign, CHRIS KING, like she was a taxi driver.

Coffee smells and chatter surrounded her like a blanket, the clattering of travelers sitting around waiting for their flights out of here, waiting to be able to endure the line through security.

A man approached her, clutching a Stumptown coffee cup. He was really tall, like almost seven foot, but he kind of matched the photo, with sad eyes and a gray business suit. She hadn't expected him to be that big. "Are you my taxi?" English accent. Looked more like a gangster than a cop, but that was London for you.

"No, I'm Special Agent Alves." She held out her badge.

"Aha. Well, I'm Chris King." He smiled. "Well, I'm sorry for making that assumption." It had been a while since Lori had heard a genuine London accent like that, nothing like the malarkey that passed for it on TV. "I suppose now that you've shown me yours, I should reciprocate?"

She just raised an eyebrow at that.

King unfolded his Met Police warrant card and it seemed to check out, though the layout had been simplified in the time since she had last seen one. He held out a hand. "DI Chris King, pleasure to make your acquaintance."

Lori shook his hand, then squirted some sanitizer and held it for him. "You got any bags?"

"Just a rucksack. I'm hoping I won't be here for long, but if I am, I can easily buy some new clothes."

Not at that height. "Come on, then." She led him through the airport toward the parking lot. "How was the flight?"

"Not bad, actually. The upside of working this kind of case is you get an upgrade to Premium Economy. Nothing like Business Class, of course, but it meant I could get some work done, and then I watched a couple of films. Still, twelve hours is a large time adjustment. I suspect I'll be flaking out later this morning."

"It's lunchtime."

"Is it?" King shook his head. There was something attractive about him that Lori couldn't quite place. His photo made him look very intense, but in person he had a warmth and an endearing sadness. Not what she imagined at all. "Here." He jogged forward and held the door for her.

Sometimes it was nice being treated like a lady, so Lori let him do it. Then again, she was aware he could be playing her. She walked through into the wind and rain. "Before we get too far down this road, I need to lay down the law."

"Ah, I fully expected this. Shoot."

"You're on foreign soil, so you need my help. It's not the other way around, okay? While this is your case, you don't have jurisdiction here. Anything you want to do, you run by me first. Okay?"

He smiled at her. Definitely had a bit of roguish charm. "Wouldn't have it any other way."

"Good."

"If things were the other way around, I'd expect it to be exactly the same."

Lori led him over to her Suburban, bumped up on the sidewalk with her official FBI sign in the window. No asshole parking attendants had tried to challenge it, at least. She opened the hatch and waited for him to dump his bag in. "Why me?"

"Why you, what?"

"You requested me for this case. Why?"

King looked away. "Lori, I asked for you because I need a liaison I can trust."

"I'd rather you called me Agent Alves."

"Really?"

"Okay, maybe not. Why do you think you can trust me?"

"My boss swore for you. You worked together in Miami."

"I see." Lori clicked her tongue a few times. It all made perfect sense now. "How is the old rogue?"

"He finally accepted his promotion, if that helps. He's in a good place."

"That business with his kid all sorted out?"

"More or less." King shrugged. "Now, I don't expect any special favors here, but I need to know that I can trust you."

"His word is my bond."

"Good. Now, I'm here because I am taking down an international human trafficking ring. Not the most brutal in the world, but still, they're connected to gangland crime both here and in the UK. I'm determined to put a stop to it."

Lori nodded. "So where to first?"

"We're going to speak to Bill Carter."

I shut my eyes and let the sun's warmth hit my skin. Could be anywhere right now, maybe on a beach somewhere. Maybe down in Brighton like when Uncle Steve took me for the day, and we ended up watching the England football match in that pub. I can even smell the sea in the air. The donkeys. The machines rattling coins as they pay out.

But I'm not there. I open my eyes again and I'm right here, outside my school, waiting. Just like every day. I kick out against the wall behind me and I swear I can hear something crumble, a tiny bit of the wall. A small victory.

"There you are."

I look up, frowning at the man who's blocking out the sun. So much bigger than me. And I have no idea who he is. "Who are you?"

"I'm your Uncle John."

"I don't have an Uncle John. I've got an Uncle Steve."

"Son, I'm your Mum's brother."

He looks okay. Not like the men Mummy warned me about. Smart coat, suit, shiny shoes. Really shiny shoes. "Where's Mummy?"

"It's your birthday, right? She's got a special treat for you. Come with me and we'll see her, okay?"

I don't know about this, but then again, if he is Mummy's brother... I look across the school playground and see my teacher, Mrs. Green. She's smiling and waving.

This is okay. I take Uncle John's hand. "Where are we going?"

"On a little adventure."

CHAPTER ELEVEN

Carter

Carter sat in his Suburban and looked out along the road. He must've driven this way a thousand times over the years, but not on any of those drives had he even spotted Ray Hill's home on Lake Washington Boulevard.

Hidden behind a tall wall he could just about see over from this vantage point, Ray had a huge plot backing onto the water. Looked like it had its own private dock and two boats. One was a speedboat worth more than Carter's car, the other a yacht worth more than his house. The house itself was a hulking place with two wings styled like a German castle, but the developers had kept adorning and adorning until it was a complete mess.

Meaning Ray Hill had a lot of money. And when people have a lot of money, they can sure do anything they want.

Carter clocked Elisha's Suburban pulling up behind him. One was fine, but two might set any alarm bells ringing. Then again, they were far enough away, and the house was secluded. He opened his door and hopped down onto the asphalt.

Elisha was already out, clutching her service cellphone. "Tyler's run the location on Ray's cellphone. As far as we can tell, it's been turned off since eight last night."

Carter mentally tossed another chip onto the pile. "Okay, then let's see if he's here." He set off along the narrow pavement until he came to the gate. Another recent case had been at the far end of the boulevard, on the other side of the road, and had the same high-end security system. A big brass plate with a mesh grille, all set into the tall stone walls. He pressed the button and wasn't sure anything had happened, so he held it down for a few seconds and got a satisfying buzzing sound.

"Hello?" A female voice crackled out. No time to answer. Almost like she had been waiting by the intercom.

"FBI, ma'am." Carter couldn't spot a camera lens, but all the same, he held up his badge. "Special Agent Max Carter and Agent Elisha Thompson. Need a moment with a Ray Hill."

A long pause, filled with crackle and the whirring drone of a Prius trundling past. "Ray's not here."

"You know where he is?"

"Nope."

"Ma'am, do you mind if we come in?"

Zoe Hill fussed around with the French press, tossing in freshly ground coffee and pouring water in from one of those fancy faucets that produced boiling water. The rest of the kitchen had that same high standard. Granite countertops, oak doors. A real stove that looked rescued from somewhere and lovingly restored. "You guys take cream? Sugar?"

Carter smiled at her. "Black, please."

"Same." Elisha was staring at her cellphone, lips pouting in that particular way, indicating to Carter that she had received an update from Tyler, but one she didn't necessarily agree with.

"Okay then." Zoe carried a tray over to the small table overlooking the lake. As much as Carter hated himself for thinking it, she was undoubtedly a trophy wife. Immaculately dressed and with the toned muscles that came from a lot of yoga, long hair tied off in a braid hanging over her left shoulder. She set the drinks down then opened the French door. "Can I get you something, hon?"

A teenage girl sat on a lounger under a patio heater, all wrapped up under a blanket. She looked around at her mom, her head bald, face puffy. She seemed wiped-out tired. Carter knew the signs of intense chemotherapy alright. Still, her piercing green eyes dazzled with vitality. "I'm good, Mom." Her smile was the warm sort that maybe was all about deflecting fear, worry, and blame from a parent, rather than indicating any genuine happiness. Strange how some kids had to be like that, knowing their time left was short and wanting their parents to be okay in their absence. "Thanks."

"Frankie, you sure I can't get you another blanket?"

"Mom, I'm good. Really." Frankie looked at them, but didn't seem to think much of two FBI agents sitting in her kitchen.

"Okay, hon." Zoe shut the door but not completely, like there was a thin thread running between her and her daughter. She walked back over and sat between Carter and Elisha. "This should be ready to pour." She plunged and splashed out three cups. "Help yourselves, guys."

"Thanks." Carter took his and sucked in the strong smoky smell. "How's she doing?"

Zoe frowned for a few seconds, taking her time to think it all through. "You know, I hate this whole narrative about fighting cancer. I lost both my parents to it. Does that mean they weren't strong enough? Hell no." Her seat looked across to Frankie. "But she's a good kid. Doesn't deserve leukemia. Nobody does, but she... she really doesn't." Her nostrils trembled slightly. "Trouble is, the chemo isn't working."

"I'm sorry to hear that."

Zoe looked at Carter. Sometimes he would get a snarky comment from a struggling parent about whether he didn't mean it, but Zoe the earth mother took it all in her stride, giving him a curt nod in response. "My husband, though... He's doing more than enough fighting for both of them."

"In what way?"

"Frankie is Ray's only daughter, but he lost his son. Deacon."

"We heard. Must've been rough."

Zoe held up her hands as if to deflect any sympathy from them. "I'm his second wife, a year younger than Deacon. But that whole thing has been tough on Ray."

"You know where your husband is, Mrs. Hill?"

"Ray's… He's… Let's just say my husband is a complex man. Didn't know that before we got involved…"

"In what way is he complex?"

"He goes off-grid from time to time. When he's involved in an investigation, he gets obsessive."

"He's a cop?"

"Was. Years ago. Ray co-owns a private detective business downtown."

"Pretty lucrative, right?"

"More than law enforcement…" Zoe sipped her coffee, but kept a long gaze on Carter. "Why do you need to speak to him?"

Carter waited for her to put her mug down. "Olivia's been abducted."

She clutched a hand to her chest. "Oh my."

"I need to know where Mr. Hill was last night."

Zoe frowned. "You don't think…?"

"We need to establish his movements."

"Okay, well, he wasn't here. He's been involved in an investigation for a very important client."

"And it's normal for him to not be here?"

"Sure."

"He wasn't meeting Gregg Ingram?"

"God damn it." Zoe clattered her cup off the table and stared at her nails like she had just broken one. "He told me he was finished with that bullshit."

"What bullshit would that be?"

Zoe looked over at the window, at her daughter staring out across the lake. "Frankie's chemo isn't working. She needs a bone marrow transplant from a close match, ideally a relative."

"And I gather Olivia Davis meets the criteria?"

"They're... it's complicated. Frankie is her dad's half-sister, but they're like cousins."

"Are they close?"

"They were."

"But?"

"But Marissa." Zoe rubbed at her fingernails. "She puts up walls."

"I understand Mr. Hill was looking for Olivia to be a bone marrow donor?"

"Listen, Ray had this test done and Olivia was a blood match for her. When Marissa found out he had gotten the blood behind her back, she shut him down. I warned him to be honest, but well... That's the last thing Ray is."

Carter frowned. "My understanding is that bone marrow donation, while painful, is safe for the donor."

"You're not wrong." Zoe picked up her cup again, but didn't take a sip. "As far as I understand it, they puncture your pelvis and extract a sample of bone marrow. Hurts like hell, but they only take a small amount." She looked out at her daughter on the veranda. "Then they culture it in the lab for implantation after they knock out the receiver's own faulty bone marrow."

While it was difficult to hear, Carter relished hearing it from her. And hearing it straight like that too, unblemished by euphemism. Raw. It was always telling when a person explained something from their point of view. He could see that as Frankie's primary caregiver, the pain and hurt rested heavier on Zoe's shoulders than on her husband's, still out doing the alpha-male thing. Meaning any plans or schemes or motives were slightly more likely to come from her.

The fact that Frankie was here was inconsequential. Olivia could be in a facility across town, a needle taking the sample. It would need at least a few weeks to culture, then Frankie would be ready for her side of the operation, which would be far riskier than Olivia's extraction.

Carter could totally understand it as a motivation. If anything was to happen to his own daughter, he would do everything in his power to save her. He didn't know if he could do anything outside that power though. But he would probably consider it.

He took a drink of coffee. "How did your husband take the decision from Marissa?"

"He wasn't exactly happy." Zoe snorted. "Way Ray sees it, this was a big 'screw you' from Marissa to Deacon." She stared at Carter, her glare only now revealing the hidden malice and anger rising above the soft exterior. "It's understandable to a certain extent. The way Marissa sees it, Deacon left her in the lurch and stopped paying for his own kid's upbringing, despite their divorce settlement. And because Deacon's family is rich, she thinks it's up to us to pay."

"How were things between you and Marissa after their divorce?"

"Good. For a while. We were friends. As hard as their divorce was, I liked Olivia. Spent a lot of time with her. She came to my yoga studio for classes, we had lunch. It was good. And Liv and Frankie were BFFs."

"But?"

Her look darkened. "But Ray disowned Marissa and Liv. And now that we need something, it's… Well, it's way too late."

"You know why they fell out?"

"I honestly don't."

"Any ideas?"

"I'd say it was something to do with Deacon."

"Care to hazard a guess? Come on, Zoe, don't hold back."

Zoe's frosty glare returned.

The patio door opened, accompanied by a blast of wind and rain. Frankie stepped over the varnished wood, still wrapped up in her blanket. "Cold." She slumped into the seat between Elisha and her mother, then frowned. "What's going on?"

"Frankie, these are FBI agents. Olivia's been abducted."

"God." Frankie blinked hard a few times, and it looked like it cost her greatly. "Will you find her?"

"We hope to." Elisha smiled at her. "You haven't heard from her, have you?"

Frankie shot a look at her mom. "I haven't heard from Liv in like a year." She snorted. "I haven't seen her since I got sick. I really miss her."

Zoe took her daughter's hand, though Carter couldn't tell if it was to show care and support, or to control and manipulate. "Like I told you, the girls used to be super-close."

"Had a cousin like that when I was growing up. We were inseparable." Elisha smiled at Frankie. "You guys talk about boys much?"

Frankie gave a side glance to her mother, then shrugged. "Sort of."

"Did Olivia ever mention a Josh to you?"

"Josh?" Frankie frowned. "Not that I remember, no. You think Josh has taken her?"

"We don't know."

Zoe let go of her daughter's hand, then gave Carter a flash of the eyebrows. "Sir, can we…?"

"Sure." Carter got up and left Elisha with Frankie, then followed Zoe across the kitchen to the sink. "What's up?"

"Look, Frankie needs to rest."

"Sure." Carter nodded. "We'll get out of here. But we really do need to speak to your husband."

Zoe turned on the hot tap and started filling the sink. "I don't know where he is."

"But it's something to do with his investigation, right?"

"I genuinely have no idea."

"Liv's life could be in danger. We need to find her quickly, and it's important that we speak to Mr. Hill. Do you have any idea where your husband could be?"

CHAPTER TWELVE

Carter

Fifth Street bustled around Carter, almost hitting its lunchtime stride. He stood there, feeling dumb.

The address for Ray Hill's company was the same as Lownds and Karevoll, not exactly Carter's favorite Private Investigation firm. Far from it. He hoped it was a coincidence.

He should've realized back at Zoe Hill's home when she wrote it down for them. But on the upside, at least the + symbol had been removed from the logo, though Carter was sure that was the fourth time they'd rebranded in as many years.

Elisha held the door for him. "You want me to lead?"

"Sure." Carter followed her inside.

The place had received yet another makeover. Gone were the beanbags, foosball tables, and PlayStations that made it feel like a frat house tech startup. Now it looked like an upmarket hair salon with minimalist tendencies. And a fetish for untreated concrete. It was everywhere—the desks, the benches, the ceiling—broke up by just some untreated wooden floorboards and the walls left as a blank white canvas. Probably cost a big pile of cash to rework it.

Carter sure was in the wrong game. Or at least the wrong side of the coin.

Elisha was up by one of the desks.

The receptionist perched on a concrete chair that seemed to be locked in place, with only leather upholstery to save her from severe discomfort. Her computer seemed like it'd come from the set of a sci-fi Netflix drama, with a brushed aluminum back with pale purple and blue lights shooting downward. "Sure, Mr. Hill works in the building. We share services with his firm here."

"And is he here?"

"Not at present."

"You know where he might be?"

"Nope. I'm new here, sorry."

"Know anyone who might have an idea where he is?"

"My supervisor might."

"Can I speak to your supervisor then?"

"She's not here at present, ma'am. Down in Portland."

Carter caught a look from Elisha that read, "Take over," so he leaned against the cold concrete desk and flashed a smile at the receptionist. "Can I speak to Jess?"

"Jess?"

"Lownds."

"Weren't you listening? She isn't here."

"Jess Lownds is your supervisor?"

"Duh."

Carter wished he could travel back to a time when federal agents got respect. "Is David in?"

The receptionist checked her computer. "I think so, yeah."

"Well, how about you point me towards his office and we can do the rest?"

David Karevoll sat behind his concrete desk, feet up, talking on the phone. "Jeff, Jeff, Jeff, would you— Please? Thank you. No, I'm saying that's too much." He looked over at Carter and frowned. "Nope." He had recently shed over a hundred pounds of fat, and had managed to keep it off since Carter had last seen him. For once he wore a necktie, so Carter was spared the usual rug of chest hair. "Look, Jeff, buddy, I got to go, some FBI assholes are in my office. Don't know what I've done. Ciao!" He slipped his feet down and slammed the desk phone onto the holder. "Maxwell of the clan Carter."

"Just Max, David. Like all this concrete. Cost a lot, I suspect."

"You don't know the half of it, buddy. How you doing, Max?"

"Doing okay, David. Looking for Ray Hill."

"Ray? Why?"

"He works here, right?"

"We're associates. One hand washes the other. But Ray isn't the kind of guy to keep office hours."

"Just been over at his place. But his wife doesn't know where he is."

"Huh."

"Fancy and expensive."

Karevoll grinned. "The house or the wife?"

"Behave yourself."

"Ray comes from money. Inherited a ton when his pop died a few years back. And he's doubled it through his business. Much fancier clients than us."

"So. Where is he?"

Karevoll sat back and restored his feet to their rightful place on his desk. He had even worn out a little groove in the concrete with his boot heels. "Ray is on a sabbatical."

"A sabbatical. Right."

"This business with his kid." Karevoll leaned forward to flick his pants leg so it sat just so. "As a father, you wonder what you'd do if it was your kid, don't you?"

"You see either of yours much?"

"When Lori doesn't dick me around on access, despite all the money I toss her every month. How is she, by the way?"

"She's good." But Carter didn't want to think about what Lori was doing. Meeting some London cop to investigate his father. "David, I need to speak to Mr. Hill. Point me and—"

"What's he done?"

"His granddaughter's gone missing."

"Liv? Shit, you should've just called me, Max."

"I would if you didn't keep changing cell numbers."

Karevoll chuckled at that. "Never change, Max."

"Bit coincidental that Mr. Hill is on a sabbatical at the same time his granddaughter, a donor match for his ill daughter, goes missing. Right?"

Karevoll sat forward again and reached into his drawer for a cheap-looking cellphone. "Right alley, wrong lane as usual, Max. He's taking time out to search for his son."

"He thinks Deacon is alive?"

"No, he pretty much knows he's dead. And with Deacon, who knows, maybe there are more offspring scattered around, another litter of potential donors." Karevoll held down the button on the top of the phone, and the screen's glow lit up his face. "Way Ray told me the tale, unless they find some random dude in Iowa or Delaware who's a match for Frankie, Deacon is their best hope."

"Except that he has a match, right? Olivia."

That pricked Karevoll's steely front. "You seriously think Ray's kidnapped his own granddaughter?"

"The way I see it, if he took Olivia, he could keep her sedated, extract the bone marrow, then return her. She'd just be drugged for a few days. In his eyes, it's no harm, no foul…" Carter left a gap, but Karevoll didn't look like he was going to fill it with anything. "Trouble is, as understandable as the whole thing is, and I do sympathize, it's not Mr. Hill's choice to make."

Karevoll looked down at his cellphone, nodding slowly. "So you need to find him?"

"I'm desperate, David. Wouldn't be here if I wasn't. As far as we can tell, his cellphone has been off since last night. Aside from anything else, it's the only way we can validate an alibi."

Karevoll held up his cell. "Just as well this bad boy has a current location on him."

"Elisha?" Carter sat back in his Suburban, low enough to see over the wheel at the navy Mercedes. "You got eyes on him?"

"Hard to tell." Elisha's voice was thin and faint in his ear, but he could see her Suburban just up the block. The lunchtime crowd was sure out in force today, flooding the pavements and making downtown Seattle feel busy like Manhattan. "That Merc is definitely his, but I can't see anyone inside it."

"Same here." Carter sat up and tried to use his binoculars to home in. Hardly subtle, a federal agent sitting by Pike Place Market with a pair of binocs, but then this case needed anything but subtlety. He focused on the car for a few seconds, at the pale leather seats, but the dark windows made it hard to keep it up for long, so he put the binoculars away. "Too hard to tell from here."

His cellphone rang out. He checked the display.

NESH WARBURTON CALLING...

"Elisha, I'll be back in a sec." He switched the calls. "Nesh, how you doing?"

"I'm awesome, Max baby, awesome." Could just about hear the ever-present toothpick being swapped from one side of his mouth to the other. "Now, what expertise can I lend my third-favorite Feebie?"

"Deacon Hill."

"Have to remind me."

"Missing person, I think. A year back."

"Remember it now, Max. And I don't work missing persons. That's a murder."

"You've got a body?"

"Okay, it's a murder without a body. Actually, the ME put it down as a suicide."

"Explain."

"Man, his apartment was like something out of a Tarantino flick. Blood everywhere. Joint was like an abattoir."

"But no body?"

"Right. And we had no reports of him. The ME thought it was pretty hard for anyone to survive that without a long stay in the ICU. No John Does in the nearest *ten* states matched his description. The clincher is we found his car, covered in more of his blood, out near the Aurora Bridge."

The George Washington Memorial Bridge. Seattle's notorious suicide spot that had claimed its first victim before it had even been completed back in the thirties. Even a five-million-dollar barrier couldn't stop the desperate from leaping to their doom. That coupled with the stories of overdoses and debts... Yeah, Deacon was dead.

"Okay, Nesh. That's helpful."

"Why you calling, Max?"

"Lemme buy you a beer sometime and tell you."

"Sure. Ciao."

Carter killed the call with a wry smile. Something in Nesh Warburton brought that out in him.

His cell rang again. Elisha. She was still hovering near the Merc. "Want me to approach?"

Carter didn't see many other options here. A navy Mercedes outside a downtown deli. Could just be getting a sandwich. Could be casing the place. Could be Ray Hill had left his cellphone in the car and been abducted himself. Too many variables. Too many options. "Go for it."

"On it."

Carter sat back again, low enough to follow Elisha's path along the street, heading toward the car.

And just then, a big guy walked out of the deli clutching a wrapped foot-long sub. The guy was muscular too, but a craft-beer gut swelled his golf shirt. He had the posture and back pain of an ex-cop. And the closer he got to Carter, the more he matched the photo David Karevoll had given him.

Ray Hill opened the Merc's driver door and got in.

Elisha sped up her walking pace but by the time she got to the door, the car pulled off into the traffic.

Carter stuck his car into gear, and he rolled off in front of a bus, following the Mercedes around the block. As he passed, he waved at Elisha to get back into her SUV.

Ray was trundling down Pike Place, biting into his sandwich as he went, his neck craning around like he was checking out the women walking past. Maybe he was looking for his son. Maybe he was looking for someone else. He hung a right onto Pine and headed up to First, then stopped at the lights. A right turn, the only way he could go for a few blocks. Eventually, that would take him on the road to his lakeside home, but Ray didn't seem to be in any kind of hurry.

Carter took it slow following him up the hill, crawling up as the pedestrians took their sweet time crossing.

Ray took another bite of his sandwich, then the lights changed, and he cut right along First. He trundled along, then shot across the oncoming traffic into the parking lot next to a strip club. He pulled up by the brick wall and got out, still chewing, but no sign of his sandwich.

A doorman in a bomber jacket and black pants sidled up to him but instead of giving him grief over parking, he caught Ray's tossed car keys.

Carter sat there, waiting like he'd done so many times over his career. Strip club visits became nightly occurrences, always searching for some dumbass. No matter what the owners said, these places had close ties to gangs, organized crime, drugs, human trafficking, you name it.

His cell rang. Perfect timing. Didn't recognize the number, but it was a Seattle area code at least, and close enough to one of those that belonged to Seattle PD. "Carter."

"Max Carter?"

"That's me."

"It's Beverley Richards."

"Okay?"

"I'm a CSI with SPD. We met earlier?"

"Ah, okay. What's up?"

"You're aware I'm running a DNA sample we found in the bedroom of Olivia Davis?"

"You got something?"

"Well, we didn't get a match from our perp's database."

"I sense a but here, Beverley."

She laughed. "But, luckily, we got a match on the database we use to exclude officers from crime scenes."

"It matches a serving cop?"

"No, an ex-cop. Raymond Q. Hill."

And Carter was staring right at him. "Okay, thanks for that." Now he had a solid reason to speak to him.

But he couldn't get across the oncoming traffic, slow as it was, and not without running the risk of being made. Still, he knew where Ray was headed now.

The strip joint was hardly the classiest joint in town, despite its downtown location. And it sickened Carter to even consider that Ray Hill would be heading into a place like that while his wife was at home with their severely ill daughter.

And places like that were mazes inside. In among the new skyscrapers, this little block of old Seattle defied gentrification and modernity, and the building was old enough to have some kooky back doors and side exits. This was the wrong end of downtown for the Seattle underground, those below-the-line floors from another century now hidden under the road system.

No.

Carter needed to get him now.

So he shot in front of a Camry and pulled in at a diagonal, blocking Ray's entry to the club. Carter shot out of the Suburban and grabbed Ray by the wrist before he knew what was going on. Sometimes FBI agent speed trumped ex-cop wiles.

"What the hell?" Ray inadvertently spat a chunk of baloney at Carter as he tried to shake him off.

"FBI!" Carter had him exactly where he wanted him. "Ray Hill, I need a word. Now."

CHAPTER THIRTEEN

Carter

Carter stood in the corridor in the field office, staring at his cell-phone, willing the other side to answer. Another look up and down the long corridor, and still no sign of her. He hated waiting, more than most people. And Special Agent in Charge Karen Nguyen was someone he had to wait for more than anyone else, even his daughter.

He tried Nguyen again, but it smacked right against her voicemail. Again.

The door was open a crack, and Ray Hill sat at the table, looking every inch the ex-cop. Knew how to handle himself in an interrogation. Must have run a million himself. You would think that most cops would know all the tricks and techniques, but very few can keep quiet longer than the golden eleven seconds. Their bravado betrays them quickly.

Yeah, Carter knew this guy was going to be a tough nut to crack. He put his hand on the door, but footsteps trundled along the corridor behind him.

"Through here." Agent Dane Rodgers, six foot three and built like a tank, showing someone into an interrogation room.

Carter squinted at the hunched-over figure, and it took him a few seconds to recognize his own father.

Bill Carter looked every minute of his seventy-two years, his face creased with laughter lines he had no right to earn given what he had done.

Carter wanted to rush over, listen in, find out what the hell Bill had done to his mom. But no, he needed to keep his distance, to let it all play out.

Lori appeared and did a double take at Carter. "Max?"

He held out his hands. "Just happen to be here."

"Right." She looked down at her shoes. "I'll keep you updated on how this goes."

"Are you sure you should?"

She shrugged. "I know how hard this must be for you, Max. I want to help."

Carter wished that he was doing it for her. Getting in that interrogation room, using his badge and role to get his father to talk. To tell the truth about what really happened back then. He wasn't the only person who had been taken, way back when, so he wanted to make sure whoever did it paid the price for their crimes. Make sure nobody else suffered the same fate.

But his priority was finding Olivia Davis. That was some hurt he could fix.

Carter smiled at her. "Just do your job, Lori. Everything else will fall into place."

She nodded, then entered the room, leaving him with an empty corridor and his thoughts.

The noise in his head was almost deafening. So many conflicting emotions. Violence, rage, fear, sorrow, loss. All of it. All of the time.

A door opened across the corridor and Nguyen appeared, her cellphone plastered to her ear. She was about a foot shorter than Carter, but he wouldn't take his chances in a fight with her. He was too soft, and she was too hard. Her dark hair was threaded with silver hair now, and she wore it like a badge of honor. She beckoned him into the room with a wagging finger.

Carter swallowed down his emotions and followed her in, then shut the door behind them. One of those meeting rooms where Carter would tear strips off junior agents like Tyler Peterson when they bungled an interrogation. The narrow-eyed look on Nguyen's face made him feel like he was going to get his own treatment. With interest.

Nguyen snapped her cell shut with a satisfying click. One of those fancy new folding-screen things that updated the old cellphone design, the kind that was still popular with drug dealers, just that hers cost a thousand dollars instead of ten bucks. "So."

"So." Carter took a seat and tried to act calm. But the reality was his blood was boiling.

All the way along First from that strip club parking lot to the field office, fifteen or so downtown blocks, Ray Hill had sat in the back, keeping quiet. Not a word.

Carter needed to chill out, to keep things level and steady. "Okay, so my read on this is that Raymond Hill fits the MO for the abduction of Olivia Davis. His daughter, Olivia's half-aunt, urgently needs a bone marrow transplant. Olivia has been tested and she fits the bill, but her mom refuses access. Ergo, Raymond could've taken her last night. Simple matter with the right medical team to keep her sedated for a few days while they extract her bone marrow, then return her as if nothing happened."

Nguyen was playing with her cell, that satisfying click soon becoming an irritant. "Okay, I buy it, but he'd need access to a clinic to perform the operation. You got any leads?"

"Could be anywhere, Karen. He just needs one of the many specialists in the city to owe him a solid. Any number of clinics in this city. Just need one."

"Do we need to monitor them?"

"That'll take a lot of manpower." Carter glanced back at the door. "And we don't know if Olivia's in Seattle. Could be Tacoma, Olympia, even down to Portland."

"Taking a kidnapped kid across state lines, Max. That's big."

"Well, Ray Hill seems the type to do anything to save his daughter."

"Anything else you've psychically obtained from him?"

Carter fixed her with a glare, but she still clicked that damn cellphone. "He's an ex-cop, so he's going to be tough to break down. He'll just sit there, soaking up whatever pressure I apply. If he or any associates have Olivia, then he just has to wait until the operation is complete."

"That's still a big assumption, Max, which you need to smash into a thousand pieces with a claw hammer."

"I intend to."

"So what's your plan here?"

"I might have to do something off books here."

"Max…"

"Nothing violent, just— Back in my service days, we had to blur the lines a bit. Go the extra mile to get what we needed from people. Psychological stuff. It's not something I'm necessarily proud of, even if it did save American lives."

Nguyen stared at her cell, clicking once. Twice. Three times. Then back at Carter. "Go for it."

The interrogation room door was still open, but Elisha was in there now, making small talk with Ray, or at least trying to. "I like that place up on Third, myself. Best meatballs in the city."

"Sure." Yep, Ray Hill was cagey as hell. Nothing given away. Even sandwich fillings.

Carter was going to have to dig deep into some dark places to get him to talk.

But did he really know anything? Could he really abduct his own granddaughter?

Hell yeah.

Carter pushed into the room like a ball of fizzing energy, strolling around the room and acting like he owned the place. He nodded at Elisha, then at Ray, but he walked past him to stand right behind him. "Heard that you're an ex-cop, Ray."

Ray had to crane his neck to look behind him at Carter. "Got my twenty years in, took my pension and got out."

"And you work with David Karevoll now?"

"Sure do. Him and Jess run a good business. There's synergy between our two outfits."

"Zoe said you own your own firm."

That should have thrown Ray. The casual mention of visiting his home, speaking to his wife. But Ray just shrugged. "My name ain't above the door, but that's the way we like it."

"Must be tough though. You're an ex-cop, put in all that service, and this is how you're being repaid?"

"Come again?"

Carter walked back to the other side of the table but didn't sit. "I've got a daughter. Name's Kirsty. It's Scottish, named after her grandmother on my wife's side. She's cute as a button. Nothing I wouldn't do for her."

Ray's nostrils were twitching, but he said nothing. Yeah, he knew there was some game going on here, and he knew the rules.

Carter gestured at Elisha. "Agent Thompson here and I met Frankie this morning. She's a good kid. What's happening to her is a tragedy."

"You don't know the half of it."

"Can't imagine what it must be like. What you and Zoe must be going through."

"Son, can we move past the rapport-building stage, skip over positive confrontation, and get right to me denying the heck out of your idiotic allegations?"

And that slight show of annoyance was exactly what Carter wanted. "Help me here, Ray. Olivia's a good kid too. If you have her or know who took her, it'll help me out a ton."

"Well, sorry. I don't know anything."

"Does 'Never forget' mean anything to you?"

"Should it?"

"Think about it."

"No, it doesn't mean anything."

"Okay. Well. The way I see it, you're real deep in this, Ray. Abducting Olivia. Your own granddaughter?"

But Ray was deadly still, like a Buddhist monk meditating.

"And you know how this looks, right? Ill daughter, who you've matched to a potential donor, but her mother won't let you. So you took her. Right?"

"Nope."

"Okay, so why were you meeting Gregg?"

Ray looked up. "What's he saying?"

"Let's focus on what you're saying, Ray."

Ray shrugged.

Carter rested his hands against the chair opposite Ray and waited for eye contact. Took him maybe thirty seconds, which was impressive.

That was enough to poke Ray into moving. "If you must know, son, I met Gregg to try and get Marissa to see sense. My daughter is *dying* and she... Marissa is preventing the only solution I got."

"Getting Olivia's bone marrow?"

"Sure. All Olivia has to do is get a needle into her hip. It'll hurt, yeah, I get that, but she'll heal in a few weeks. Frankie..." His breathing quickened. "Every day that passes, we lose a little bit of her. A little bit of hope, a little bit of her life. And Marissa can help us, just like that." He snapped his fingers, loud and sharp.

Carter held his gaze, nodding slowly. "You see why I think it's a good motive for Oliv—"

"No!"

"Ray. You're saying it yourself. How the operation would be pretty much risk-free for Olivia, so you can—"

"That ain't what happened!"

"You're a wealthy man, Ray. I've seen your home, know the circles you work in, know how well it pays. Hear you've got a lot of inherited wealth. Someone like you, I'm sure you've got the money to pay a surgeon, right? Or maybe you hushed up a DUI for someone back in your day? Some kind of favor, am I right?"

"This is bullshit."

"Ray, I just want to find Olivia. What if I told you a member of the medical team ratted you out?"

"If you told me it was sunny outside, I'd get my umbrella. I'm telling you the truth here, son. Marissa's got it in for my side of the family. My son's side. Deacon. But when I finally spoke to her, she was too caught up with the steps I'd taken to get that blood test, and she just pulled all hope away from me and Zoe. We'd started dreaming again of seeing Frankie with kids of her own, or god knows what, living in a lesbian commune in Iowa. Anything. Just… Surviving. Living. And Marissa took that away from us."

"So you spoke to Gregg?"

"Sure. Gregg's a good guy who only wants to help. He doesn't like the idea of Frankie suffering. He was playing peacemaker, trying to get Marissa to see sense, to help us out."

"He wasn't taking any money?"

"Of course he was. The boy ain't stupid."

Carter could see it all with so much clarity. Ray and Gregg collaborating to save Frankie's life. It made sense to them, but obviously not to Marissa.

"Truth is, it triggered Marissa. Her marriage to that piece of shit son of mine… It ended real bad. And I could've helped her. Marissa used to be a good person. Kind, gentle, honest. But my son… What he did to her, it twisted her until all she could think of was herself. If she'd told me Deacon was in any trouble, I could've helped."

"What kind of trouble was he in, Ray?"

"Don't ask me. That lousy son of mine didn't own up to anything. Not as a kid, not as an adult."

"You know where he is?"

"He's dead. SPD have a murder book on him. Know the dick leading it. Total asshole, but what can you do?"

"So why are you taking time out hunting for him?"

"You really want to know? I'm looking for Deacon because I've got to have hope. Olivia's a closed door, fine. I accept that."

"You think Deacon's alive?"

"No, my deadbeat boy is dead. I just want to see if he's got any other family. Kid put it out a bit before Marissa tied him down. One of them can maybe donate to Frankie. Hell, I'm paying Gregg, could pay any one of them. Even thought of taking a big check to Marissa's. Still might. That's why I've been searching for him. When you picked me up, I was chasing down the only lead I've had in months."

"At a strip club?"

"Calling me a liar?"

"So, why don't I believe you?"

"Don't be an asshole. I wasn't speaking to one of the girls there. The guy who runs the door, Gerry, he used to be a cop. Used to work with me. It's easy money kicking assholes out of a strip joint, but one of those assholes talked to him. Used to know Deacon. So Gerry called me up."

"Any idea what the lead is?"

"No idea. It's why I was going there just now."

"Huh." Carter gave him a smile. "You ever been in Olivia's room?"

"Why do you ask?"

"When? Why?"

"Of course I haven't."

"Well, now that we've proven that you're a li—"

"A liar? Hold on a minute, son."

"Anything else you want to admit to?"

"If you say there's evidence, then there's no cause to lie."

"And here you thought we just ask questions at random, right?" Carter sniffed. "You being an ex-cop is a good thing."

"Why?"

"You know all about the exclusion database, right?"

"So the DNA traces of cops on the case don't get flagged as a lead."

"Well, you haven't been a cop for a while, and you're obviously not working Olivia's abduction. And yet your DNA is in her room."

"Damn it."

"A few strands of hair, Ray. In her room, Ray."

"I haven't been there in weeks."

"You weren't supposed to have been there in a year, Ray."

"Look, okay. Fine. One night, I dropped by after dark to speak to Marissa. That's when she told me that Olivia wouldn't be donating her bone marrow."

"How did you take that?"

"How do you think?" He sighed. "Olivia is my granddaughter, so I asked to see her one last time, and she let me. But that's it."

"I don't buy it."

"It's the truth."

"We believe Marissa had her drink spiked. Gregg gave her the wine. Lo and behold, Marissa was out of it when Olivia was taken."

"This has nothing to do with me."

"Did you supply Gregg with the Rohypnol?"

"Rohypnol? Are you crazy?"

"No, the complete opposite, Ray. I'm following the evidence, and it all points to you and Gregg conspiring."

"Listen to me, you asshole. I spoke to Gregg, he said he was going to speak to Marissa. That was it. Then I was looking for my lousy son all night."

"But nobody can back that up?"

"Check my phone records—the GPS will show you where I was and where I wasn't." Ray dropped his phone on the desk and slid it across the surface. "Be my guest."

"Okay, Ray, let's just pretend that I think you're telling me the truth here. What was Gerry going to tell you?"

"That's the thing." Ray smashed the desk. "Because you grabbed me and brought me in here, I have no idea what he wanted to tell me."

CHAPTER FOURTEEN

Carter

At least the rain had stopped. The wind, though—that was another matter.

Carter peered inside Ray's Mercedes, still in the parking lot next to the strip club. Immaculate, like Ray had just driven it off the sales lot. Cream leather interior that must've cost a couple extra bucks. Or a couple thousand. Yeah, any way he looked at it, Ray Hill was loaded.

"Hey, buddy, you want to step away from that?" The club's doorman was walking over, hands stuffed in the pockets of his black bomber jacket.

But Carter just leaned back against the car, arms folded. "You Gerry?"

He got a shrug for his troubles. "Depends who's asking?"

"FBI's asking, Gerry." Carter unfolded his badge. "Special Agent Max Carter. Pleasure to meet you."

Gerry had the look of a man who wanted to run, but he seemed to realize that shifting his three-hundred-pound body down a back alley was not a good idea. "What do you want to know?"

"Talk to me about Ray Hill."

"Worked with the dude. SPD. He got his twenty, I… didn't."

"Why'd you leave, Gerry?"

"Being a cop wasn't for me, man."

"And running the door at a strip club is?"

"Sure. I make bank here. Run the door at three nightclubs too. Good money in it."

"Smart guy. So you hear about Ray's kid?"

"He mentioned it."

"What did he say?"

"Look, Frankie's sick, right? But Ray. Man, Ray was here, pleading with me, trying to find out what happened with his son."

"You know him?"

"Deacon, sure."

"How well?"

"We weren't close, exactly. Ray took us to a Seahawks game a couple times. He's got access to a box. Great view, as many hotdogs as you can eat. And beer."

"Sounds good."

"Swell, man. Could see everything too. Anyhoo, me and Deacon got chatting—we're about the same age, knew some of the same people."

"You ever see him again?"

"Nah, man. Just that and another game. Couldn't even tell you who the Seahawks were playing."

"You look like a football guy."

"Nah, I'm a hockey guy."

"So, these same people you and Deacon knew, that why you called Ray?"

"Kind of. Turns out one of the guys we know, Jimmy Yates, he worked at the deli I got my sandwich from one lunchtime. Went for a beer after his shift. He told me the last anyone heard of Deacon was he was with someone called Angry John."

"Angry John?"

"That's what he said. Jimmy thinks that's who killed Deac."

"Any idea who this Angry John might be?"

"Not on me. I was just going to pass it on."

"To Ray?"

"I was going to. Then you came, and the rest is history."

"Why didn't you go to the cops?"

"I, ah, might not be particularly welcome in those scenes…"

"So, this guy in the deli, Jimmy Yates, how—"

"Good luck finding him. He texted me this morning, said he was feeling the heat. Caught a bus out of town. Wouldn't say where he was headed neither."

"You know what kind of heat?"

"Guy like Jimmy? Could be anything, man."

Felt a lot like he was giving Carter the runaround. But Carter didn't have any grounds to make this any more formal. And Gerry was so tangential to this case.

Then again, he ran the door for nightclubs, seemed to know some shady folks. While he wasn't likely to be the party who had taken Olivia, given his huge bulk, he would sure know some people who could do that without blinking.

But Carter didn't have any direct line to Gerry. No real reason to think anything, just a suspicion.

"Is there anyone who knows about this Angry John?

"Look, I want to help you. I want to help Ray, but I just can't."

"Seriously?"

"Seriously, man." Gerry snorted. "Given how much shit Deacon was in, I imagine his wife might know."

CHAPTER FIFTEEN

Marissa

Marissa was sitting in a room with a kid who looked about twelve, but who wore the official windbreaker and aviators. The type who usually fetched coffee for the real agents, but every so often got to sit with a witness or guard a dog. Or certainly, that's how the TV shows she watched portrayed them. Even so, she felt trapped like a fly in a web. She was stuck in the mobile command center while the FBI combed every inch of her home, searching for evidence that she was involved.

That was it, wasn't it?

This was a prison, and they were going to frame her. She was stuck in here while Liv was… While she was… God damn it.

The door opened and Carter entered the room. He took the seat next to her. "Can you give us a minute?"

The junior agent got to his feet. "Sure I can't get you that cup o' joe, Marissa?"

"Sure." Marissa kept staring into space. "Thanks."

Carter waited for the door to shut, then focused on her with a searing intensity. "I've spoken to Ray. Gave us quite the tale."

"He's blaming me for this, isn't he?"

"Why would you think that?"

"It seems obvious."

"Marissa, Ray said you declined to let Olivia help Frankie."

"He what?" That lousy asshole. "You want to know what happened between us? Fine. When Deacon left, Ray cut us adrift. Ray has the means to help, to play a role in his granddaughter's life, but he didn't. And instead of asking me for help, he bribed a nurse or some lab tech? There's no way I am subjecting Liv to his bullshit."

"Even though it's a relatively minor procedure?"

The balls on this guy... Marissa returned his glare with similar intensity, or so she hoped. "You can go into the dentist with toothache, only to find you're having an aneurysm. There's no such thing as a minor procedure, especially if it involves a *needle piercing bone.*"

"You know what's going to happen to Frankie though."

Where did this asshole get off?

"I just can't..." Marissa slumped back on the sofa, wishing it could swallow her up and she would wake up again this morning and none of this had happened. "Look, I read about this on the internet, okay? There was this case in Florida where they missed the spot and severed a nerve, and now this kid is paralyzed below the waist. I can't take that risk with Liv. I know how hard it is for Ray and Zoe. I *know.* But Liv is all I have left, and I can't risk her health like that."

"Did you talk to Olivia about this?"

"How could I? She loved Frankie like a sister. She'd insist she got it done. And she's a child and it's my choice. I won't have her used for spare parts..."

"Did Gregg ever speak to you and try to persuade you?"

"A couple times. Why?"

"Marissa, we recently learned that Gregg wasn't at the school last night. He was meeting Ray to discuss—"

"That *asshole.*"

It physically hurt her. She felt it burning away like a candle on her skin. That betrayal of trust.

Lying.

Marissa had been on the receiving end of enough lies to last her six hundred lifetimes. She thought Gregg was one of the good guys. She thought she could trust him. She did trust him. And this was how he repaid that trust?

"You're angry with him?"

"Of course I am! I'm pissed! Gregg went behind my back to speak to Ray? God damn it."

"Did he ever—"

"Of course he did." Now she thought about it, it made the burning on her skin feel that much hotter. "Greg... He would try, try to get me to change my mind about it. Guilt trips about Frankie, about what Olivia would want. All that BS. What if something went wrong? How could any of us live with ourselves?"

"Marissa, Ray's in the field office right now, speaking to my agents."

"Did he take her?"

"It's one possibility. Do you think he could do it?"

"Honestly?" Marissa sucked in a deep breath. The burning sensation was worse, but she knew the only way to cool it down was with full honesty. "Yes. I do. I *know* Ray would take her to save Frankie. In a heartbeat."

"Do you think Gregg would help him?"

"I don't know. Clearly I'm not an expert on what Gregg would do." Marissa looked around the room, and it felt a little bit less like a prison cell. "I've been sitting in here for hours now. I can't do anything, other than tell cops and agents who my daughter might be in touch with. If Gregg was meeting Ray last night? It all makes sense, doesn't it? Gregg bought that wine. He opened it, then he got the call."

"You didn't tell us this before."

"Sorry. I just realized it. Gregg's OCD about letting wine breathe." Marissa squeezed her eyes shut. It all felt too raw right now. "All he had to do was drug my wine then take her out of the house and make it look like an abduction. Then Ray… Ray can take her marrow. And in some backstreet place where her safety isn't guaranteed."

"Ray told me he was here a few weeks back."

"Right."

"Slipped your mind, did it?"

"That was… I forgot. I was drugged, and I'm still barely holding it all together. I'm trying my best here, and the puzzle pieces are still all jumbled. Okay?"

"We found his DNA here. It would've been useful to know that."

"I'm trying. You try being your best after someone drugs you."

"Marissa, you forgot that you brought Ray here to tell him you weren't letting him have Olivia's bone marrow?"

"I just thought… I thought it was elsewhere. Or… I don't know. Things have been crazy recently. I just can't remember it."

"He was in her room long enough to leave a DNA trace."

"I let him see her. It was… It was my way of letting him down gently, you know? He could see her and…"

"Was she asleep?"

"She was."

"Okay."

She looked right at Carter. "You don't think he took her, do you?"

Carter shrugged. "The trouble is that Ray also said he's looking for his son."

"Why would he do that if he had Olivia?"

"It's a good cover, isn't it?"

"Does Ray think Deacon's still alive?"

"Says he's got a lead."

Marissa shook her head. "If Ray told me the sky was blue, I'd have to go outside and check."

"Ray says if he can find Deacon, maybe he'll be as good a donor as Olivia. The way I understand genetics, maybe he'll be better given they're half-siblings rather than aunt and niece."

"Look, people need to accept that Deacon is dead."

"Why do you insist that's the case?"

"Because I *know*. I just know."

"Talk to me."

Marissa sat back and stared up at the ceiling. This room had ceiling tiles just like at the school. "The reason we divorced is Deacon got into deep debt."

"What kind of debt?"

"What do you think? It wasn't to Wells Fargo."

"Gambling?"

"Drugs. Cocaine, heroin—you name it, he'd taken it. I didn't know, then one day... He told me we'd lost our house. Hadn't paid the mortgage in months. Lost our savings. I didn't know how bad it had got. He'd raided Liv's *college fund*. Who does that?"

Saying it all over again made it burn that much more.

Carter didn't seem to have any cut words for this level of honesty.

"I had to protect Liv, get her out of there. I moved out with Liv into my friend's house. Here. I was so lucky. Things have been tough. Bringing up a teenager on a high school teacher's salary is tough in this city. And she's a college-grade kid, so I'm trying to save for her to go. But I don't regret a thing. Deacon was toxic, and he was getting worse. He made sure the divorce was really hard on me. And it was worse on Liv. She idolized her dad, but he was a very flawed man. No way I could tell Liv about it."

"When did Olivia last see Deacon?"

"When we left."

"How old was Olivia?"

"Thirteen. I had to shut him out of her life. The divorce... He tried to get access, but I kept trying to block it. Liv suffered from depression afterwards; it was really tough on both of us. I had to watch her every night, worried she'd take her own life."

Saying these words out loud to someone other than her therapist, it made Marissa feel lighter than air, but it also made her feel wrung out, like a dirty cloth squeezed of all the water.

"That must've been tough."

"You have no idea." Marissa rubbed away the tears. "Liv blamed me for what happened. For the divorce. For everything. But she didn't know how bad he was. How much I protected her. I took Olivia to therapy, and it all cleared up. She became healthy again, but she still hates me."

Voices thundered from the hallway.

"Just a second." Carter walked over and opened the door.

A male agent stood there with Gregg. "I want to speak to her."

He was the last person she wanted to speak to, but Carter tilted his head to the side. "You mind giving us a few?"

"Sure." Gregg frowned, then the door shut again.

Carter took the armchair next to the sofa. "Marissa, we've been trying to track down Deacon."

"And I told you, he's dead."

"All the same, there are any number of reasons why—"

"Deacon is dead. He *can't* have taken Liv."

"Okay, but maybe someone connected to him has—"

"No!" Marissa sat back, arms folded, legs crossed. "I just…"

"Marissa, why do you believe he's dead?"

"Because there's a murder case against him? Because my lawyers paid a private investigator to track him down? He's dead."

Wait.

No…

Carter thought she had killed Deacon, didn't he?

"Look, I haven't seen him in a long time, okay? I didn't kill him, if that's what you're thinking."

"Marissa, nobody is accusing you of anything like that. Okay?"

She looked at him, and it at least looked like he didn't think she killed him. "Okay."

"But the thing is, Marissa, I can't help but wonder if Olivia's abduction doesn't have something to do with your husband's death."

She looked away from him.

"I get paid to ask the dumb questions, Marissa. You'd be surprised how frequently they yield me smart answers. Marissa, I don't believe that he was in debt to a drug dealer. And it's worse that you're lying to me while your daughter is missing."

"I'm not lying!"

But Carter just sat there, playing dumb. She knew what he was doing, but her anger was rising in her throat.

Such an asshole. Marissa should speak to his boss. But that wouldn't bring Olivia back, would it?

"I want to find Olivia, Marissa. If your husband was in debt to people involved with the drug trade, then there's no limit to what they'd do to recover their debt. Even after they kill him. A big-enough debt, they'd definitely consider kidnapping Olivia. Why? Well, they can extort Ray's family. He's rich, right?"

"Ray wouldn't pay..."

"Sure about that?"

But she didn't have an answer. Ray was a law unto himself.

"Marissa, you've got to help me here. As hard as this is, if Olivia's disappearance relates in any way to your husband, you need to talk to me."

"I have been, and that's all I know. As soon as I found out about it, I severed all ties. Got my daughter away from him."

"You got a name for his dealer?"

"Nope."

"What about Angry John?"

"Angry John? What?"

"That means nothing to you?"

"No. And I still feel like you think I killed him."

"No, it's just… Most drug dealers wouldn't let a user build up a week's debt, let alone enough to lose your house over. And I know your house was a big place."

"My house?"

"A colleague visited your old family home and spoke to the current owner."

"I loved that house. Thought I'd grow old there. Thought Liv would take it from us, raise her kids. But that asshole—"

"The current owner said the home was foreclosed? That means a mortgage." Carter was frowning again. "Deacon was a moving man. How could he afford to buy a home like that?"

"Deacon's family is rich. Like you already know." Marissa brushed some tears from her eyes. "Okay, so Ray gave us some money towards a deposit, but we had to get a mortgage. Turns out Deacon had remortgaged it behind my back."

"It takes both parties to—"

"The mortgage was in his name. Our marriage was complicated. Then we lost the place and all my savings were gone. A whole life's worth, gone. On his goddamn drugs."

"You know anyone who might know who this Angry John is?"

"Listen, Deacon was a teacher at the same school as me. He lost his job when the principal found out what he was up to…"

CHAPTER SIXTEEN

Carter

For a day of such urgency, Carter was finding it full of waiting. Another room, another no-show.

He looked out of the principal's office across the parking lot, crammed full. The teachers had their mature sedans near to the school building, while the student lot held mostly beat-up scrap that could barely pass inspection. But, it being Seattle, there were a couple in the students' section that looked like they cost a bomb. Sports cars that belonged in the parking lot of a start-up that had just vested.

He got out his cell and tried Elisha's number. He was glad *someone* was picking up his calls. "You getting anything on Jimmy Yates?"

"Just been with his supervisor at the deli. Gerry's tale checks out."

"So he's cut and run?"

"Sounds like Jimmy Yates has been dealing to customers. SPD caught wind of it, tried to implicate the owner, but she isn't involved. Meanwhile, Jimmy's bolted and she's no idea where he's gone."

The door clattered open behind him. "Sorry about the wait."

"Better go." Carter ended the call and turned around.

Iona Harrison crunched into her office chair with all the weight of a woman who had no time for this. "Hell of a day."

"Know the feeling." Carter didn't take the offered seat, just stood by the window. Despite the earlier rain, it was bright enough that looking at his silhouette would irritate Iona. "So. It turns out there's something you've been hiding from us."

"Listen, I want to find Olivia as much as you do, but I don't have the time to play games with you."

Carter felt that tingling in his wrists, the fire building up. "Why didn't you tell me that Deacon Hill was a teacher here?"

"That's in the past. Why is it relevant?"

"Because his daughter has been kidnapped."

"So? I'm an educator, how do I know what you need to know in an investigation?"

The tingling became full-on fire. Rage burnt at his arms and neck. "You've got a duty of care to your students here. If one of your teachers is—"

"What the hell is this about?"

Carter took a deep breath, swallowed down his anger. Snapping at her wasn't going to find Olivia. Sure, someone needed to investigate this place, but that wasn't Carter's responsibility. "I'm guessing that you found out about Deacon's drug use and you asked him to resign?"

She wouldn't look at him. Couldn't. "Listen, you don't know what you're talking about."

"Try me."

"I suggest you try finding Olivia Davis and don't—"

"You know what happened to him, don't you?"

She shook her head. "Mr. Carter, this is a tough school, and I didn't want any blowback on the hard work me and my team are doing just because a douchebag teacher was bumping coke."

"That must've been a lot of cocaine to lose his home over."

"As far as I know, it was everything. Grass, X, coke, heroin, meth."

"Did you know about his debt?"

Her head dipped low, and she took a deep breath.

"It's possible the drug suppliers Deacon ripped off are extorting the family for Olivia's safe return. They don't care if Deacon is alive or dead, they just want their money back. Whatever it takes." Carter let it sink in, tried to watch for any telltale cracks. "It's also possible that her abduction has nothing to do with that, but it could. I need you to work with me here."

"Whatever, just whatever."

"Whatever?" Carter was shouting now. That instinctive bark that he struggled to control, that deep connection with his trauma. He clenched his jaw and tried to control his feelings. "Deacon Hill's daughter is missing. That's not a whatever. That's a lead I need to trace and get right to the bottom of."

Iona dipped her head, eyes shut. "How can I help?"

Carter chose that moment to take the seat in front of her. He had broken her down now. "Look, I need to know the full story about Deacon's drug use."

"It wasn't just drug use." Iona stared at the floor, then the door, then up at the ceiling again. Anywhere but at Carter. "The way I've heard it, and this is from stuff I've pieced together from speaking to staff members, is that Deacon's dealer ripped off his own supplier. He stole another guy's stash, and they split it. Deacon was dealing to schoolteachers, parents, kids, you name it."

Stealing the supply, dealing to teachers and parents. The whole nine yards. That all made sense to Carter. But something else didn't add up. "So you just fired him?"

"Deacon went quietly. His descent afterwards wasn't my fault."

"You hushed it up, didn't you?"

"What?"

"A teacher smacked out of his head, dealing to parents and other teachers. You covered it up. Why didn't you take it to the police?"

"That wasn't my place to."

"Okay. I've got buddies in the DEA. They can be in here like a shot."

"But I stopped it! Deacon was one bad apple!"

"Dealing heroin and cocaine to students, teachers, and parents? Come on."

"I don't appreciate being threatened."

"Well, you tell me what you know and, *maybe*, I can find Olivia before it's too late. I'm looking to speak to his supplier. Or his dealer."

"I wish I could help you. Really, I do."

"I believe the dealer goes by the name of Angry John."

"Angry John? Couldn't you be more imaginative?"

"I play the cards I get dealt. Did that come up during your investigation?"

"There wasn't an investigation. Deacon just kept quiet. Didn't say anything to me. Wrote out his resignation letter by hand right in this room, signed it, and walked out the door. Last I saw of him."

"So all this about you stamping out the drug problem in this school is just hot air?"

"You can never stamp it out. It comes and goes in waves. Right now, we're in a good place. Grades are up, don't have street dealers hanging around nearby."

Carter wished he could reassure him. He pitied the poor kids who attended, and the poor parents who trusted her. "Is there anyone here who was close to him, who might've known Angry John?"

Iona turned and looked right at him. "Well, there's someone."

CHAPTER SEVENTEEN

Carter

Carter walked through the school past the long walls of lockers. Felt like just yesterday he would have been storing his books in one. Probably a lot of drugs in them these days. He hit dial, put his cell to his ear, and carried on.

"Sir?" Tyler sounded breathless. "What's up?"

"I didn't see you in the mobile command center back at—"

"Sorry, sir, I've been hella busy." Where had he picked that up from? Kept on using it. "What's up?"

"Need an update on Olivia's cellphone and laptop."

"Okay..." Tyler paused. Sounded like he was climbing a stairwell somewhere. Probably at the field office. "The honest truth, sir, is that I'm struggling with both."

Carter had to wait for a pair of teachers to come in through the door at the end of the corridor. He had to ease their frowns with a flash of his badge. Whether they were the kind of teachers who had been buying from Deacon Hill, well, that was someone else's issue. "Thought you were brute forcing the laptop's security?"

"I did. But it's on the latest version, so they've fixed the bug I was trying to exploit."

"You're such a hacker, Peterson." Carter passed through the door and caught a mix of perfume and secondhand cigarette smoke. Hard to believe anyone still smoked in this age of vape sticks. He set off toward the parking lot. "You got a timeline?"

"You want me to bore you with the details, because it's complicated?"

There it was again. He needed to have a word, when things were less complicated. "Just give me a timeline."

"Could be hours, sir."

With all the possible threads, all the possible explanations that Carter was juggling, homing in on the actual reason for Olivia's abduction would be made a ton easier by having access to her cellphone. "Can you prioritize her cell for me?"

"Will do."

"Thanks, Tyler." Carter ended the call. That kid was one of his best agents, but the trouble was he knew it. All the times he had saved Carter's ass with something straight out of left field. Well, Tyler knew it, and he wanted to climb the greasy pole.

Speaking of left field, the baseball diamond was empty. But there was noise coming from behind the bleachers.

Carter left the parking lot and climbed the steps. At the top, he saw the girls' soccer team in the middle of a drill, split into teams of red and blue.

Halfway along the bleachers facing the soccer field, Gregg Ingram sat on his own, looking out. Hands clamped to his thighs, his face twisted in concentration.

Carter sat down alongside him. "Thought you'd be out on the field with them?"

Gregg did not even look over. "You follow soccer?"

"Not my game. I was born in England, so—"

"Seriously?"

"Seriously. My dad… brought me over here. And you'd think I'd be all over soccer, but a combination of growing up stateside and my father's love of it turned me away from the sport."

"Well. Soccer's a tough game to master, and so different from other sports. They're all stop-start, maybe with the exception of basketball, but even then. All those time-outs? Give me a break.

And hockey, I guess, but who cares about that?" Gregg motioned his hand to the twenty-two teenage girls lined up across the grass. "Soccer's free flowing for the most part. See how they're lining up in three banks. Well, four if you count the goalkeepers."

Carter could kind of see the pattern. Both sides had four girls guarding the goals at either end from two attackers, with eight in the middle split fifty-fifty fighting over the ball.

And it was sure dirty. One girl in blue slid in to take the ball and an opponent's legs. The referee blew her whistle and held up a hand, pointing to where Carter thought the blue team's goal was.

"If I sit up here, it lets me see how well they're adhering to the formation." Gregg chopped his hand in three motions, each one taking in a particular cut of the field. "This is a four-four-two. They don't use it so much in Europe, but I like it at this level." He pointed at the girl nearest to them. "Shania there, the left back, see how she's too deep?"

Carter could. Maybe three feet behind the line kept by her three teammates. And it was the girl he had spoken to earlier, Olivia's classmate. She looked very different on the sports field, her hair tied back in a ponytail.

Gregg picked up a notebook and wrote something down. "The girls in blue are the first team, and they're playing down in Olympia next week. I need to have a word with Shania and get her to push up." He put his notebook down. "I take it you're no closer to finding Olivia?"

Carter watched one of the midfielders launch a diagonal ball toward them, but it angled down quickly and Shania, the defender Gregg was so interested in, intercepted it and started a lung-busting run down this side of the field. "Not yet."

"How's Marissa?"

"She's not in a good place, I'd say. A mixture of guilt and fear. We're doing the best we can to recover Olivia, but sometimes it's not enough."

"I hear you." Gregg stood up and cupped his hands together. "SHANIA, GO ON!"

On the field, she clipped in a cross toward the two attackers, but the goalkeeper snatched it out of the air like a basketball player. One fluid motion and she launched the ball back upfield.

"You see?" Gregg was jabbing a finger at the field. "Now she's out of position there."

Shania was rushing back, but a teammate had dropped back to cover her.

"Back at work. You seem to be taking this well."

"I'm distracting myself is what I'm doing." Gregg sat back down with a sigh. "I got a text. Marissa says it's over."

"She say why?"

"Oh yeah. She found out about me meeting Ray last night." Gregg shook his head. "I know I should've told her, but I was just trying to help, trying to do the right thing. Frankie's a good kid. I'm not saying Marissa's overreacting, it's her right to refuse, it's just... disappointing."

"I understand."

"Why are you here?"

"I was just speaking to your principal. She said you and Deacon were close."

"We were."

"Funny thing is, I'm only finding out now about how he was a teacher here. And I've only just found out about the drugs. You want to talk to me about either?"

"I told Iona she should go to the cops about it. Only way to eradicate the scourge from here."

"Even though that would've put Deacon in jail?"

"Sure. Least he deserved, for what he did."

"And what did he do?"

"It's more what he didn't do. I thought for months he was off his game, but he insisted it was just some bug they'd picked up on their vacation to Aruba last summer. But he just kept getting worse and worse. And then, I started hearing stories about him."

"What kind of stories?"

"About him dealing drugs. I mean, taking them, sure, that was one thing. Who hasn't smoked some pot, right?"

"How did he get into dealing?"

"Hard to say. It's not something we talked about."

"You know who the dealer he was working with is?"

"Deacon and I weren't friends like that. Go for a beer, talk about the game, sure. But he didn't talk to me about his drug deals. God."

Carter's cell rang. Tyler calling... "Need to take this." He stepped away to answer it. "Shoot."

"I'm assuming you're with someone, sir, so I'll make it brief. I've got access to her cellphone."

"Good work, Peterson."

"Hella lucky, sir. She used a *basic* passcode. Thought I'd try it and, bingo, got in."

"What have you found?"

"Just working through it, sir. Most of it seems to check out, but she barely used it for calls and texts. Lots of internet searches, but mostly stuff for homework and some stuff about K-pop."

So, Olivia had the usage of a teenage nerd. Swap the K-pop for *Star Trek*, and that could've described Carter back in the day.

"Thanks, Tyler." Carter killed the call and sat down. Part of him hoped that Tyler would've found some smoking gun, some string of texts between Olivia and Gregg, or maybe to her grandfather or to Frankie. But no, he had nothing. So far.

Carter still had some sick feeling about Gregg, that he was grooming Olivia. Who knew how far it had gone? Dad was a buddy, so he must've known her for years. Then Deacon was out of the picture, he could move in. Still, it wasn't concrete. Not yet.

"So, I gather Deacon was working with someone called Angry John."

Gregg looked over at him, frowning. "Angry John?"

"That mean something to you?"

"Pete Wasilewski." Gregg waved a hand at the sports field. "He was a student here, good football player—a running back—but got busted for drugs."

"Know where I can find him?"

CHAPTER EIGHTEEN

Lori

Lori found it strange to be interrogating Max Carter's father in the room Max himself liked to use.

Sometime in the recent past, the clock on the wall facing the door had developed an irritating click. Not too loud, and it didn't seem to have a repeating pattern, at least not a solid one. It felt like it was into a cycle, then it would change, which made it even more irritating.

While Max seemed to be able to block it out, anyone he brought into this room never could, and he had fought tooth and nail with Karen Nguyen about replacing it.

Lori wanted to grab it off the wall and smash her boot heel into it. But she sat back and tried to ignore it, tried to focus on the body language, because there was none of the verbal kind happening.

King was next to her, body forward, head up, sitting still like a statue, but with the open posture that encouraged speaking. His nose in profile was slightly larger than she had expected and showed the kind of kinks you got from having it broken a few times. She knew the way the police department worked over there, how he would have joined up as a beat cop, then transferred over to being a detective. Tough way up, but it would have its benefits. "There's nothing to be gained from keeping quiet."

Bill Carter sat under the ticking clock, his liver-spotted hands splayed on the table, his oversized thumbs scratching at the wood. He looked up at Lori like he was pleading with his son's colleague to stop this. His shriveled-up face was all twisted, but Lori couldn't tell if it was from guilt, shame, or anger. His dull eyes, hidden behind glasses, didn't give much away. His hair had grown back since Lori had last seen him, though Carter had not told her whether that was from his chemo successfully ending, or just slowing. "I don't know what you want me to say." His London accent was usually hidden behind the softer Seattle, but being in a row with a fellow Londoner had somehow brought it back out into the light.

King sighed and it sounded wearier than just from a long flight from the UK. "I've just stepped off a plane from Heathrow. I suspect you know how long that takes, yeah?"

Bill kept scratching the wood.

King held up his hands in apology. "Actually, you wouldn't, would you? You don't take normal airlines, Bill. You've got mates with private jets. Right?"

"Ain't a crime."

"Not saying it is, mate."

"Son, I don't know what you're expecting me to say here. If you write it all down, how about I read it out loud, then you can get on the next flight back to London?"

"This isn't that simple."

Something in Bill's frown struck Lori as strange. Up to now, he had been humoring them, playing along. Being his usual jovial self. But that frown betrayed some inner turmoil. "I see."

"I really hope you do, Mr. Carter."

"Listen to me, you little prick." Bill sat back and stuffed his hands into his pockets. "I've been honest and open with my son about… about what I did. I'm here voluntarily. So if you don't stop all this macho bollocks, then I'm out of here. You understand me?"

King nodded, but he was smiling too. "Let's get down to brass tacks with this." He sat back, mirroring Bill's body language, hands in pockets, head tilted to the side. "You paid for a hit on your ex-wife to stop her going through the courts to try and return your son to London."

"I've been through this with my boy. We've come to an understanding over it. I did what I had to."

"Huh."

"Huh, what?"

"What you had to." King snorted. "It's not just about you, Mr. Carter, it's about a lot of parents. A lot of kids. A lot of other parents. Mothers and fathers in England separated from their children by an ocean and all those states."

"This is bollocks."

"Do you remember the name of the assassin you paid to kill your ex-wife?"

"I didn't pay any assassin, son. And whatever you think happened, it was a different time. It was all legit, least as far as I'm concerned. And as far as my lawyers in this country are concerned."

"The man who killed your ex-wife, Mr. Carter, you know that he died a couple of years ago. It's why I'm here. We've spent a long time unpicking the evidence, getting to the bottom of it all. I'm here to investigate a few similar cases to yours, Bill, people who paid these men to bring their kids over here. Like you did with Max."

"You've got nothing on me."

"No. You paid a fee to the men who brought Max here to make sure your ex-wife's court battle went away, didn't you?"

"It all went through my lawyers, son."

"So your law firm arranged this accident?"

Bill shrugged, but he had the air of a man who thought he was untouchable. "It was a tragedy, sure, but it was an accident. And I can't be held responsible for what happened. I was here in Seattle when she died in London."

"Your son was taken from the only home he knew to a new life on the other side of the world. No friends, no relatives. Then a while later, his mother died. Could be an accident, could be a hit. Either way, he grieved for her. He never saw her again."

"Listen, my son's an FBI agent." Bill pointed a large thumb in Lori's direction. "Works with her here, rescuing abducted kids."

"Interesting, isn't it?"

"What is?"

"How Special Agent Alves here was assigned to be my shadow on the Seattle leg of my North American tour."

Bill sat still in the silence, his gaze switching between them. "What's that supposed to mean?"

"It's not sinking in, is it?" King chuckled, but it looked pained to Lori. "Mr. Carter, it's not just you I'm speaking to. I'll be here in the United States for a couple of weeks at least. Got a lot of work to do, sharing my time between federal agents like your son and with local law enforcement, as necessary. As far as we know, there are others who were taken from London to this country. Five in the Pacific Northwest, seven in California. All of them left behind tragedies. Murders, usually. Gangland hits."

"I don't know anything about that."

King leaned forward, casting a dark shadow across the table. "Mr. Carter, the worst part of this is that the people you paid to bring Max to this country are still operating."

Lori felt a jolt in her gut. All this time, she had been helping Max deal with this, including using her old contacts to dig into the past in London. But she had thought it was ancient history.

Bill sat back again. He was sweating now, betraying some fear at what might come of all this. Until now, he'd been all bluff and bluster, but this derailed his strategy. If it was still an ongoing concern, then there were witnesses, records maybe. People who would talk in exchange for some leniency. "Let's cut the crap, yeah? What do you want to know?"

"I just want to know what happened, Bill. If you tell me everything, I can add that to the picture I have of their operation.

Because there are other kids going through the same trauma as your son. Not all of them will be okay. Not all of them will be high-functioning FBI agents. Most will have suffered some loss as a result of this."

"My boy hasn't suffered! I gave him everything he needed!"

"I've flown thousands of miles to argue with whatever delusions you tell yourself to help you sleep at night. Believe me, every kid in that situation suffers. No question." King paused, waiting for Bill to look at him. "Now, I haven't met him and, while Max might be an FBI agent, the very fact he's out there rescuing abducted kids shows he hasn't healed from this. He's reliving his own trauma. I'm asking for your help here, Bill."

Bill looked over at Lori and she saw the glistening in his eyes. King was getting through to him, and it was hurting him. "Okay, I'll help."

"Good." King was nodding. "First, you're going to tell us precisely what happened, then you're going to show us. Where you met these people, where you paid, where you collected Max from."

I get out of the car and the place is like something out of a film. A fancy airport, but not busy like when I went to Majorca with Mummy, just the two of us. Mummy bought a tea towel that was spelled Mallorca, and I still don't know if that's a different place from Majorca. There's a Minorca, so maybe it is different. I just don't know.

But it isn't busy like when we flew from Heathrow. There's nobody around. And it's so quiet. Just me and Uncle John.

"Where's Mummy?"

"She's on the plane, son, waiting for us. She's got a special treat for you."

I don't like this, but I need to pee, so everything feels odd. Stressful. "I need the toilet."

"There's a toilet on the plane." Uncle John's holding out a hand. "Come on, you should taste the hot chocolate. It's to die for."

CHAPTER NINETEEN

Carter

"Earth to Max."

Carter opened his eyes and blinked away the harsh sunlight, then looked over at Elisha as she opened her door. "Huh?"

"Looked like you were having a little nap there."

"Something like that." Carter hadn't even noticed her pulling up. He let his seatbelt go and opened his own door, but didn't get out immediately. His daydream still lingered with him. Made him want to call Lori or Bill.

No, he needed to do his job. Find Olivia.

He settled for texting Lori. *How's it going with Bill? Anything I should know about?*

Carter hopped out of the SUV and looked over, relieved to see that Ray Hill's Mercedes had been driven away from the strip club, even though he was still in custody at the field office. One good use of a beat cop, though he expected some blowback on him for it.

"It's needling you, isn't it?" Elisha led over to the entrance.

Carter felt the deep bass thudding out of the strip club's basement through his feet. Like a heartbeat, but the echo was slightly off. "What is?"

"The fact that Ray hadn't been honest with you."

"Don't give up the day job." But she was right. Ray had been hiding information from them. Stuff he knew, but maybe didn't expect anyone else to. But Gregg did.

Carter needed to cast all that aside and focus on the here and now.

"My friend, you got a real taste for this place, huh?" The doorman took a look at Carter, then at Elisha, then back at Carter. "And bringing the little lady here? Mm hmm."

"You know we're federal agents, Gerry."

"You ain't the first feds I had in here today. Won't be the last, either. Some just can't get enough of my girls, know what I'm saying?"

"Know full well." Elisha gave him a sly look. "Looking for Pete Wasilewski."

"Huh."

"Come on, Gerry, don't dick us around. We know he's working in the kitchen here and we know he's on shift."

Gerry got out a fancy cellphone and tapped the screen, then frowned. "He's on a smoke break." He pointed back into the parking lot, then stepped away from them, returning to his door.

Elisha led the way. "Guy gives me the creeps."

"He'd say he's just doing his job."

"Yeah, wish that job wasn't exploiting people though."

Carter followed the column of blue smoke to a recess in the brick wall.

A man stood there talking into a cellphone, cigarette perched carefully between thumb and two fingers, sucking deep. Sure matched the description of Angry John. Pete Wasilewski. Tattoos climbed his neck, a pair of dragons fighting in the clouds. He looked their way, and Carter saw it in his eyes.

That fear.

That guilt.

Wasilewski was like a wolverine, or just a wolf. Had a real nasty look about him, that way of looking at the world you only got from one too many prison showers. And he looked fast, too, like he could outrun Elisha in a block, Carter in half. "Got to go, Emilio." He nodded at them as he pocketed his cell. Deep in the pocket too, like he was protecting it from damage during an unplanned run. "Whassup?"

Elisha held out her shield. "Looking for Pete Wasilewski."

"That's me."

"Hear you work the kitchen here?"

"I wash dishes, if that's what you mean. Dudes that come to this joint like to eat their chicken wings off porcelain, know what I'm saying?"

"I hear you."

Wasilewski blew smoke out of his nostrils. He held his cigarette like he was going to flick it. Hot ash in the eye would only take out one of them though. "What's this about?"

"FBI, sir. Investigating a child abduction."

"Girl or boy?"

"Why do you ask?"

"Well, if it's a boy, he ain't working here."

"It's not, but thanks anyway."

And there it was again, that nervous twitch that could signal a run.

Carter stepped forward, hands up. "Just want to ask you a few questions, that's all."

"Never just a few questions."

"Promise."

Wasilewski's eyes shot around the parking lot. Blocked off on one side by new office buildings, but open to First on the other side. Clear run into Pike Place, and Carter knew from bitter experience that the market was a rabbit warren.

Carter fixed him with a stare. "I know you want to run, sir, but I recommend you don't. For one, I suspect your employer either doesn't know about your recent history, doesn't care, or, most likely, doesn't want any more heat placed on them. Either way, you'll lose your job. And that'll be tough for you, Pete. You're just out of jail, trying to go straight. You've got a job and you're putting all those drug deals behind you. Be a shame to lose that over a simple misunderstanding, wouldn't it?"

Wasilewski took a deep suck on his smoke. "What do you want to know?"

"Deacon Hill."

"Him." A long slow smoky hiss. "Dude's bad news."

"His kid is the one who's been taken."

"Shit. Olivia? Seriously?"

"Know where we can find him?"

"Dude's dead, man. Keep telling his old man."

"Ray's been here?"

"Well, he ain't here for the chicken wings or the pussy." Wasilewski tilted his head to Elisha. "No offense, ma'am."

"None taken." Some frost in her eyes though. "You know anything about his son's death?"

"Just that Deac's dead. And I was inside when it happened, before you ask me."

"You want to tell us about it?"

Another flash of that fight-or-flight instinct, but Wasilewski just took another drag. "Deacon seemed like a good guy, okay? He was one of my teachers at school. Then he heard I was dealing to other students, okay? And I was trapped, man. He could've taken me to the cops, or whatever. Instead he got me to supply to him. Coke at first, then heroin. Man, never trust addicts."

"Why didn't *you* go to the cops about him? Maybe to the principal?"

"Who they going to believe? Me or him? I'm clean now, but I was using my own supply. Nobody's going to believe a junkie."

"Worth a shot, surely? Especially if you felt trapped."

"Man, Deac was part of this drug taskforce at the school. I mean, how messed up is that? Dude was smoking H, man. Next minute, he's meeting the cops, telling them all kinds of noise about how they're cutting drugs from the school."

"That how you ended up inside?"

"Nah, man. My supplier, Vic Jordan. He... What happened was, I knew these other dealers who worked for him, okay? Knew where their stash was. Me and Deac stole it. Used his taskforce contacts to make it look like the feds had taken all of it, but we had like 95 percent of it. Lot of crack, lot of smack, lot of coke. And pills too. So Deac knew teachers, students, parents even who were after some stuff. And he started dealing too. Deac was smart, got me to do all the action while he filmed it. Anyone ratted to the cops, their life was over too."

"So how did you get caught?"

"Let me tell you a little story. When I was inside, I studied economics, high school level, but one thing they teach is supply and demand. So Vic, he had the supply to that school, that neighborhood, all sewn up. Then we start meeting that demand with another supply, and the demand goes down. And it ain't due to the Seattle PD taskforce, let me tell you. Vic figured out that we ripped off the stash, and he screwed us both over."

"They caught you though?"

"Nah, man. I ended up inside for some other shit I did for Vic. Had me kicking in doors and teeth to get back his bad debts, man. Got caught. Eighteen months inside, now I'm out and I ain't going back."

"Did they catch Deacon?"

"Nah. Someone like Vic Jordan, when you take a hundred grand's worth of drugs, they notice, and they hold it against you. Trouble is Deacon used his own product and made deals with people while he was high, so how do you recover what you fronted when you don't know who you sold it to? Plus the mystique cuts both ways, he can't go to the cops and he doesn't exactly have his own crew to lean on people. So largely everyone ignored him and the debt grew. Vic wanted every cent back, and his interest was steep. Deac emptied his savings account, took out a second mortgage, but still wasn't any closer to paying it off."

It backed up Marissa's story, for sure, but it also backed up one of the many theories nailing Carter's skull. That this supplier, Vic Jordan, this drug kingpin, had taken Olivia to extort the debt out of Ray's family. Forget about bone marrow transplants, it also made sense that Ray would be hunting Vic Jordan down to rescue his granddaughter.

But Wasilewski was not finished yet. "When I was inside, I heard Deac was doing well. Straightened up, got another job. Deac and Vic came to an arrangement. Pay it off real slow, man, but he lost his house to the bank. That pissed off Vic, so Vic started asking for more, but he couldn't. Then Deac got angry, man, and thought he could take out Vic, kill him and clear his debt. So Vic broke his legs. Deac lost his job, then spiraled out of control, man. On that real death kick. Heard about it a lot inside, man—dudes getting stronger and stronger doses of heroin, inching closer to death each time. Heard Deac died. Overdose."

"This what Ray wanted to speak to you about?"

"Beats me, man. Haven't heard from him in a long-ass time."

"But you told Gerry?"

"Sure."

"You know where we can find Vic Jordan?"

"Man, that's all I heard. Keeping myself clear of dudes like Vic."

"But you still hear from people, right?"

"Shit, man. Heard he lives in the Jungle."

A place Carter hadn't heard of in a long time. A tent city in the Seattle greenbelt, full of unfortunate homeless people, but also gangsters who wanted to leave no trails. "That's shut down though?"

"This is like the New Jungle? A mile from the old place."

CHAPTER TWENTY

Carter

Pete Wasilewski was right. In among the crossover between interstates I-5 and I-90 was a greenbelt, a buffer zone between the freeway and the homes, newish places that had been put up in the last decade at most. An expected consequence of town planning, when nobody expected a small city like Seattle, stuck as far from DC and NYC as you could get, to become a sprawling metropolis.

But calling it a jungle was not right either. In other cities, this would be a park, like Central Park in Manhattan. The rattle and drone of the heavy overhead traffic on the freeway could be drowned out by fancy headphones, the music's tempo matching a jogging pace.

But the tents were hard to ignore. Even at this time, they were still occupied, pairs of feet poking out, covered in sores and wounds. A lifetime spent on your feet was no fun, despite what some people thought.

Sergeant Ricky Johnson led a small team of guardians. SPD's finest, two bulky men and two women with fierce looks. Johnson looked at Carter as he caught up. "That poor woman. Think we'll find her kid?"

Carter didn't know, but he'd do everything he could to find out as much as possible. "Your guys haven't found anything in the neighborhood, right?"

Johnson shook his head. "It's like nailing Jell-O to the wall, but you're using chocolate nails."

Carter gave him a smile. "Whatever happens, we'll do our best to find her."

"Over there." Johnson was pointing through the forest, but didn't seem to want to follow his own direction. "But we don't call it the New Jungle. It's the Triangle. On a map, the interstate interchange is like a triangle."

"Come on, then." Carter set off, but Johnson didn't follow. He stopped and swung around.

"I was stationed here when the sweeps were going on two years ago." Fear swelled in Johnson's eyes looking up at the mess of freeways and train bridges towering over the trees. "Every day we had reports of gunfire and drug abuse, then we got support. Big squad of cops and feds of all stripes descended. We found this large tent in the middle. Dudes were selling crack, meth, heroin. You name it. Seven arrests, all on arraignment."

"Good work."

"But they're still there, still selling, just different dudes now." Johnson stomped off along the path, clutching his belt tight. Whether he was reaching for his gun or his baton first wasn't clear.

Carter got a knowing flash of Elisha's eyebrows before she set off along the path after Johnson. A thin curving line of asphalt covered in twigs and leaves, but with a heavy enough footfall to prevent much overgrowth. And the farther he progressed, the fewer tents there were. He would have expected the reverse, some sort of aggregation effect.

The path led around to the right, following the arc of I-95 above their heads, but Johnson led them left through a clearing.

Carter smelled smoke, and sure enough, some homeless people huddled around a brazier, toasting their hands. Poor souls.

Johnson bowed his head as they neared, showing no malice, and soon passed by without incident, just concerned looks and low chatter.

The traffic drone got louder, now punctuated by blasts of horn, but Carter started to feel the throb of deep bass, just like back at the downtown strip club. The trees hid its source, but he could smell roasting meat. Beef, and heavily spiced.

Johnson pulled a tree branch out of the way.

In the middle of a clearing, almost directly under the interchange, was a large pavilion tent. Beige material, but not the kind you would see at any Seattle wedding during the outdoor months. Much more of a military thing, like Carter had slept in on duty in Iraq and Afghanistan. Either way, it was big enough to host a good-sized event.

A man worked at a barbecue, grilling some steaks and burgers. His beard was long enough for any hipster and was dangling low enough that it could catch.

A woman wearing a kaftan, with beads in her hair, tossed some fish onto the fire.

The music was louder here too, drowning out the din of a diesel generator. The lazy roll of dub techno, a constant heartbeat with swooshes of melody hidden under atmospheric noise.

Didn't seem to be too bad a place, certainly nothing like what Carter had expected from Johnson's fear. More a hippie commune than a drug den.

The woman waved at them with the cheery smile of someone high on ecstasy. "Hey guys!"

The man looked at them with vacant eyes—Carter could now see he was skin and bone, the physique of a long-term junkie. "You guys hungry? We got enough food to go around." His voice sounded alive though.

Johnson led Carter over. Inside the pavilion, it looked like a kitchen—big hot plates steaming against the far wall, with the smell of Indian curry catching on the breeze. The rest was a bedroom with sleeping bags all over the floor, most of them empty. And boy, the food sure smelled good. "Sir, we need to speak to Vic Jordan."

The bearded man smiled at them, his eyes full of delusional love. "Vic held us under a spell, my friend. Under the iron boot of hate. But he is no longer here."

Johnson bit his lip, looking at Carter.

Carter took it as an opportunity to take over. "Sir, we needed to speak to him in relation to a possible child abduction."

The man frowned. "You should speak to The Savior. He will enlighten you."

"Who is The Savior?"

The hipster pointed inside the tent. "The Savior is guiding a meditation. He won't mind if you interrupt."

Carter smiled at the man, but he could not figure out how drug dealers were now involved in meditation. He followed Johnson through the tent flap.

A big ring of people sat on the floor cross-legged, hands on either side at head height, thumbs touching forefingers.

In the middle, a big man in his mid-forties was talking in a low, soothing voice, his eyes closed. "Hold on to that ball of light in the pit of your stomach." Shaved head, with a bushy beard streaked with white. "Now imagine the ball of light expanding out, further, wider, until it's at the size of the Earth's orbit around the sun." He opened his eyes, and his gaze lashed across Johnson and Carter like a whip. He eased himself up to standing, then shook an acolyte sitting next to him, and got a nod in return.

Carter followed The Savior back out into the smoky air.

Now that he wasn't meditating, The Savior looked a lot more earthbound and less spiritual, like he had lived a hard life, and he gazed at them with bloodshot eyes. "How can I help, my friends?"

Johnson stood in a standard cop pose, chest puffed out, holding the top of his soft body armor. "Place has changed a lot since I was last here."

The Savior nodded at Johnson. "I owe you a debt of gratitude, my friend. You cleared out the worst of our problems for us. Gangbangers, you got to love 'em." He bared his teeth. "Dealing drugs here in the forest, a place of enlightenment and enchantment. Of growth. Of spiritual prosperity."

Carter took control of the situation. "We're looking for Vic Jordan."

"Well, you're too late for him." The Savior smiled with the same dead-eyed love as the hipster. "Vic used to live here, but he's gone."

"Where is he?"

"Our group is called the Limbs. Arms and legs cast off by modern society. *They* call me The Savior. It's not a self-given title. And I know what you're thinking. You're wondering why tree-hugging hippies are cooking beef, aren't you?"

Carter frowned. "No, sir. I just want to speak to Vic Jordan."

"We're an omnivorous society here, my friend. We're trying to live a hunter-gatherer diet. Not that we hunt much around here, but sometimes we find meat that the modern consumer deems unfit for their consumption. An animal has died for their sustenance, and to throw it away is entirely wrong. So we cook it all up ourselves." He picked up a fork and pressed it into the beef sizzling on the grill. "Nothing is wasted."

"A noble aim. The reason we're here is related to a needless death though. The death of Deacon Hill."

The Savior laughed.

"Why's that so funny?"

The Savior clapped the arm of the thin man barbecuing meat. "Because Deacon is standing right here!"

CHAPTER TWENTY-ONE

Carter

Carter looked into his favorite interrogation room, the one with the clock.

Ray was still here, still in the same room, being grilled by two agents. Looked like the interrogation had reached some kind of impasse, and he didn't know his son was alive. Ray Hill was glaring at Elisha. "I won't speak to you anymore."

Carter cracked his knuckles and opened the door. "Got some good news."

"You've found Olivia?" Something sparkled in his eyes, maybe the potential that he could get her bone marrow. Or maybe it was just relief that a family member had been recovered.

Carter took the free seat next to Elisha and waited for Ray's attention. "Deacon's alive."

Ray frowned. Then looked around the room, like he could follow the words through the air and check them for lies. "What?"

"He was living in a commune in the south of the city. Place you'll probably know as the Jungle. Maybe the Triangle?"

"It's definitely him?"

"We believe so."

"Can I see him?"

"That depends."

"What on?"

"I don't know, Ray." Carter shrugged. "I just thought you deserved to know."

"I appreciate it. How is he?"

"Hard to say. He seems fine. Completely fine." Carter took a long look at him, but decided there was nothing else to get from him. "Okay, Ray. I'll do you a solid if you're honest with me. You can speak to your son, but you need to tell if it really is him. We're testing blood, DNA, dental records, so I'll know if you lie to me. Those things take time, Ray, so if we're to find Olivia, we need to be fast."

"Okay, sure. Whatever." Ray still had the look of someone who was days from even accepting the news. But he got to his feet and played along. "Where is he?"

"This way." Carter led across the corridor and opened the door.

Deacon Hill was sitting there, eyes shut, his breathing slow and regular. Meditating away the wait. He wore a gray FBI T-shirt and matching track pants, but still looked like a shadow of his former self.

All the photos Carter had seen of Deacon, he had looked healthy. Athletic, even. Maybe too thin, but he knew agents who did far too many marathons and ended up that way.

Deacon frowned into the light. "Dad?" He got up and limped over.

"Deac?" Ray rushed over and wrapped his son in a bearhug. "Deacon!"

Well, that didn't need confirmation.

Deacon Hill *was* alive and well.

Arms folded, Carter stood in the corridor and took a few minutes to process the news, assess the implications of what they had versus what they expected to have.

He had gone to the New Jungle—or the Triangle or whatever it was called—thinking they'd get a lead on Deacon's death, maybe find Vic Jordan. All that would have backed up one of the more solid motives for Olivia's abduction—that Vic had taken Olivia to extort Ray and recover the drug debt.

Instead, Deacon Hill was alive.

"Max Carter." Nesh Warburton was pacing along the corridor, a toothpick away from the movie cliché of bad-ass detective. Stubble, lank hair. Leather jacket, hood, jeans. A city detective, no doubt about it. He wore a guest pass lanyard around his neck but seemed to have slipped away from anyone looking after him.

Carter held out a hand. "Good to see you."

"Not that this is a beer in my fave bar." Warburton looked around the place. "Anyhow, Bob Johnson told me you recovered Deacon Hill?"

"That's right. You can rest easy now."

"Wish I could." Warburton adjusted his gray hood so it sat just right. "It's definitely Deacon?"

"Had my doubts, but Ray Hill just confirmed it's him."

"Huh."

"Blood type matches. We're planning a DNA test, just to make sure. And dental records, but if he's been a heroin addict, that can be less reliable."

"Is he high now?"

"Doesn't seem like it. Looks like he's a changed man, in fact. Meditation and all sorts of stuff."

"Don't believe that for a second." Warburton shook his head. "I mean, I assumed Deacon might still be alive. Just the sort of trick people like that would play."

"Was Vic Jordan on your radar?"

"He had Deacon working to pay off his drug debt, then he broke both his legs. Dude lost his job, hit skid row."

Which matched the story Pete Wasilewski had told them.

Almost word for word, which made Carter wonder if ex-cop Gerry was a source for Warburton. Or just a barroom buddy.

"So you never spoke to Vic Jordan?"

"Tried. Failed. Several times."

"Even though Pete Wasilewski's your source?"

"Wasilewski? What? Who?"

"Admit it."

"Who the hell is Wasilewski?"

Carter stood up a little bit taller. He did not like being shorter than anyone. "He gave us the lead on Vic Jordan's whereabouts. Didn't find him, but we found Deacon."

"News to me." Warburton seemed off his A-game. He exhaled slowly. "I want to speak to him."

Carter nodded. "You know our case takes precedence here, right?"

"Sure, I get that. Ticking clock and all that. I mean, I don't have a case now. I just need to check a box, then I'm done. How about we do this together?"

"No way."

"The reason I'm here isn't to investigate your apparent murder, Deacon, it's to investigate Olivia's abduction."

Watching the reaction was a revelation to Carter. What looked like genuine fear for his daughter's life. "What?"

"She was abducted from her home sometime last night. Her mother reported her missing first thing this morning."

"God damn it. Who's taken her?"

"That's the trouble, Deacon. I've got a list of suspects a mile long. What's worse is you're high up on that list."

"Me? Why would I take her?"

"Because she's your daughter. Your estranged daughter."

"You asshole... if my kid's been taken, you should be out there looking for her."

"I have a team of fifty agents who have been doing that around the clock, and all I've gained is finding out that you're alive and well. Now, that seems mighty suspicious to me at the same time as your kid gets taken. Stands to reason, doesn't it?"

"I have no idea what's happened to her. Man..."

Carter caught a glimpse of something in there, some shred of humanity, of fear and worry and concern that his kid was missing. "Marissa wouldn't let you see her, right?"

Deacon let his head slump. "I had no choice there. Condition of our divorce. Supposed to pay all this alimony out of a lousy paycheck from a job at a moving company. How the hell was that supposed to work?"

"You never tried to see her?"

"Nope. Didn't know they were still in Seattle."

"Okay, so I hear you lost your job at school because of your drug use."

Deacon bared his teeth. "Total BS, man. Total BS."

"That's not what we've heard."

"You don't know shit about my life. You should be out there searching for Olivia."

"Deacon, to do that I need you to open up to me here."

"All I'm saying is..." He frowned. "Look, either you let me out and I can do my own investigation, or you do your job, asshole."

"This is me doing my job, Deacon. Like I said, you're top of my list of suspects. Especially now that you're alive."

"I didn't take her."

Carter slapped a hand off the desk. "Case solved, then. Thanks, off you go."

Deacon shook his head at him.

"Where were you last night, Deacon?"

"At our camp. The Happy Place, we call it. We had a group meditation."

"You know how that sounds, don't you?"

"I'm serious." His stern gaze betrayed it. "At least thirty who'll vouch for my presence there last night."

"And that's whether you were there or not."

Deacon looked away, his mouth pinched. "I don't know what you think goes on there, but it's not... Just let me get out of here and let me find my kid."

"Where did you take her?"

"I didn't."

"Somebody else, then?"

"You've got your militarized police force tossing the place, haven't you?"

"Is she in another camp?"

"You tell me."

Carter knew he was getting a reaction from Deacon, but sustaining that level of irritation was only likely to recover Olivia if Deacon was involved in her abduction. "Talk to me about Frankie."

Deacon frowned. "What?"

"Your half-sister. Olivia's half-aunt, but they're the same age."

"What about her?"

"You hear she was ill?"

"No?"

"Leukemia."

"Shit." Deacon shut his eyes. "I had no idea."

"That's why your father was so angry earlier. He's been hunting for you to see if you can donate bone marrow."

Deacon looked away. "Man..."

"You really had no idea?"

"None." Deacon looked back at him. "Thing is... Shit." He swallowed again. "I'm HIV positive. Can I still be a donor?"

As much as it made sense to Carter, it hit him hard in the guts. He had grown up during that AIDS era when it was a death sentence, even for Hollywood actors and rock stars. "I'm sorry to hear that. How about you tell us what happened to you?"

Deacon's gaze darted around the room but kept settling back on Carter. "After he bro— After *I* broke my legs in an accident, and I, uh, cut my stomach, the pain... It was... I got these pills off that vet. Don't know where he got them. I'd smoked H before, but these were... Probably ketamine. They dulled the pain. Dulled everything. Until they stopped. Smoking wasn't enough anymore; the pills were harder to get hold of. So I started injecting heroin. I was out on the street, and I took the heroin when I could get it. It meant sharing needles. Dumb, I know, but..."

It explained the state of the man. How gaunt he looked. "Are you gettin—"

"I take all the required antiretrovirals, but there's no way anyone should risk Frankie getting my tainted blood."

"There is another alternative donor."

Deacon frowned. "Olivia?"

Carter nodded.

"Let me guess. Ray had a blood test done and found she's a match for Frankie?" Deacon ran a hand through his hair. "You think Ray has her?"

"You tell me."

"I haven't spoken to my father in a long time. A long, long time. I mean, we just saw each other, but that's the first time in years. Taking Olivia... that's the sort of bullshit he could do if he was desperate enough."

"Explain."

"My father is an arrogant man. Grew up with money. Became a cop, couldn't hack it. Blamed the system, so he got out and used his inherited wealth to run this private eye firm for rich assholes like himself. Made a bomb. And all he's learned is he can take what he wants. You see what happened after my mom died? He shacked up with some piece of ass my age. I mean…"

Carter was edging away from Ray as the abductor. Something about it just didn't stack up. Mainly Ray's reaction, his continuing desperation, his continuing hunt for his son—his last hope. He still didn't know it was dashed, did he? "Could Vic Jordan have taken her?"

Deacon sat back in his chair, arms folded, sighing. "Why?"

"It makes perfect sense to me, Deacon. You owe a huge drug debt to him. You're someone with a rich family. Classic abduction blackmail MO."

"No."

Carter sat back and reached over to the desk for a paper file. The oldest trick in the book, a file filled with blank pages. "The doc who checked you out just now, she found a ton of scar tissue on your stomach. You want to talk to us about that?"

"Nope. I just want to find my kid. Am I going to get out?"

"I can't imagine how sore those cuts must've been. Doc reckons they were deep."

Deacon's jawline kept pulsing, like he was clenching his teeth.

"There was a lot of blood in that apartment house. Only one blood type, but it matched yours. Must've been taken to an ER somewhere, huh?"

Deacon swallowed hard.

"Let me guess, a friendly corrupt vet?"

A light nod. "You have no idea how painful it was. Not during the operation, because animal tranqs work on humans too, but afterwards… Well, there was no TLC."

"Deacon, Seattle PD have been searching for your killer for months now. Leaving your car near the George Washington Bridge. Was that your idea?"

"I just want out of here." Deacon's voice was calm and level.

"Make it look like a suicide?"

Back to nothing.

"I want to understand, Deacon. Talk to me about it."

Deacon put his fingers deep into his beard, and it was like he was knitting with the hair.

"So, you're not going to talk to us. I get that. People in your situation don't feel like they can talk. Someone's got something on them. Pressure, blackmail, leverage. Don't know what it is in your case, Deacon, but it's always there, isn't it?"

His left eye twitched. He blinked hard a few times and seemed to get it under control.

"So how about I put the words in your mouth, Deac. You can agree or disagree with what I say."

Deacon shrugged.

"Okay, Deac, so the way I hear it is, you were working a job, paying off your debts little by little."

Not quite a nod from Deacon, but definitely not a no.

"Then some asshole breaks your legs, right?"

"It was an accident."

"What kind of accident?"

"I tripped."

"Give me a break, Deacon."

"It's true."

"But it meant you couldn't work anymore, right?"

"Through no fault of my own."

"So you couldn't clear your debt, right?"

Deacon jerked his head back and stared up at the ceiling.

"Was this debt to Vic Jordan?"

Deacon nodded.

"We know all about Vic Jordan. He runs that camp you're living in. Selling narcotics. Heroin, X, coke, crack, meth. Human trafficking too. Stop me if I'm missing anything."

"He doesn't live there anymore."

"Where is he?"

Deacon shrugged. "You need to let me out of here."

"You want to get out of here, tell me what's really going on there."

Deacon stared hard at Carter, his eyes all steel and fury. "Listen, asshole, if you think I'm talking about anyone or anything, you can stick it up your ass. My kid's missing, so if you want to stop me from finding her, that's your lookout, but it'll be on your head if she's dead."

"Why would you think that?"

Carter had hit a wall. Maybe it was too neat. But all Carter knew about Vic Jordan was he wasn't a sophisticated man. Frontier justice. Breaking legs was right up his alley.

Carter waited for eye contact. Took him maybe a minute, but it felt a lot longer. "Deacon, I'm going to offer you a way out of this. You had your legs broken. Your stomach sliced. If we can get some evidence, we can put Vic Jordan away. Then your debt won't even exist. He's had you working hard to clear it, but it'll always be there unless he's away for a long time."

"You don't understand."

"Try me."

Deacon just shook his head.

"Listen to me carefully, Deacon, because I won't repeat it." Carter leaned across the table. "Right now, we can use your testimony to help put Vic Jordan away. If he's taken Olivia—"

"What?"

"It's a possibility, right?"

"Dude…"

"We've got a friend of yours spilling his heart out."

"Pete, right? That how you found me? Through Pete?"

"I can't say. We weren't looking for you, but the man who we believed killed you. Then you were there. Serendipity, they call it. But both of you will be enough to put Vic Jordan away."

Deacon shook his head again. "Your big problem is that Vic is dead."

CHAPTER TWENTY-TWO

Carter

Warburton held out a tablet computer showing head-mounted video feed from the gulch below, where six CSIs worked away.

Through the wet long grass, the screen showed two corpses, rotten and decayed. Mostly skeletons now, but still hopefully enough flesh left to test DNA.

One of the corpses wore green scrubs faded almost to gray and soaked with dulled blood.

The other wore biker-gang gear, torn-off denim over a leather jacket. The name tag read VIC JORDAN.

Warburton put his tablet away. "Might be convenient."

"Sure, but it's most likely them." Carter looked around the officers fanning out to continue the search. "Looks like two gun-shots to the back of the head. All the hallmarks of an execution."

"What I'm thinking..." Warburton sighed. "Think this is legit?"

"Could be."

"Going to take a long-ass time to process an autopsy, but time is something my case is blessed with."

"And mine ain't."

"Man, I thought I'd lucked out. A corpse turns up alive and well, now I've got two unsolveds. In the old Jungle too. Damn it, thought we'd combed that place." Warburton looked like he wanted to punch the walls, if there were any around. "We had Vic on our radar, but the focus was on the raids here, clearing this place out. We just lost track of him when we shut down this whole place. We thought Vic had slipped into the mist. I heard stories of how he was in some prepper hideout in Wyoming, but he was here all along. In the shade of the I-5."

Carter looked over at the freeway through the heavy downpour battering his umbrella.

Vic Jordan. A drug supplier, dead but not quite buried. Supposedly.

And The Savior had taken over the remnants of his band of men, Deacon Hill among them.

Deacon stared at Carter. Guarded by two SPD cops, so he wouldn't run. "You going to find my kid now?"

"What we're trying to do here."

"Well, Vic's dead. He didn't do this."

"If it is him down there."

"It's him, man. Saw him die with my own two eyes."

"You know I don't believe junkies. Did you kill him?"

"Nope. But I was living with him at the camp in the Jungle. Before the cops came and seized the place, these dudes from a rival gang came in, shot the place up, and took Vic away. We heard the gunshots."

"I'm supposed to believe this?"

"It's the truth. It was brutal, man. I saw it. Three of us followed Vic, trying to stop it, keeping a distance."

"Who were they?"

"I don't know. Big dudes. They tortured Vic and the vet, then they shot both of them. Bang, bang, in the head. I think Vic knew them."

"But you don't?"

"I recognized a couple of them. They were the ones who had found me in my apartment and attacked me."

All that blood, Nesh Warburton's crime scene.

"But I got away."

"How?"

"They left me for dead. A buddy came around; he took me to this veterinarian. He was a user too. I could tell. Someone like that, they're helping Vic Jordan because they need to get high. Then the guys who attacked me, they got to the vet, made him tell them where Vic was. He was there when they killed Vic, so yeah…"

Carter didn't know whether to believe it or not. Down below was a human body. Could be Vic Jordan, could be someone else. Either way, that was a long-term objective for Nesh Warburton. DNA tests, all that jazz. Right now, Carter had to find Olivia. "Deacon, you've got as good a motive as anyone for Olivia's abduction."

"Dude, no way."

"Think it through. You were denied access to your daughter. Take her, be reunited. Or maybe you heard about Frankie. Extort her to your father, a desperate man."

"There's no way I could've done either. I need you to find Olivia."

"What does 'Never Forget' mean to you?"

"Nothing."

"Sure?"

"Sure. Why do you ask?"

"It was written on the mirror in Liv's room."

"Her name's Olivia."

"Okay. But does it mean anything?"

"No. But have you asked Gregg Ingram?"

Carter said nothing, but his heart was thudding now. Strange to mention his name. "Why him?"

Deacon shook his head in disgust. "I heard he's shacked up with that bitch ex-wife of mine." He snarled. "You should be looking at him as a suspect."

Carter's heart was doing double time now. He really needed to make sure he was not tumbling down a rabbit hole. "Why?"

"I worked with Gregg at that school. I know a lot about him. When you mentioned 'Never Forget'... The soccer team used to have that as a motto. 'Heroes are never forgotten.' He used to get them to shout it before a game."

"So why would he write it on the mirror?"

"You heard about the trouble he had?"

Carter frowned. "No."

"Easier to hush things up than confront them. Dude has a taste for fresh meat. He was almost fired for banging the captain of the girls' soccer team."

CHAPTER TWENTY-THREE

Lori

Lori settled back in her seat and looked around the damp parking lot in the shadow of a mountain she should be able to name, but could not. Not too far from Seattle, but it felt like she had traveled a million miles, and back a couple hundred years. Logging country, and it was still going on, Washington state's old history alive and well in the twenty-first century.

The truck stop was almost empty, just five or six long eighteen-wheelers sitting apart from each other. A couple had dudes sitting in the cabs, most were empty. Either asleep in the bunks in their cabs or getting something to eat. Long journeys on the road, crossing the nation. Washington was usually the end of the route, or the start. Picking up lumber to take it where it would be used, where it would be spun into gold. A truck stop this near to Seattle meant one thing—these dudes would be using it to break a long journey, not to start it. They'd be heading from California up through British Columbia to Alaska, and all the way back. Long, treacherous trip.

King sat in the passenger seat, scanning around the parking lot.

The wooden restroom sat in the rain. Bill was still inside, but he'd been a long time.

Gave her a flash to earlier, sitting in an interrogation suite with Bill Carter. Seeing him squirm like that. Cover up the past, his misdemeanors, and try to wriggle free by offering them an olive branch.

None of that sat well with her.

And the olive branch, it just felt like an empty gesture.

Lori wondered if Bill's olive branch was exactly what he came all this way for.

King crunched a mint and swallowed, then tore another strip off the roll and offered a fresh mint to her. Some British brand she didn't recognize, but boy were they strong. Big white lozenges.

"Thanks." She sucked on the mint and it tasted almost medicinal. "You know that phrase about America and England? Two countries divided by a common language?"

"I've heard it."

"Well, these mints are another division."

"Lori, if you don't like them, then you really shouldn't have taken one." King was smiling. "My suitcase could only hold so many."

"No, I love them. That's the problem."

"They are addictive." King narrowed his eyes at the truck stop, focusing on the small restroom, the kind you would see anywhere across the state. Wooden, with a stone foundation, and not exactly shielding anyone from the elements. "What *is* he doing in there?"

"You want to follow him in?"

"Men that age like their privacy as much as small children."

"How many you got?"

"None. But my nephews stay with me fairly often."

"Just you?"

"I'm single, yes."

Lori swallowed down the last of the mint. "This is weird, right?"

"What is?"

"Well, I've been helping Max deal with what happened to him. Being abducted by his own father. I mean, Bill's an old man now, but those selfish acts as a young man, they traumatize kids."

"They do. The law of unintended consequences." King tore another chunk of paper and offered her another mint. "Take two, they're better that way."

"Thanks."

"I told you how my boss's daughter was abducted. Took eleven years for him to find her. Not the same thing as what Max Carter went through, obviously, but both men have thrown themselves into their work. Curious, isn't it? That whole child abduction rapid deployment business. A psychologist would have a field day with Special Agent Carter."

"Every time I speak to him, Max just clams up."

King laughed. "Now, where have I seen that before?"

"Your boss, right?" Lori put the radio to her ear. "Mimi, can you send your buddy in?"

"Roger."

The other car door opened and a big state cop got out. He put his hat on and walked over to the bathroom just as Bill walked out, whistling a tune and drying his hands on his pants.

"Come on, then." Lori opened her door and hopped down onto the cracked asphalt. "You were a while in there, Bill. Beginning to think you'd run off. We were just sending a search party in."

Bill raised his eyebrows. "I tell you, going to the bathroom these days needs serious logistical management." He looked at King. "Getting old, mate, it's bloody awful. You wouldn't believe the struggles I have with my waterworks these days."

"I can imagine." King held out his pack of mints to Bill. "So, where are we headed next?"

Bill took a mint and crunched it. "We're here."

King looked around the truck stop. "This is the place?"

"Yeah, sorry. Maybe I should've explained." Bill crunched again, then pointed over to an old diner. Sure looked run down, with the neon lights half out and grass growing on the flat roof, but the steam coming out of the chimney showed it was still open. "This is the place."

King frowned. "Rosie's Diner?"

"Yep." Bill set off toward the door.

But King grabbed his arm to stop him. "Mr. Carter, I want to make one thing abundantly clear here. You've been keeping things from us. I don't appreciate that. Before we go anywhere near that place, I need to know precisely what happened here. Now."

"Mate, it's better if I show you." Bill wrestled free and walked across the parking lot toward the set of steps leading inside.

"Lord save me." King followed him over.

A truck hissed as it rolled past with a loud rattle.

Lori kept a pace with him, following him up the creaking steps. The bell rattled when she entered. It'd probably had a nice clear ring at some point. Maybe in the seventies.

Bill was already seated at a table by the window, but the glass was too dirty to show much of the parking lot outside. "I sat right here."

King let Lori sit first, but his dark expression revealed maybe a bit too much worry that this was a wild goose chase. Could just be jet lag or travel fatigue, but it felt like it was something more.

Bill opened the menu and had a look at it. "Had to sit at this table for three hours. Ordered a burger and chips." He grinned at Lori. "That's fries to you." Then back to the menu. "These fellas kept coming in and looking to me, but not talking. Either they were truckers and I was in their favorite seat, or they were checking me out in case I was with the law." He set the menu down. "Ironic how Max turned out, isn't it?"

Lori took her own menu, scanning it like she was just another diner, though her pant suit probably screamed "FED" to the three other customers in there. "You recognize anyone?"

"This was over thirty years ago, love. If this is still running, then I doubt it's the same blokes."

King was examining the menu like it was fresh evidence. "It very much is still a thing."

"Anyway." Bill shut his menu and nodded at the waitress. "I'm going to have a Right-Hand Burger."

The waitress looked harassed. Maybe early fifties, and if she'd been in that line of work her whole life, it was a wonder how she hadn't shot the place up. Her name badge read KATH. "Fries with that?"

"You got any sweet potato ones?"

"Sure do."

"That'd be great. And a Coke?"

"Pepsi?"

"Fine, Pepsi it is, love."

The waitress looked at Lori. "Ma'am?"

"House salad and a water."

"I'll bring you a plate. Salad bar's over there." The waitress waved over at the other window. "Sir?"

King smiled at her. "I'm vegan."

The waitress smiled at him. "They shoot vegans here. And eat 'em."

King laughed. "I presume there's nothing I can have?"

"I'll put you down for another salad bar. Egg in the mayo, but otherwise everything is kosher, or whatever it is. Be surprised how many truckers are turning vegan these days."

"Thanks."

"Coffee?"

Three hands went up.

The waitress scribbled again. "That everything?"

Bill winked at her, then sat back, frowning. "Thanks, love."

"Okay." Kath the waitress walked off toward the long counter. A dude in plaid and a ball cap looked back at them as she slid the order through the hatch.

King returned his menu to the holder, easing it in place. "Why should she have remembered you?"

"Because she served me that day. Right-Hand Burger, like I said, then a coffee which I kept going on their free refills all afternoon. Definitely her, but this was a long time ago."

King sucked in a deep breath through his nostrils. "Go on."

"Anyway, after a few hours of waiting, this bloke came in. Tall, olive-skinned. Nodded at me, said my name, then hotfooted it out of here. I left a fifty for a ten-dollar check."

Another waitress came over with their coffees and set them on the table. "Anyone for cream or sugar?" She seemed maybe too interested in them.

Lori shook her head with a smile.

"Not for me, love. Take it black."

King gave a polite English smile.

"Okay, well Kath will be back with your meal soon."

Bill watched her depart and picked up his coffee and blew on it, then slurped at his cola instead. "These blokes took me in the back of a car. Mask on, couldn't see anything. Must've been an hour we were driving."

"Were you alone?"

"Hard to say. They stuck the mask on before I got in the car." Bill pointed to his mouth. "I was gagged too."

"Where did they take you?"

"A private airstrip." Bill ran a hand down his face. "Max was there."

Lori sat there sipping her water, looking around the room. The jukebox played an old Queen track. The deepest of deep cuts too, some noisy live recording. That or the speakers were blown. The coffee machine bubbled away. Frying sounds came from the back, accompanied by a wave of greasy meat smells. She looked back at Bill. "Then what?"

"They brought me and Max back here, and I paid the man."

"No blindfold?"

"Not this time. I was too focused on Max to pay attention to where we were."

"And you were alone?"

"I'll come to that in a minute."

Lori caught King's frown, but didn't want to lose her train of thought. "Why do it that way though? Why not bring him here?"

"I've wondered that myself over the years." Bill popped an ice cube into his mouth and crunched it like one of King's mints. "Only thing I can think is because they'd kidnapped a child from London. Brought him over here, thousands of miles. What if it was the wrong kid? No matter how much money I'd paid them, I'd kick up a stink, wouldn't I? Better to do that on their land than here."

"You never looked into it?"

"Why would I?" Bill finished his drink, leaving the ice cubes. "I had my boy. And I had a ton of hassle from my ex-wife. She was trying to recover him." He stared into space. "And you know how that went."

King swallowed his water in one gulp. "Is that everything?"

"I swear."

"Bill, if I find out that you—"

"I swear that's it. And put yourself in my shoes, mate. I'm risking a lot coming here with you two. This whole place could be filled with geezers who work with them. People trafficking is deadly, as you well know."

King sat back. "This is a waste of time."

"Look, there's something else I need to let you know." Bill took a drink of his coffee. "There was another kid at the airport."

King looked over at Lori, then at Bill. "From London?"

"Can't be sure. From England, certainly. He was on the flight with Max."

Lori frowned. "But there wasn't a parent to meet him?"

"That's the thing I've been trying to remember all this time. I *think* there was another bloke at the airport. I can't say for sure if he was in the car with me."

"This *is* a waste of time then."

"Mate, I don't know what you're expecting to find." Bill exhaled slowly. "You've got the same hero complex as my son, ain't you? Travel all this way to uncover some big conspiracy."

"This is a criminal act, Mr. Carter. You arranged for the abduction of your son, not to mention the murder of your ex-wife."

"Mate, you're talking—" Bill shut his eyes. "I've been over this so many times. In my head. All these things I've done. I've got so many regrets. Part of me thinks that's why I've got this cancer."

"I didn't know."

"It's almost in remission. It's justice, though, isn't it? For what I've done."

"It doesn't work like that."

"What's your end game here, King? You going to arrest me?"

"No, this is merely to gather intel. I have no jurisdiction. Special Agent Alves here does, but I can't arrest you, can't prosecute you, as much as I'd like to."

"Listen, Lori. A few years back, I paid your husband's firm a packet to do some digging into this."

That stunned Lori. All those wounds from her divorce welled up. "You hired David?"

"No, not him. The woman."

"Jess?"

"Her. Yeah, she did some digging for me. Came out here, even."

"Why?"

"Trying to track down that other kid. I felt guilty, wanted to see if he was okay."

"She find anything?"

"All she got was—" Bill looked over at the approaching waitress, carrying a plate with a burger and fries stacked on top of two salad bowls. "That waitress told Jess that she knew the boy's father."

I step up the ramp towards the airplane, and it's like when we were at the shopping centre, but the escalators were all broken so we had to walk up them. They're too big to walk up, too big for my short legs.

Uncle John notices and picks me up under the armpits, but it's not sore like when Mummy does it. He carries me, then puts me down at the top of the steps, then takes my hand again. His hand is strong and reassuring.

A pretty lady smiles at us, then points into the door. She's wearing a fancy uniform, like when we went to Majorca.

But I can't smell Mummy's perfume. I don't want to go in. "Where's Mummy?"

Uncle John crouches low. "Your mum called me when we were driving here. She says she'll see you at the other end. The surprise is even better now too."

I don't know now. This feels bad. And I really need to pee. I wrap my arms around my torso, and I'm going to stay here like this.

"Come on, silly billy, let's get you inside." Uncle John holds out his hand.

I don't want to take it, but I need to pee so badly. "O-kay." I take Uncle John's hand and he helps me into the plane.

The pretty lady takes me to a chair, and there's a big TV with a Nintendo! She helps me buckle up, but I can't take my eyes off it. "Does that work?"

"Sure. What games do you want to play?"

"Have you got Mario?"

"Which one? We've got three of them, I think."

Oh man!

I pick up the boxy controller just as Mario starts jumping around on the big screen in front of me. "Is this my surprise, Uncle John?"

"No, son, this isn't your surprise." He laughs. He's kneeling on the chair behind the big TV, smiling. "Now, you be a good boy for Alice here, okay?"

"Will do." But I'm focusing on that first level. I played it at Andrew's house, but I wasn't very good at it. Andrew won't believe this, though! Playing Mario on an airplane!

She puts headphones on my head. The tingling music makes it feel like I'm actually in the Mushroom Kingdom!

Uncle John waves, then steps out of the plane. Alice locks the door and we start moving. It's called taxiing, but I don't know why. Uncle John is down on the tarmac, still waving as we move off.

Alice leans down and smiles. "Can I get you a hot chocolate? It's so good."

"Yes please!"

"Can I get you anything else?"

"What else is there?"

"Whatever you want. Cookies, potato chips, soda. Burgers, hot dogs. Anything."

"This is the best day ever."

CHAPTER TWENTY-FOUR

Carter

This was the third time Carter had been to the high school that day, and it was like he was getting farther away from finding Olivia. Her life remained a mystery, but it felt a heck of a lot like that was because everyone in it seemed incapable of telling the truth.

At least in person. Nobody seemed to think anything of laying their soul bare online, but when it came to face-to-face? The spoken word was edited and redacted, each tiny omission building up to a fiction.

Elisha was outside the principal's office, thumbs bashing away at her cellphone.

A teenage boy sat next to her, bigger than her already and looking like he was in serious trouble.

Elisha looked up at Carter. "Hey. I've got an appointment with the principal. You want to sit in?"

"It's why I'm here." Carter nodded over at the door. "She busy?"

"Tad here's parents are in with her just now."

Tad rubbed his neck, burning red.

Carter decided that maybe a little FBI attention might help Tad focus on his future, rather than whatever he was doing to make the present seem okay. "What did you do, Tad?"

He kept staring at his sneakers.

Elisha sat forward, clutching her cellphone tight. "Tad decided to post a message on his class WhatsApp that Hayden Primrose had murdered Olivia."

"Said I'm sorry." But Tad didn't seem like it. Seemed like an entitled douchebag, probably one of the kids with a hot rod in the parking lot.

Carter's cellphone rang. He checked the display. *LORI CALLING...* He got up to answer it, keeping one eye on the principal's door. "Hey."

"Max, will you stop texting me?"

Carter was barely aware of it. He pulled his cell away from his ear and, sure enough, there were five messages to Lori, all asking for an update. He thought he'd sent one, but that really didn't look good. He put the phone back to his ear. "Lori, I'm sorry. I shouldn't have done that."

"I get it, Max, just stop it."

"Fine."

She exhaled down the line. "I'm with Chris King and your father at a diner."

"A diner?"

"Long story." She paused, but Carter knew that she was not going to start telling the tale to him of all people. "Look, I need to ask you something."

"Shoot."

"When you were brought here, do you remember another kid on the plane?"

That threw Carter. Made him feel dizzy. Something clawed at his skull, hauling him back to the distant past, when he was a little kid with a London accent, stuck on the other side of the world. Tad was frowning at him, so he walked down the corridor. "I can't remember much, no. Why?"

"Bill reckons there was another kid there."

"I can't recall, Lori. Sorry. All this therapy I've had has been opening up these fragments of memory, but I can't... I... How important is it?"

"Not sure."

"How's Bill doing?"

"Having a whale of a time." She sounded distracted now, maybe because people were listening in. Wherever she was, an old Prince song played in the background.

"Do you need me to speak to him?"

"No, Max. That wouldn't be appropriate."

"Is King there?"

"He is."

"Can I speak to him?"

"Same, Max."

"Lori, your English friend got him involved. Please."

"Don't guilt me, Max."

"I'm not. This is—"

The door opened and a soccer mom stormed out. Despite there being a school principal behind her and two federal agents in front, she grabbed Tad by the hair and hauled him up to standing. "You lousy, lame-ass *jerk*." She smacked him on the butt and pushed him away down the corridor. "Get!"

Carter turned a blind eye to it. "Got to go, Lori." He ended the call and pocketed his cell.

Principal Iona Harrison watched Tad and his mother recede down the corridor, Tad's mom's heels clicking off the hard floor. "I wish that was an isolated incident, but technology and kids are like water and oil. But on fire." She shook her head, then opened her door wide. "Please, come in."

Carter let Elisha sit first, but she knew how to play this. See what that Tad lead shook out. So they both stayed silent.

"Tad Hetfield thinks he's gotten away with it, but he is in for a whole world of hurt. I spoke to Sergeant Johnson, a good buddy of mine, and he says he's sending a few of his bigger, badder dudes over to speak to him."

"I take it there's nothing in that rumor?"

"Never likely to be. Hayden Primrose was playing basketball last night when Olivia went missing. Poor kid shares a bedroom with his brother too, so we know he was at home all night." She stared at Carter. "So what brings you back here?"

"Some good news for once." Carter sat back in the chair. "We found Deacon Hill."

Didn't seem anything like good news to her. Her face twisted up like she'd been told a parent had died. "Oh."

"He was living in the greenbelt just off—"

"The Jungle?" Iona's eyebrows shot up. "Maaan." Her reaction showed that she knew how big a descent that was.

"We don't believe that he is involved with Olivia's disappearance, but he made some allegations we do need to investigate."

Iona's eyes narrowed. "Pertaining to what?"

"Gregg Ingram and someone called Jennifer Huston."

She shook her head. "That's bullshit."

"Before you get too far down that path, let me point out that we've got agents over in Cambridge, Massachusetts, picking her up right now. I'll get a feed of the interrogation. Be interesting to see what she says to my Boston colleagues."

"Damn it. Deacon is stirring the pot because I fired his ass for selling drugs."

"I thought you—"

"Okay, I didn't technically *fire* him, fire him, but I told him to get out of my school, and he graciously resigned." She snarled. "Can't believe he's still alive."

"Is there anything in this allegation?"

Iona stared up at the ceiling, then back down at them. "There's everything. Sadly."

"So Gregg was sleeping with the captain of the soccer team?"

"That's correct."

Carter looked out the window behind her. While the soccer field was empty just then, he couldn't help but think of Gregg getting on the case of that player. Shania? Sure did make him wonder how many others there might have been over the years. "You need to walk us through what happened."

"Not much to tell. Wait, you don't think Gregg has anything to do with Olivia's disappearance?"

Carter gave her a shrug. As much of a coincidence as it seemed, he wanted to let her stew in it.

Iona stared at her desk like it had all the answers she needed. "But Gregg's with Marissa now?"

"Indeed. The way Deacon told it, Gregg has a taste for 'fresh meat.' Olivia's fifteen. Stands to reason, doesn't it?"

"Oh my days."

"It's a bit absurd that you can bust Deacon Hill for dealing drugs, but Gregg Ingram gets off with rapped knuckles for sleeping with a student."

"That's a false equivalency and you know it."

"So you're sitting here, pretending you're responsible for the welfare of all of these children, but you've taken the school's reputation over their safety."

"How dare you."

"Did you ever tell Marissa?"

Iona shook her head. "I should've gone to the cops with this."

"Of course you should have. It's your responsibility. Legally. It's designed to take discretion away from you. Teachers, doctors, police officers, FBI agents, anyone in a professional capacity who has knowledge of potential child abuse or exploitation. Why didn't you?"

"Because there wasn't a thing any of us could've done about it. When Gregg was in a relationship with Jen, she wasn't a student here anymore."

"This was after?"

"Sure. She was eighteen and there was enough of a gap between her graduation and them stepping out together to make it all aboveboard, at least legally. I didn't like it, but I was powerless to do anything against him."

"And you're certain that this wasn't happening when Jen was a student here?"

"No. I can't be certain about anything."

Carter pulled up outside Gregg's apartment and took a look around. Four-story building, modern and tasteful, perfect for a bachelor. Six blocks away from Marissa's place.

Elisha was at the apartment block already, pressing her thumb against the entry buzzer.

Carter stayed back, with the engine running. Normally, he would turn it off while he waited, but the last thing he needed was Gregg Ingram escaping because he was trying to cut his emissions.

He couldn't figure out if there was anything in this story about Gregg. Felt like he was tying himself in knots, and all the while Olivia was still missing, at the mercy of whoever had her.

Could Gregg really have taken her?

Every way Carter cut it, Gregg sure had a lot of items in his column. The wine bottle, the clandestine meeting with Ray Hill, and now this.

But did any of that mean he could abduct Olivia?

And why? Why would he do that?

So many reasons Carter could think of, and none of them had that same tinge of hope that Ray Hill's MO had. With Ray, at least he could cling to the possibility of Olivia's release once they had harvested her bone marrow. And that her physical suffering would be minor.

But Gregg… It could be anything.

Knock out the mom, and he'd have a clear path to the daughter. In his head. The trouble with fantasies like that was, soon as rubber hit the road, nothing went the way it was supposed to in reality. Instead of a night of passion, maybe he killed her and had to bury the body.

And Carter needed to find out. He needed to speak to Gregg, see what Deacon being alive brought back to him. Then hit him with a full-frontal assault. A guy like Gregg, no matter how highly he regarded himself, he would crack under extreme pressure. He was just a high school sports coach. Carter had left enough meat on the bones of the interview, questions not asked, answers that didn't match up. Yeah, he'd crumple like a fender in a pile-up.

Elisha turned back, shaking her head at him.

So Gregg wasn't there, or he wasn't answering his door. Neither seemed palatable to Carter.

He got out his cell and found Elisha's contact in the call log. Just as he was about to hit dial, a German sports car pulled into the parking lot, taking it nice and slow.

Gregg Ingram was behind the wheel, wearing wraparound mirrored shades.

Carter hit dial and put the cell to his ear.

"What's up, Max?"

"Gregg's turned up. Hide." Carter killed the call, but didn't like just sitting there. He wanted to drive over, catch Gregg, but all he had at the moment was "he said, she said." Nothing concrete.

Except, Gregg's passenger door opened and flowing blonde hair stuck out of a gray ball cap. Dark shades, black tracksuit.

Took Carter a few seconds to recognize her, then it hit him.

Shania. The soccer player. Olivia's classmate.

God damn it. Gregg was hitting on her. Inviting her to his apartment.

Carter had to act now.

He let his Suburban trundle across the asphalt toward Gregg's car. Every inch cut down Gregg's escape vector that little bit more.

But Gregg clocked him. He swung the BMW back and just missed Carter's front left fender.

Elisha had her handgun out, aiming inside the vehicle. "FBI! Get out of the car!"

It took Gregg a few seconds to process just how screwed he was. Carter could see him playing it all out, all the options. Running, driving, smashing into Carter's Suburban. All of it. But in the end, he just got out, hands up.

Carter joined them. "On the ground! Now!"

"What the hell is this about?"

Carter stepped closer and wrapped a cuff around his wrist, too tight. "I'm arresting you for the abduction and murder of Olivia Davis." He nodded for Elisha to take Shania away.

"What the hell are you—"

"We've found Deacon."

That shut Gregg up. For a few seconds at least. "Who killed him?"

"He's alive, sir."

Confusion flooded Gregg's face as he collapsed back against his car. "What?"

"Not quite well, but alive." Carter joined him by the hood. "He told us about you and Jennifer Huston."

Gregg looked at him like he might try to deny it.

"Don't. And don't even think about telling us that Shania Anderson is here for some sports coaching."

Then he shrugged. Guy like that, sometimes people finding out their darkest secret made them feel lighter than air.

"Okay, Gregg, here's what's going to happen." Carter nodded at Elisha. "You're going to accompany my colleague here and you're going to give her a full account. Nothing missed. Because if there's so much as a misplaced comma, I will make sure you never see the light of day again. Do you hear me?"

CHAPTER TWENTY-FIVE

Carter

Carter watched Elisha take Gregg Ingram inside the mobile command center. It would be hours before he would be out of that interrogation suite again. Shania was sitting in a room with a trained child-exploitation investigator. Jen was doing the same over in Boston. Who knew what they'd spill? But Carter didn't necessarily think Gregg was Olivia's abductor

Or was that just hope that someone else had her?

Someone with a motive to return her?

Carter had to hope she was okay. It was all he had.

He got out his cellphone and called Nesh Warburton.

"Yello."

"Nesh, it's Max Carter."

"Mad Max. Whassup?"

"Wondering if you've got any news for me?"

"Well, the good news is that corpse is a match for Vic Jordan. Vic had no DNA in the system, but we found a brother. Would you believe, he's an accountant in Clovis, California? Suburb of Fresno, been there a few times. Hell of a place. Anyway, the DNA confirmed Vic's identity. And Deacon and The Savior's description of the perp matches some dude we've got serving hard time upstate. My guys are in with him now, and I don't want to jinx it, but I do believe that we're minutes away from a confession."

"You *believe* this?"

"If this was you telling me, I wouldn't. But this dude, he's been in stir so long and so many times. It's real easy for them to take the hit. What's another life sentence on top of five? Know what I'm saying?"

Carter knew, but all he gave him was a grunt.

"So when this guy takes the rap under extreme duress, it must mean something. Says he's found Jesus in jail and started worrying about his immortal soul. So he's been confessing about all these other murders we didn't even know about. And he's looking good for Vic Jordan."

"Good enough for me." And it was. Carter had seen the corpse, the name tag. The hurried burial. It all stacked up, especially with the science.

The door to Marissa's home opened and Tyler shot out, his gaze sweeping around the street. He focused on Carter with the look of a man who had spent too long staring at a screen, blinking hard and not quite focusing. "Sir!"

"Got to go." Carter put his cell away and jogged over. "What's up?"

"I've got something you need to see." Tyler led him into the mobile command center.

Elisha stood inside the interrogation door, opposite Gregg. She gave Carter a nod before she shut it.

"So…" Tyler sat at the big built-in desk, a long bunker that let ten agents work away, give or take some accidental elbowing. "I got into her laptop, sir."

"We're looking for emails and—"

"I can go one better. Ten better, in fact." Tyler was beaming wide. "I've found a snooper app."

"A snooper app?"

"Sure. It sits there in the background and hijacks her webcam, then sends the video over the internet. As far as I can tell, there's a queue of files sitting on a server somewhere."

"Somewhere?"

"All I've got is an IP address in the Netherlands, but that's probably been masked and covered up, so it could be anywhere."

It would sound like garbage to other people, but Carter could turn the technical malarkey into words. Emotions. Feelings. And none of them were positive.

Someone was hacking her laptop's camera and sending video files over the internet. He had one guess, but no proof it was Gregg.

But Carter's mouth tasted like he had drunk a quart of gasoline. "Is this being broadcast?"

"That's what I'm trying to assess, sir." Tyler was hitting the keys hard. "I've recovered a couple of files. Here." He clicked on a play button.

Timestamped the previous morning, the screen filled with high-resolution video of Olivia getting dressed after a shower. Damp hair, wearing a towel.

Tyler hit the button and froze it. "It's being sent out over the internet. Someone has been snooping on Olivia."

"Was it Gregg?"

"Don't know, sir. But I'd put money on it."

Carter had encountered this kind of depravity on a case before, but something about this time made it feel even worse. Aside from the premeditated grooming of a minor, there was a whole secret world being built up.

All those casual acts Olivia would do every day—getting dressed, doing homework, listening to music, talking to friends on her cell, going to bed at night—as long as the laptop lid was open, it was being recorded and transmitted.

Carter had to get out of there. It was like the atmospheric pressure was getting higher. He kept getting flashes of the stale smell of used coffee cups and yogurt tubs from the trash. All made him feel like he was going to throw up.

Sure, it was just that. An oppressive temperature. Rancid food containers. Nothing more.

No, he needed to get to the bottom of this whole mess.

He grabbed a chair and sat down next to Tyler. "Is there any proof it was him?"

"Well, I was in the house hooking into the router directly. It looks like it was accessed by someone in that house."

Carter sat back in the chair. Assuming Gregg had done all that, he knew as much about Olivia as she herself did, probably much more than her mother did. He would know all her blind spots, her weaknesses, and how to exploit them.

Carter leaned forward and focused on the surveillance video from the interrogation suite next door. Gregg sat there, looking calm and rational, while Elisha and Mimi interviewed him.

Gregg was now prime suspect by some distance, but there were so many possibilities.

Maybe Olivia found out about the spying.

Maybe there was some sort of consensual intercourse. Or non-consensual.

Either way, Olivia could be pregnant.

Or maybe she was just threatening to talk to her mother or the guidance counselor at school. Maybe another teacher. Maybe the principal.

But still, why would Gregg take her away? Unless he was doing something much, much worse.

Carter pushed up to standing and stared right at Tyler. "Okay, Peterson, here's what I need from you. I need you to dig deep into this snooper app. First, I need you to find out who it was. Second, I need you to unpick the chain of evidence. Where do those files go? Who else has access? What else is there?"

"On it, sir."

Carter almost laughed at that. "Get up to the high school, would you? See if Gregg's been accessing that video remotely."

Tyler was leaning over his laptop, already lost to the cause. "Sir."

Almost too competent. Carter stepped over to the door just as it flew open. He caught a blast of cool, damp Seattle air that almost hauled away the room's stale smell.

A Seattle PD CSI stood in the doorway. Beverley, though Carter barely recognized her out of the crime-scene suit. Flame-haired and with an intense stare. "Tyler, you'll want to see this." She was holding up a clear evidence bag containing an envelope.

Tyler swung around and smiled at her. "Hey." He got up and joined them by the door. "What is it?"

"My guys have just found a package in the neighbor's trash." Beverley stared at the evidence bag with a frown. "Had to move heaven and earth to get him to allow us access. Here you go."

Carter took it from her. To anyone else, it was just an empty padded envelope. But to Carter, seeing the name DEACON HILL written in Sharpie, well that changed everything. "What was in it?"

"That's the thing." Beverley shrugged. "There's no sign of the contents."

Carter spun it around, trying to restore the deformations and bends and shaping that, yes, a bottle would do to the envelope. "Looks like a container, right?"

"Drugs too. And it more than looks like it. I tested it and found some traces of Rohypnol. It matches what we found in the wine."

Carter took another look at the envelope. Postmarked Seattle. Gregg had gotten someone to send him this, then he injected it into the bottle of wine, knowing Marissa would drink it. Then she fell asleep and he tried to make it look like Olivia had been abducted by someone else.

Tried and failed.

CHAPTER TWENTY-SIX

Lori

Lori gripped the wheel tight as they trundled along the back road marked with puddles and broken asphalt. Felt like every foot they traveled, she had to make some micro-adjustment to the wheel. Usually it would be instinctive, second nature, but this road was in such a bad state, and their prey was just up ahead.

Any backward look and Kath the waitress would spot the Suburban coming.

King was in the passenger seat, grabbing the handle above the door tight, his other hand with an even tighter grip on his cellphone. He pulled it away from his ear and thumbed the screen. "Well, that was our friendly patrolman. Bill's on his way back to Seattle."

"Good." Lori didn't know what they were heading toward, but she didn't want any civilians nearby. "He going to come back over?"

"Sounded like it."

"Either he is, or he isn't. Which is it?"

King shrugged. "I don't know the lay of the land over here. Sheriffs and cities and state cops and federal cops. Is he the correct type to come over?"

"He is." Lori had to slow to ease around a bend.

Up ahead, Kath was signaling left to take a dirt road lined on both sides by pines—the forests that had attracted so many people to this part of the country in search of work in logging and the lumberyards. A lot of it was growing back now that people no longer needed so much pine.

Lori slowed down even more.

A few hundred yards down the dirt track, Kath got out of her beat-up Chevy and walked over to the chain-link fence surrounding a wooden house. Peeling paint and misted-up windows.

A man stood up out of nowhere. Must have been crouching behind the fence. Wild gray hair, stooped over.

The waitress said something to him, but Lori couldn't hear it. Then Kath got back in her car and drove on up the road.

Whatever she told him, it needed to be done in person rather than over the phone.

Interesting.

The man shuffled back to the house, with a twitchy look back in their direction. Out here there would be guns and plenty of them, no doubt about it.

"We're out in the boonies here, so we could really use some backup."

"Let's just speak to the man, shall we?"

"Okay." Lori rolled down her window and caught a blast of a rooster crowing. In the garden, white hens swarmed the man as he reached into a bucket and tossed a spray of something over the dirt.

No other sounds, just that pressing silence.

No more houses in sight, just trees on all sides. No cars for miles. Back at the diner, any of those guys hanging around could have been involved with Bill's conspiracy, but out here, it looked like it was just this guy. Lori liked those odds much better.

She drove along the track and parked, making sure the Jeep was boxed in. "Let's do this. I'm leading."

"Wouldn't have it any other way."

Lori got out and walked across the dirt track. The gate was rusted all over, but still seemed strong enough. Tall enough to prevent any predators from getting at the man's flock. She tried opening it, but it was locked tight. A bell was mounted to a wooden post, so she rattled that.

The rooster stood in the middle of the mud, his head jerking around as he assessed these new threats to his hens.

The front door cracked open and the man stepped out, wearing jeans and a plaid shirt. A real frontiersman, scratching out a living in rural Washington. And yep, he had a shotgun. Remington 870, the kind of home-defense weapon Lori had seen a bunch of times. But at least he wasn't aiming it at them. Yet. He was squinting, so his eyesight was failing. Lori hoped that meant his aim was similarly afflicted. "Can I help you?"

"FBI, sir." Lori held up her badge. "Need to ask you a few questions, if that's okay?"

"And if it's not?"

"Well, we'll just have to see."

The man lowered the shotgun, his squint replaced by a frown. He mumbled something, but she missed it.

"Can I take your name, sir?"

"Albert Blackhurst. Friends call me Al, but you can call me Mr. Blackhurst. What's this about?"

"It's easier if we do this inside."

"Not for me, it ain't." But Blackhurst was stepping over the mud toward them. "Names, now. Or I swear to god, I will shoot you."

"I'm Special Agent Lori Alves." She gestured to the side. "This is Detective Inspector Chris King from the London Metropolitan Police."

Blackhurst raised his shotgun again. "London, England?"

"That's right." King smiled, broad and kind. "I'd really rather do this inside."

"And I'd rather you get off my property."

King stared at his feet. Looked to Lori like he was going to use that old "I'm not on your property" line, but he stepped back from the fence, hands up. "We're not here to investigate you, sir."

"So why are you here?"

"I'm investigating a series of people-trafficking crimes dating back to the 1980s."

Blackhurst sighed. "Again, why are you *here*?"

"Because we gather you were one of the parents who may have benefitted from this operation."

Lori looked at the man, and he seemed a million miles away from Bill Carter and this plot. Maybe they had been played.

Blackhurst snorted, but something seemed to be breaking through his defenses.

Lori held out her cellphone, showing a photo of Bill Carter. "You recognize this man?"

Blackhurst looked over at King. "Should I?"

"Do you?"

"Nope. Who is he?"

"His name is Bill Carter."

"Why should I remember him?"

"Because he was collecting his son the same day you were collecting yours."

Blackhurst lowered his gun and rested the barrel against his leg. He looked up the long dirt track. "You'd better come in."

Mario jumps into another pipe, and I don't know where he'll end up, but boy am I getting good at this game. This'll show Andrew!

I look out of the window and we're above the clouds now. I didn't even notice us taking off!

"Here you go." Alice rests a white cup on my armrest, slotting it right into the hole. Perfect fit. "What about some potato chips or snacks?"

"Thank you. Are potato chips crisps?"

"Sure are."

"Then them, please."

"Coming right up." She tries to move away. "Anything else?"

"Is my mummy definitely going to meet us?"

"As far as I know, she is." She goes now.

I really wish she was here with me, holding my hand and pointing to the big city below and telling me what was where. But she isn't. I'll just have to wait.

I can see across the aisle.

There's another boy there, wearing headphones just like mine, but the boy is watching a film. Might be The Goonies, *one of my favourites. But the boy looks sad. Maybe he doesn't like* The Goonies?

I reach down and unbuckle my belt, then walk over to him. I wave hello to the boy, but he won't even look at me.

"What's your name?"

The boy looks right at me. He is crying and I don't know why.

"Why are you sad?"

"Hey, hey, hey." Alice rushes over and picks me up under the armpits and it hurts just like when Mummy does it. She carries me back to my chair and buckles me in.

"Alice, who is that boy?"

"He's your new friend."

"Why is he crying?"

"He's… Because he doesn't have a Nintendo."

"Oh, that's sad. Can I share mine with him?"

"He doesn't want to share. And he's watching a movie."

"He can have mine."

"Your friend doesn't like flying. He hasn't been on a plane before."

"Oh."

"You've been on a plane, haven't you?"

"I went to Majorca with Mummy." I frown. "Is that a different place to Mallorca?"

"No, it's the same place. In Spain, they say a double L as a Ye sound, but they can spell it with a J. It's like in Welsh. I'm from Wales."

"Oh. Uncle Steve took me to Cardiff once. It was nice."

"It is." She twists something on the buckle. "Now, you just drink your hot chocolate and play your Nintendo, okay?"

"Okay." I reach over and the hot chocolate is at the right temperature now. I take a drink.

And Uncle John was so right, it's AMAZING.

CHAPTER TWENTY-SEVEN

Carter

"Okay, Gregg, how about instead of what you haven't done, you tell me what you have done. Okay?"

Gregg sat in the field office interrogation suite, sweating hard like Deacon had been. His pale polo was soaked through, and his hair was like he had just stuck gel on. "There's nothing to say. You're wasting time talking to me when you could be out there looking for Olivia."

"Gregg, it feels very much like I'm in the right place."

"I've done nothing wrong."

"Except, you have. You omitted the fact you knew Deacon Hill."

"I didn't think it was relevant."

"No, you were worried we'd start asking about your behavior at the high school. Find out about Jen."

"I knew you would find all this shit out about me, but it wouldn't lead you to Olivia."

"Talk to me about Shania."

"Shania?"

"What did you call it?" Carter frowned, but it was entirely for show. "Oh yeah, the full-back in the girls' soccer team. She was there to get some extra coaching, right?"

"What are you talking about? I was just driving her home. She lives a few blocks away."

"So why not drop her at her home? Looked like you were inviting her into your apartment."

"I was going to share a DVD about Trent Alexander-Arnold."

"And who is he?"

Gregg looked away. "The best right-back in the world."

"He's a soccer player?"

"Plays for Liverpool. I wanted to show her how he positioned himself."

"Shania is fifteen."

"So?"

"At the best, it's inappropriate."

"It's entirely innocent."

"Fifteen, Gregg. Perfect age for you. Just like all the rest, huh?"

"The rest? What?"

"Gregg, we have been talking with Jen and with Shania. They've both told us details. We know all about you now. There are a hundred agents in this city, and I am one of three who actually understands why this happens. I am not going to get mad at you or judge or intimidate you, but it's time you were honest."

And he collapsed. All that meat fell off the bone. "I'm a pervert." His focus stayed on the table. "I'm sick."

"You prey on girls, underage girls, watch them getting dressed, watch them sleeping. Move in on traumatized mothers, then you groom their daughters and you—"

"Grooming? What?"

"You install your software on their computers, so you can jerk off to videos of teenage girls getting dressed."

"This is bullshit!"

"Admit it. All of it. And you'll feel better. You need help. You've been carrying this by yourself for too long. Telling another person will unload all the guilt and fear you've been feeling. It must be scary never knowing when someone is going to tell, or what will happen next. Living with that constant fear must be real hard. But, you're talking with someone who understands."

"This is bullshit!"

"We have gone past all the bullshit now. We know. People are talking; the truth is out."

Gregg sat there, rocking slightly.

"Who made the first sexual move, was it you or was it them?"

"Always them."

Could be truth to that. But also, someone like Gregg would have done so much preparation to put them in that situation. "Did you love them?"

He didn't answer.

"Did they lead you on? We know what teenaged girls are like, right?"

He swallowed hard. "Sure."

"Gregg, neither Jen nor Shania said that you hurt them, and I am glad to hear that."

He shut his eyes and ran the back of his hand across his eyes. It looked slicked with tears when he rested it against the table again.

Carter was close to snaring him now. In order for Gregg to trust him, to confess to his crimes against the other girls, and to bring back Liv, he had to know the agents understood his way of thinking... his cognitive distortions, his stinking thinking. All the common defenses. "So did Jen come on to you?"

"She did. If I'm guilty of anything, it's being weak."

"I understand." From the bitter experience of sitting with countless similar men. "Shania wore you down too, didn't she?"

"She did."

"And Jen and Shania, they were students of yours, right?"

"They were."

"And you knew they wanted you, right?"

"Absolutely."

"And the temptation was way too hard to resist."

"I never hurt them. I loved them."

Carter let the words sit there. He'd flipped the tale now, so Gregg could take over. "I understand."

"You've got to listen to me here. I tried to get them to stop."

"I understand."

"I wasn't in control of this. I told them it was wrong, but they wouldn't listen. They just… They… But I didn't rape them."

That part was true. Neither Shania nor Jen had said anything about not consenting. Statutory rape, sure, but not actual rape.

"But you let them do things to you, didn't you?"

"I did."

"Even though they were underage?"

"This was out of my control."

"Sure." But Carter had him now. Admitting to sexual abuse of two minors in his care. That was going to be a long prison term. Time to bring it home, time to find Olivia. "And Liv was like the others, but different."

Gregg frowned. "How?"

"Well, Liv was under the same roof as you most nights. Gregg, we just want to bring her back. You can help; we know you love her but…"

"I have no idea what happened to her."

"Okay, but you might be able to help. See, someone installed an app on Olivia's laptop that recorded video from the webcam and transferred it to a server in the Netherlands."

"That has nothing to do with me."

"Do you know who it has to do with then?"

"No."

"You should be doing everything you can to help me recover Olivia."

"And I have been!"

"No, you're trying to save your own ass. And it's not working. I know exactly what you've done. How you've done it too. It's over, Gregg. All that remains is helping me to recover Olivia."

"I don't know who took her. I swear."

"You did, Gregg. You."

"No!"

"That message in the mirror, that could easily apply to you. To your actions. Never forget. What aren't you forgetting though?"

"I've done nothing!"

"What about heroes?"

"What?"

"You used to get the girls in your soccer team to shout 'Heroes are never forgotten' before a game, didn't you?"

"I did, but I don't understand what point you're trying to make."

"What was Shania Anderson going to forget at your apartment?"

"What?"

"You have an MO. You drug women." Carter reached over to the box at the side of the desk and picked up the evidence packet. "You recognize this?"

"It's a padded envelope."

Carter tossed it onto the desk, but out of reach. "It's addressed to Deacon Hill, which is even sicker. At Marissa's current address. Deacon never lived there."

"So?"

"This was found in her neighbor's trash. We found traces of Rohypnol on it."

Gregg sat there, struggling to breathe. Shaking his head, faster, wider arcs. "No!"

"Is that 'No, you've caught me red-handed,' or—"

"No! This has nothing to do with me!"

"What does Jen not remember?"

"Jen?"

"Jennifer Huston."

He scratched at his neck. "Not my proudest moment."

"Dating a student is pretty low."

"The principal knew all about it."

"Not what she told us."

"You've been checking up on me?"

"Of course I have. It's called doing my job."

"Listen to me. Jen and I dated for like nine months, then we broke up. This was all after I coached her."

"Sure about that?"

"Uh huh. Maybe I'm a bit young for it, but I had a mid-life crisis. I'd just split from a long-term relationship and I wanted to move on, so I bought that stupid car. Typical bullshit. And then I bumped into Jen. And stuff just happened between us. She had graduated high school the year before. And she had 'daddy issues,' you know? And I was too weak to knock her back."

"How did it end?"

"She went to college, but I'd grown bored of her. It seemed pretty sexy at the time, dating this nubile young thing, but man. Her dad isn't much older than me. He likes the same music as me. I mean, it's tough when your girlfriend says her old man's favorite band is Pearl Jam, you know?"

Carter had him talking now, spilling. "So you went from an eighteen-year-old college student who'd been captain of your soccer team, to a teacher in her late thirties?"

"I didn't plan any of it."

"Sure it wasn't you moving in on her daughter?"

"No, man. No!"

"Going to need a bit more than that for me to believe you."

"The truth is, I grew up. With Marissa, I can't explain it, it just happened. I realized I wanted the wife and kids thing, you know? Missed out on that, but she's given me a chance to reclaim it."

"Gregg, you installed a video surveillance app on Liv's laptop."

"I can't believe you think that was me." But it was a plea, almost to himself.

"These are videos of a minor. I'll let you do the math on that."

Snot bubbled in Gregg's nose. Carter was getting somewhere, close to breaking him.

"If we don't find Olivia, Gregg, or we only find her dead body, you can bet your bottom dollar that you'll be adding a life sentence onto that."

"I haven't taken her!" Gregg sat there, shaking his head. He looked up at Carter with tired eyes ringed red from the tears. "Of course I love Liv. She's a beautiful girl. I'd never hurt her."

He was talking about her in the present tense. Either he was deluding even himself, which Carter had seen, or he genuinely had nothing to do with her abduction. Still a long way from figuring out which was true.

"Jen's talking to agents based out of the Boston Field Office. Sounds like a good kid."

Gregg sat back, arms folded. "She is."

"She's talking about why she ended it with you."

His eyebrows twitched twice in quick succession.

"You installed something on her machine, didn't you?"

"That's bullshit."

"No, Gregg. The files went to the same server. Why the Netherlands?"

"I don't know. It's just where it goes."

SNAP. Snared in the trap.

"Gregg, what is this video fetish? Is it about the fear of getting caught?"

"Partly."

"And the rest is about control, right? About knowing their movements and seeing into their private world. Makes you feel powerful and in control."

Gregg ran a hand across his nose. "I've got a sickness." He bowed his head. "It's an affliction. I can't handle it. It's an attraction to… and… Olivia knew."

"Knew what?"

"Knew I liked her." Gregg was panting like a dog now. "She used to leave her door open while she changed after a shower. Knew I was watching her. I am the victim here, not her."

"So why did you install the app?"

"Because I needed to control this. I was afraid of what other people might do to her. I was trying to protect her."

Always came down to control, didn't it?

These beasts justified their actions by wanting to own a situation, to foist their deviance onto others, then they complained the second someone else might be in charge.

"I know I'll pay for my sickness and my thoughts and my actions, but I swear…"

"I'm asking you one last time. Where have you taken Olivia?"

"I keep telling you!" His voice echoed around the room. "I haven't taken her anywhere!"

"The man who admits to installing a snooper app on a fifteen-year-old girl's laptop denies using Rohypnol to drug her mother and then kidnap her daughter?"

"No!"

"Did you use the Rohypnol on Olivia as well?"

"No!"

"So what is it, Gregg? What did you do?"

"Nothing. That's the truth." Gregg swallowed hard. "There is *no way* I would do any of that to Olivia. It's all about consent. I'm not a rapist. I want these girls to want me. Jen, Olivia, it's what it's all about."

"Shania?"

"Yes."

"Did you have sex with Olivia?"

Gregg looked away. "No."

"Did you try?"

"No."

"Did she offer?"

Gregg looked back at him. "That's what her leaving her door open was all about. So I thought."

"But Olivia never invited you in?"

"No."

"Is that why you killed her? Couldn't handle being—"

"No!" Gregg was on his feet, tears flooding his cheeks now. "I'd never harm her!"

"You know I don't believe anything you say, Gregg. This is all looking really bad for you. Snooping on a teenaged girl, drugging her mom. History of snooping on an ex, who you may or may not have been sleeping with while she was Olivia's age."

"That's not true. You've got to believe me."

"You're the last person I've got to believe. You've lied about a lot of things, omitted others. You lied about meeting Ray Hill. You wanted money from him, didn't you? That to pay for your sports car?"

"No!" But something sparkled in his eyes, behind the tears and the anger. "You think you know all about that, don't you?"

"Gregg, if you're just going to lie to me, spare it."

"Ray got in touch with *me*. He found me at school, knew about my relationship with Marissa. Thought I could influence her to get Olivia's bone marrow."

"And you took the money?"

"No. There was no persuading Marissa. But Ray offered me money to take Olivia."

"Abduct her?"

"That's right. It's what we were talking about last night."

"Do you have any proof of this?"

CHAPTER TWENTY-EIGHT

Carter

Ray Hill was in a field office interrogation room, guarded by two agents. Good ones too, people Carter could trust.

Carter took a deep breath and started counting to ten. He tried not to think of Gregg Ingram preying on Olivia. On Jen. On Shania. On other girls he didn't know about yet.

And he lost count. He started again, taking it nice and slow, matching the count with each breath.

Okay. Here goes.

Carter put his hand to the door. His cell thrummed in his pocket.

Damn it.

Any longer, and he would've ignored it. He fished it out of his pocket and checked the display. Unknown caller, but a British dialing code—0044.

He stepped away from the door and answered. "Hello?"

"Max?" A man's voice. That R.E.M. song played in the background, "Shiny Happy People" maybe?

"Speaking."

"Max, it's Chris King." The London cop. "Lori's given me your number."

"Why?"

"There's something I need to speak to you about."

"I'm kind of busy, Chris. Can't this wait?"

"It's about your father."

"It's never a good time, but fire away."

"I'd rather do it in person."

"And I hate waiting, especially when I've got an interrogation to run."

"Well." King paused just as the music switched to The Bangles. "Hard to say this out loud, but I'm afraid that he's just confirmed something. A suspicion, maybe, which is now a fact."

Carter gripped his phone tight. "Go on?"

"Max, I think you've been operating under the illusion that your father was perhaps not so directly involved with your mother's death."

Carter felt his gut clench. "But?"

"It's an illusion. He paid for a hit on her."

"You're sure?"

"Positive. His movements on a date in question validate some transactional evidence and three phone calls. He paid to have your mother killed."

Carter had spent years knowing the truth, then stupidly let Bill back into his life. For months, he had lived with him and his family. Carter had put all those doubts into a box and ignored it, but now all his doubts were clinging to his skin like stinging jellyfish. And it was true.

Bill Carter was more than an accessory to murder.

Bill might as well have pulled the trigger of a gun. Instead, he paid some lowlife to do it for him.

And Carter had forgiven him. Such a dumbass.

"Thanks, Chris."

"Max, if you need to talk to anyone about it, then—"

"I'm fine." Carter killed the call, but something stopped him from entering the room.

All Bill's lies, all his bullshit, and Carter was using his own savings to pay his medical bills. Prolonging the life of the man who had paid to end his mother's. Who had selfishly abducted Max as a kid.

Despite Bill's wealth, he was just as bad a father as Deacon Hill. Hell, he was just like Ray Hill, believing that money solved all problems.

Carter patted his jacket pocket, checked *it* was still there, then stormed into the interrogation room and didn't stop until he was by the chairs, where he whispered into Elisha's ear, "Leave him to me."

"Sir." Elisha got up and left the room, leaving Carter with Mimi Yu.

Mimi didn't look like she'd been having fun, her razor-sharp cheekbones even tighter.

"You're the boss of these assholes, right?" Ray was sitting back like he owned the place, or at least had the guy who did on speed dial. "You know how long I've been in here?"

"To the second, Ray." Carter sat opposite him and didn't let his gaze leave him. "I brought you in, remember? You were outside that strip club."

"And I ain't done nothing wrong. I'm *sick* of being treated like a criminal. Whatever you think you're doing here, you're fishing and that's it. Well, you're fishing in the wrong pond, pal. I've got nothing to do with Olivia's abduction, and you know it."

Carter sat back and mirrored his body language.

Ray spotted it already. Seasoned ex-cop like him, he'd know all the tricks. Know all the responses too. "I just want to get home to my kid. Way things are going, Frankie hasn't got much time left, so every second is precious."

"It keeps on going back to her, doesn't it? The strongest of all motives."

"Bullshit.

"Gregg Ingram's across the corridor right now, Ray."

Ray was frowning. He was wondering what Gregg was talking about. Wondering what Carter knew. "So what?"

"So, Gregg's been talking about your meeting last night, Ray. About how you tried to pay him to abduct Olivia."

"Bullshit."

"Nope."

"What? You believe that asshole over me?"

"No, I don't. I don't believe either of you, Ray."

"So what the hell are you talking about?"

Carter reached into his jacket pocket for the folded-up sheets of paper. This was a trick Ray would know, alright. That last-minute presentation of evidence. Still, he hadn't seen it coming. And another trick—Carter kept the pages folded, unseen. "You know about encrypted messaging, Ray?"

"Don't dick me around here."

"Been a while for you since you left the force, so let me explain how it works." Carter got out his own cellphone. "I can type a message into something like WhatsApp or Signal. The service scrambles my message, then sends it to your cellphone. Thing is, you're the only person in the world who has the key to unscrambling the messages. It's a huge problem for law enforcement. Drug dealers and terrorists can use it. Congress keeps trying to get service providers to install a back door so we can get access to the messages. Congress's problem is that it's not just bad actors who use it. No, journalists use it. Whistleblowers. Victims of crimes. Joe Public too. So people still have the privacy of encryption. And our technology lets us see that a message has gone from my cell to yours, Ray, but we can't see the content of the message." Carter left a long pause. "Until we get one side of the conversation. And here it is, Ray. Gregg's side." Now he laid out the messages. Twenty-three short text exchanges.

"So, is this supposed to impress me or something?"

"No, Ray. I'm disappointed that an ex-cop who works with David Karevoll would leave himself open to this."

"You tell me what I've done, seeing as how you're so goddamn smart."

"You know a few things about Gregg, don't you?"

"Like what?"

"Ray, it's better if you tell me."

"There's nothing to tell. This is your fantasy, not mine."

"These messages." Carter tapped the page. "They talk about meeting up in the Safeway parking lot in Capitol Hill. And then you obviously met, right? No mention of what you talked about, except for Gregg asking for more. More what, Ray?"

Ray bared his teeth.

"That got you real pissed, didn't it?"

"Cut to the chase, asshole. I don't have all day."

"You're a rich man, Ray. Your old man was a sage investor, earned a bundle, but you decided the noble path was to join Seattle PD, to serve your community. But your family is well-connected. You move in certain circles, Ray, so you must know a few surgeons who would take some cheddar to turn a blind eye at a hospital somewhere."

"Bullshit."

"So you paid someone to abduct Olivia, knowing that Gregg had drugged Marissa's wine. Hell, you probably even decided to frame him if worse came to worst. Like it has now." Carter left a long pause. "You didn't expect him to have any kompromat on you, did you?"

Ray gave him a weary look. "Kompromat. Jeez, get a load of you."

"It's a Russian term, meaning—"

"I know what it is, son. And I'm not that kind of man. I'm clean. You find anything on me? You've found a lie."

"So what are these messages about?"

"Gregg is an asshole is what. I wanted to save my daughter by fair means. Looking for my lousy son was my first port of call, not that he can save her." Ray stared off into the distance. "His blood is dirty. But I needed a backup, anyway. Olivia. And Marissa wasn't playing ball, so I met Gregg to discuss him helping out. Only, he wanted payment."

"How much?"

"Ten grand."

"How did that make you feel?"

"How do you think? I felt lousy. My kid's dying and that piece of shit wanted money from me. But I didn't have a choice, did I?"

"You do much digging into his background?"

"Of course. He's clean."

"Interesting."

"Why?"

"Well, it's just that he'd installed an app on Olivia's laptop to watch her getting dressed."

Ray took a few deep breaths. Obviously a man trained in the art of anger management. "God. Damn."

"Not his first rodeo either, Ray. He was sleeping with a previous student of his, captain of the soccer team. Swears it was after she graduated, but I don't believe him. She's in the Boston Field Office right now, talking to agents like you are to me, but they haven't been able to get a confirmation yet. And Gregg is probably doing it again to another kid. And who knows who else over the years?"

Ray gritted his teeth and locked eyes with Carter. "I admit I was trying to pay Gregg to get Marissa's consent, but that's it. Just to do the operation, legally, at a clinic. I'd pay, get the best care, the best surgeon. Barely even... He was just supposed to persuade her. The money was to go on a vacation, maybe, something to sweeten it. Now Olivia's gone...? And he's... I'm... He was really snooping on her?"

"That's right."

"Man..."

Carter let him sit with his rage for what felt like a minute. Hard to tell without a clock in this room. "Ray, I'll be honest with you.

I have far too many possible motives here. You're still very much in the frame for her abduction. Saving Frankie is a strong motive, and you don't seem to be able to disprove any of your actions. Trouble is, I've got nothing to prove you *did* take Olivia. Or if you paid someone to do it; I can't find anything. But I know you offered to pay Gregg, so I'm open to that."

"I want that son of a bitch put to death for what he's done."

"That won't happen, but he's going to prison for a long time, Ray. Sure you'll know how long as an ex-cop."

"Not long enough. Nowhere near long enough."

"If you've got anything on Gregg, anything at all, then now's the time."

"I… I got nothing. Wish I did."

Someone knocked on the door and Elisha stuck her head in. "Need a word, Max."

Carter got to his feet, all the while maintaining eye contact with Ray. "Think it through, please. Anything at all. Anything he said."

"Oh, don't you worry about that."

Carter gave a conciliatory smile then left the room. He had no idea what was up, what was down.

Did Ray have any involvement? Hard to say.

Gregg? Still harder.

Elisha was talking on her cellphone. She noticed Carter and pressed it against her chest. "Sir, it's Tyler Peterson. He's got an issue at the school."

CHAPTER TWENTY-NINE

Lori

The house was warm, with a stove burning away under a brick chimney. Needed work to repair a lot of it, but it seemed to get a lot of love from Albert Blackhurst. A comfortable couch and a small TV mounted on the chimney, playing an old spaghetti western.

Blackhurst leaned over from his chair and poured coffee out of the French press into three cups. Smelled even stronger than the stuff back at the diner, and Lori would take strong over good any day. Blackhurst sat back and kicked off his work boots, then rested his feet on the table. His socks were covered in enough crisscross stitching to pass for a cadaver after an autopsy. "My feet swell up from all that work. Not sure how much longer I can do this for, but all I've got is my hens. And Cobalt, my rooster."

"That's a nice name."

"Didn't pick it myself."

King reached over for his cup. "Did your son?"

"Listen, son, whatever you think's going on here, there's nothing much I can tell you."

King blew on the surface of his coffee. "So you've invited us in and made some fantastic-smelling coffee just to tell us that you don't have a son?"

Blackhurst shook his head. "You're not from London, are you?"

"Correct. Cambridge, as it happens. Moved down to London six years ago when I transferred to the Met. You know London?"

"Lived there for a few years. Moved back here."

"You miss it?"

"Some of it." Blackhurst smiled. "But what you're looking for, there's nothing here."

"My intelligence says they're still doing it."

"They're doing nothing. Whoever your source is, this Bill Carter, whatever he's saying to you, it's bullshit."

"Does that mean you have spoken to him since that fateful day back in the distant past?"

King held up his hands. "We're just here for the truth. Nothing more, nothing less."

"I'm telling you the truth, son. Whatever you've heard is complete BS. That man is a fantasist."

"Unfortunately he's not." King rested his cup on the table. Somehow he had already drunk it. "Bill is on official record recounting his story of how he paid some people to bring his son over from England."

"Bullshit."

Lori leaned forward, trying to attract his attention. "Mr. Blackhurst, my colleague, Max, he was one of the kids taken from England."

"Max?"

"Max Carter. He's Bill's son." Lori picked up her own coffee cup, and it seemed cool enough to drink. "We're out in the wild here. Anything can happen. It's not like in the middle of Seattle. Nobody can hear you talking to us."

Blackhurst slurped his coffee, but it was like he was chewing it. "Nothing to talk about."

"Max has had a hell of a time. Trying to sort his head out because of what happened to him as a boy. Taken from his home, from his friends, his *mother*, over to a new country with just his father."

It still bounced off Blackhurst's steely resolve.

"Mr. Blackhurst, it's not just about what happened to Max, that was tough enough. It's what happened to his mom. The men who brought him here, they killed her. They didn't mean to, as it turns out. They were supposed to just scare her off. But she died, all the same."

Blackhurst rested his cup on the table, but his hand was shaking. "This is Bill's kid?"

"Mr. Blackhurst, we need your help. They're still doing this, aren't they?"

Blackhurst shut his eyes. "Okay, so here's my story. I was born in this shack and grew up here. Pop ran the local sawmill. Closed down now, but it was a good business. And I hated living here. I was a kid, full of dreams. Then my mom died. Last thing she said was to not live the life she had. She was a Chicago girl, somehow ended up over here." He stared into space. "This was the late seventies, and I had this big thing about London, about punk rock. The Clash and the Sex Pistols. So I saved up enough for a plane ticket and I moved over there."

"When was this?"

"June 1978. I was eighteen, didn't have any qualifications. Mom had homeschooled me. But I got a job in a bar." He smiled. "A pub as they call it. Place on Fleet Street where all the newspapers are. Supposed to be the oldest pub in England, but I don't know if that's true."

King smiled. "The Cheshire Cheese?"

"You know it?"

"One of the finest establishments in the city. And the cheapest, with some of the best beer."

"Well, I had a lot of fun living there. Met this girl, Rachel. She worked at a newspaper, and we fell in love. Trouble was, when she got pregnant, Rachel didn't feel the same about us. Said it was just a bit of fun, not love like I thought it was. But I persuaded her to have the kid. And she changed. She was angry. Started beating me, then did all this mental torture. So I ran. Tried to take my boy with me, but it was too hard. Came home here, to this place; not much now, but back then…"

"What happened to your son?"

"He was six when I left—1987. And I missed him. Rachel's mom, she was looking after him, and she was okay, but still, the thought of Steven being brought up by Rachel… Turns out my father knew these guys, they said they'd get Steven for me." Blackhurst shook his head. "I thought it was legit. They had lawyers, and I had to sign this NDA. I tell myself I was doing the right thing, but… It came down to my dad paying these assholes to abduct Steven from Rachel, just like what happened to your buddy. Max, did you say?"

"I did. Did Rachel ever contact you?"

"She found out what had happened. Somehow. Tried contacting us through the courts, but she kept getting denied. Then she died."

King sat forward, clasping his hands together. "How?"

"Car accident." Blackhurst frowned at him. "Sounds familiar then?"

"It does." King got up and walked over to the window like there was a sniper outside, ready to take them out. "Go on."

"We had a tough life out here. My dad sold the sawmill, but he just drank all his money away. Died twenty years ago, left me with nothing except this place and some goddamn hens. I've got a few hundred, all free ranging. Supply a few local businesses with all the eggs they can eat. But it's hard labor, and I worked hard for Steven, for us. And he wasn't an easy kid."

"Where is Steven now?"

"Haven't heard from him in months."

"Are you worried about him?"

"Always. But I didn't file a police report, if that's what you're asking."

"Why?"

"Don't trust them." Blackhurst looked defeated and broken down. "Besides, I doubt they would be able to find my lousy son."

"But Steven lived with you?"

"Typical modern kid. Living in his folks' basement into his late thirties."

"You know where he could've gone?"

"Could've gone anywhere. See, Steven worked a job driving trucks interstate. As far as Chicago sometimes, where his grandmother came from, god rest her soul. When he got back from a long drive, he'd just sit down in the basement in front of his computer."

"What was he doing on it?"

"Playing stupid games or talking to assholes about those stupid games. Like having a zombie down in my basement."

Lori could see the possibilities spread out like branches on a tree. So many connections, both from trucking and from his virtual life. But her role here was to supervise King while he gained intel. She caught his eye and thumbed over to the kitchen nook, then walked over. "You know about this Steven Blackhurst?"

King kept his gaze trained on the armchair, at the old man sitting with his feet up. "This is news to me. I've got a lot of cases to look at here, like I've told you. Max is one of them, but this is another new one. Another unknown death."

"Do you want to keep tracking Steven down?"

"It's not a case of want. I need to, Lori. I need to speak to as many of these children as I can, no matter their age now. One little detail could pair with another one and, bingo, we've identified someone we can prosecute."

Lori nodded at him, then looked over at Blackhurst. "Sir, do you mind if we take a look at that computer?"

Something thumps and screeches. I open my eyes and the Mario game has gone back to the title screen. I look around and my head is sore. Out of the window, it's raining, but we're on the ground and moving over some tarmac. Taxiing. I must've been asleep, but I don't know for how long.

Alice is sitting up at the front of the plane by the two doors, facing towards me. One was where I came in, but the other must be where the... where the man who flies the plane sits. When Mummy took me to Majorca, I got to see inside the cockpit. That's it! There were two men in there, but maybe a small plane like this only needs one man. I don't know.

The other boy is still sleeping.

I sit up and try to take the buckle off, but it's stuck.

Alice smiles at me, then gets up and walks over. "Hey, little man, how did you sleep?"

"I'm still tired."

"Isn't that always the way?"

"Where's Mummy?"

"It won't be long now. Okay?"

I don't know if it will be okay. Will it? I have slept, and Mummy's usually there when I wake up. Feels strange not having her wrap her arms around me and call me her special boy.

The cockpit door at the front opens and a man in a uniform comes out. The pilot! He walks up the aisle and rests his hand on Alice's back. "That's us parked up and ready to go."

"Good, good." Alice crosses the aisle to wake up the other boy. "Hey."

He lashes out with a hand and catches her in the nose.

Her hands cover her mouth. "You little shit!"

The pilot leans in to me, but it's like he's trying to distract me from Alice and the other boy. "You want to see the cockpit?"

"I'd love to!" I let the pilot release my belt, then he helps me up and carries me down to the front of the plane.

CHAPTER THIRTY

Carter

The school sports office was a dark space tucked away in the bowels of the football stadium. While they played baseball, soccer, and basketball here, it was approaching the level of college football. Someone had invested heavily, but Carter could not see them getting their return, at least not legally.

As he approached Gregg Ingram's office, the beige walls started to fill up with rows of rosettes and other pre-match niceties, looking like they went back to the seventies, all preserved for posterity. Not that anyone but Carter would notice them, at least not on a regular basis. A pair of large trophy cabinets sat on either side of an office door marked with COACH in a large graffiti font. The cabinets had barely enough trophies to fill one, but the sparse collection was spread across both. However, the girls' soccer team did seem to have won the state championships five years running.

Raised voices came through the door, so Carter opened it. And saw the problem. The big issue.

Iona Harrison stood in front of a computer, arms folded, an immovable object.

And Tyler Peterson wasn't the unstoppable force Carter needed him to be. Strange how adversity often revealed gaps in armor. Tyler was so good at manipulating technology, at hacking into data sources or finding surveillance cameras in unexpected places.

Trouble with this job was that people got in the way most of the time.

And Carter knew people. Knew them all too well. "What's the issue here?"

Iona stood her ground, hands on hips, but didn't drag her gaze away from Tyler. "Your *man* here is illegally trying to access one of my teacher's machines."

Carter walked over and got between them. "That's correct."

"You can't just do that."

"So you're saying I need a warrant?"

"Yes!"

"I've arranged for one." Carter fixed her with a long stare. "Problem is, these things take time. In normal circumstances, say a murder case, there's less pressure to provide the information immediately. Sure, SPD detectives will always use the line, 'What if the killer strikes again?' but you and I both know that the vast majority of homicides are one-time things. The cops can wait for their warrants, do things by the book, build their evidence trail."

Iona straightened up. "I'm waiting for the 'but' here."

Carter gave her a smile, even tried to put some warmth into it, but inside he was boiling with rage. He had to take a couple of seconds to make sure his voice came out precisely how he wanted it. "But this isn't a murder case, ma'am. We're not Seattle PD detectives. This is a child abduction. Now, Olivia might or might not see herself as a child anymore, but she is legally a minor. In all abduction cases, we in the FBI have primacy and investigate. We've got a standard playbook and authority. And I'll be honest with you, ma'am, I'm struggling to figure out what the hell is going on here."

"You don't think Gregg took her, do you?"

"I have at least three, maybe four concrete explanations for why she's been taken. Gregg Ingram is key to two of them."

For a moment, Iona looked away, seeming unable to accept the reality of the situation.

Carter pounced on that doubt. "Ma'am, you know what happened with Jennifer Huston before. It's happening with Shania Anderson now. We're searching for others. Gregg will hopefully see sense and spill, but hopefully you'll help us. After all, you put him in a position of trust and authority, and you kept them there. There's a clear pattern of targeting minors here."

"There something you're not telling me?"

"I'm being completely honest with you, ma'am."

"So why do you have this big palooka here trying to access his computer?"

Yep, she was going to hold her ground, prevent anyone getting anywhere near that machine.

"Because Tyler's one of my best agents. He's got experience in data extraction and manipulation. If there are any clues as to where Olivia is on that machine, he can find it."

"Why do you think there might be?"

"Because… We found something on Olivia's machine at home. Her laptop." Carter knew he had to be careful here. She was sensing blood, and he knew the full story would blow everything wide open and let Tyler in, but he just couldn't give her everything. "We understand Gregg was tracking Olivia's movements electronically."

"Surveilling her?"

"It's possible there's some tracking mechanism at play here."

"Mr. Carter, you know the number of parents here who have some sort of surveillance on their kids' cellphones?"

"That's not what I'm talking about. Besides, Olivia's cell was still in her room."

Iona flared her nostrils.

Carter knew he was nowhere near winning her over. "Ma'am, I understand what you're going through here. Having a missing student must be tough on you. You've got a responsibility to every single one of your kids."

"You have no idea."

"No, I do. I've worked so many cases. Spoken to so many people in your situation. But I need to monitor Gregg Ingram's online actions."

"Why do you need to get at his work machine?"

"Sexual offenders like to relive their fantasies or engage in their behavior at all times, in all ways. Doing it at work would be no different than having a bottle hidden in his bottom drawer."

Tyler had more though. "I've been to his apartment, but his computers have all been emptied. The hard drives are gone. He's a very careful man. And we have no idea where the drives are."

But Iona still didn't look reassured. "You aren't being completely truthful, are you?"

Tyler looked over to Carter, passing the buck to his superior.

"No, we're not." Carter stared into her eyes. "But that's because we can't be completely honest with you."

"Oh my god." Her face slipped, revealing a human being beaten down by her experiences here. By Deacon Hill's drug dealing. By Gregg Ingram's child abuse. "What has he *done*?"

"He won't be your problem for much longer, ma'am. Put it that way."

Iona collapsed into Gregg's chair and reached into her pants pocket. She held up a yellow-cased smartphone. "I've got his credentials here."

"Thank you." Tyler took the note and started logging in to Gregg's machine.

Carter gave Tyler space to work in, but he didn't want Iona here when—and if—the expected payload landed. "Need you to come with me, ma'am."

She looked up at him. "I've always had my doubts about him. With Jen Huston, he assured me it was all aboveboard. He didn't touch her when she was a student here. And I believed him. Such an asshole. Now… Shania? Olivia? Whatever he's been doing, he's still doing it. And it's my fault."

Tyler looked over from the machine and gave Carter the nod. He had something.

"This is on me, isn't it?" Iona collapsed in on herself, arms folded tight around her shoulders. "All this, what's happened to Jen, what's happening to Olivia, it's all on me."

"I need you to come with me." Carter helped Iona to her feet and caught a flash of Tyler's laptop screen.

It looked like Tyler had found more of the Olivia files, probably stored in a cloud drive.

Iona stopped by the door. "Please, just tell me what he's done to her."

"I can't. And you both don't want to see this and *can't*. But you'll find out in time."

She shook her head. "Okay."

Carter shut the door and twisted the lock. "What have you got, Peterson?"

Tyler was working away at his machine, the high-end equipment that would act as a second pair of eyes, provide an audit trail for his work when this all came to trial. Should it ever come to trial. "Well, this is the cloud drive he's been accessing. The Netherlands one. At least a hundred nude videos of Olivia on here."

"That's a *lot*."

"It's one every three days, by my reckoning. So maybe there were more, and he's just picked the best. But I don't know."

"Okay, this is a good start. But what else do we have?"

Tyler gave a brief flash of a smile, a tiny nugget of hope in an avalanche of horror. "Nothing."

That little nugget of hope trickled away down the stream toward the river.

Carter felt it all collapse. Sure, they could prosecute Gregg for manufacturing child pornography, but it was not finding the girl. She could be anywhere. Dead, even. And Gregg was not going to tell them.

No, she was gone.

Carter collapsed against the wall. He had failed yet another missing child.

"Sir?"

Carter couldn't even look at Tyler. "I'm fine."

"I found something." Tyler held up a USB drive and attached something to it. "If this is what I think it is…"

Carter pushed himself up to standing. "What is it?"

"Remember when I checked Olivia's laptop, the files were missing?"

"Right."

"Well, this is where it all lives." Tyler plugged the drive into his machine. "The motherlode." The screen showed a directory filled with messages. "In addition to the videos, it appears that Gregg has stolen all messages Olivia sent on Instagram, Twitter, Facebook, you name it. He's really getting inside her head, right?"

"Social engineering as they say. Hackers' toolkit 101. Being inside their heads is the easiest way to manipulate them."

"But those hacker guys are using it to get inside databases. Gregg's using it to groom his partner's daughter. Sick."

He was right. This was sick.

And Carter did not want to even think about the fact that Gregg had returned to Marissa's home while she slept to steal Olivia's USB drive.

"So what have you got?"

"Well, that's the big issue now, sir. They all seem to be deleted and wiped. Kids these days are so smart. It's going to take time to recover them. A lot of time. But there's a message from Olivia that he hasn't looked at yet, sir. It hasn't even been read, let alone deleted."

"Open it." Carter walked back to his spot against the wall, the better to focus on the text.

"Okay, here goes." Tyler cracked his knuckles. "Hey Josh, how you doing? Did your dad take you to the ball game like he promised? I got an A on a test, so Mom's buying me that dress. And I started *Cobra Kai* on Netflix. Holy shit!"

"Tyler, can you cut to the chase?"

"Sure. Okay, so she says, 'Man, I don't even know if this will get to you. Mom might've blocked this message. Maybe got that creepy psycho to do it. When he's not spying on me. Gregg. Such a douchebag.' That's not good, is it?"

"No." And it deepened the hole Gregg Ingram was in.

"The good thing about having a drunk for a mom is she never has any bottles in the house. Gregg brought over a Californian Merlot for tonight's dinner. Heard him giving her it, and she was gushing and cooing over it like a new baby. It's got a cork! Perfecto! All I've got to do is inject this stuff in the bottle and wait for her to drink it. Then she'll be out like a light."

Carter jolted forward. "What?"

"That package turned up, Josh. The syringe and the bottle."

Carter felt sick to his stomach. "She ran away?"

"I think so, sir. 'I could just run away or make it look like I'm dead, but even Mom doesn't deserve that sort of shit. You're such a genius. Make it look like I've been taken and, I don't care who she thinks has taken me, but it could be, like, a million people. And she doesn't know about you.'"

"This is all to get back at her Mom?"

"I think so. She ends with, 'I want that bitch to understand what it's like not to know if someone you love is dead or alive. She doesn't feel anything for Dad, but I still do. I'm Olivia **Hill**, not Olivia **Davis**.' The names are in bold, sir. 'Dad was my whole life, and now that he's gone, there's nothing left. I'm absolutely, completely crushed. I want her to understand the depth of my feelings, then maybe we can be close again. Maybe. Not knowing where I am will give her one iota of what it's been like for me with my dad. But one thing I'm sure of, she will never forget.'"

CHAPTER THIRTY-ONE

Marissa

Marissa tugged at her hair, straightening out the kinks then letting them go again. She stared at the pages, her lips moving as she read the words again. Then she rested them on the table, like they were a handwritten note from her daughter rather than printed pages, and looked right at Carter. "You believe this?"

That was the only way she could think of this.

If this was genuine, then she had let her daughter down. Trying to protect her from her asshole father, but instead she had pushed her away.

If this was genuine.

Or was it Gregg pretending to be Josh? The tide of bile climbed her throat. Letting him in her house was bad enough, but letting him take her daughter?

And why would Carter lie to her?

She looked at him. He was a parent too. Some parents would own up to their shortcomings. Others would be angry, maybe blaming each other. Or themselves. But they'd both want to do whatever they could to recover their child.

Marissa knew this was shock making her feel like she was in denial about Olivia running away.

Blaming everyone but herself. Gregg, Ray, Deacon, even Carter.

But if she accepted it, then what it came down to was that she'd run away.

Carter was leading this because it appeared to be an abduction. Had all the hallmarks, all the signs. Even had suspects. But that's all it was, just the appearance of an abduction.

God. Marissa had pushed her baby away. All she wanted was to protect her daughter from her father's deviancy.

But she saw something in Carter too. Beating himself up for not spotting what was happening. The FBI special agent who had done hundreds of these cases. Outfoxed by a teenage girl.

"If only Olivia knew…" Marissa coiled her hair around her finger again and picked up the pages with her free hand. "She talks about how I stopped her from seeing her father. I mean… Deacon was *toxic*. Still is. All the dark shit he'd done to us—losing our home, stealing her college fund, ruining our lives. I was protecting her from that. How can I make her see that?"

"I want to help you get her to see things your way." Carter sat there, nodding slowly. It was like he was letting her know he understood, but was waiting for that moment when she *knew* he understood. "But two wrongs don't make a right. And I have to find Olivia."

"You mean, find this Josh kid?" Marissa pushed the sheets away. "I'm still completely in the dark about him. She never mentioned him to me."

"What about to Gregg?"

"Liv didn't speak to him much." She snatched the pages up again. "How did you find this?"

"I can't say."

"Please, I need to know." And she did. After Deacon, she could not believe she had fallen for another toxic man. And a buddy of Deacon's too. God, she was so dumb.

"Marissa, this isn't something I can share with you, and I'm not sure you want to find out."

"You expect me to believe you without proof?" She flung the sheets of paper on the floor. "That could all just be made up."

"But it matches how Olivia speaks, right?"

"Kind of." He was right, though. That was Liv. Her Liv. Her baby. "But I can't understand why she would run."

"We've found some things about Gregg."

"What?"

"He was snooping on Olivia."

"Snooping?"

"He installed an app on her laptop."

"I told him to. I wanted to know who she was talking to on the internet."

"Well, the problem is he went one step further. That service seems to have forwarded this message on to a server. The other side of it, though, was Gregg using her laptop to record video of her getting changed."

"What?" Marissa looked at him, but it was like Carter wasn't there anymore. Just a ghost. Then there were two of him.

Marissa felt herself collapse in on herself. All that rage, all the anger, it found a focus now.

And it wasn't Gregg.

It was Marissa herself for trusting him.

"Marissa, do you have any idea who Josh is?"

"None. I told you. Could it be Gregg?"

"Why would you think that?"

"I'm just worried it is. Please. Find her."

CHAPTER THIRTY-TWO

Carter

Gregg was still in the field office's interrogation room. "I won't talk to you."

"This isn't like on TV." Carter sat opposite, arms folded to mirror him. "You can't just sit there and wait this out. And I'll explain why. Gregg, if we never find Olivia, if this Josh kid kills her, then forget this sickness you're suffering from, because your silence right now will eat away at you. Every second of your life, it'll be whispering in your ear, 'You could've saved her life.' Is that something you want to live with, Gregg? Is it?"

"I can't help you."

"Sure? Because, I wonder if you might know more about Josh than you've told us so far."

"I've never heard of him."

"Right, and I'll just believe that?" Carter pulled out a sheet of paper and passed it across the table. "That's a message Olivia sent to Josh."

"Never seen it before in my life."

"No, that's actually the first true thing you've said to me, you son of a bitch. Because you didn't get around to it, did you? Know where we found that?"

"No?"

"It was on a USB drive we found in your office at school."

Gregg's face lost all color. "My office?"

"Right. One of my best agents is going through your stuff right now, Gregg. He's relentless. He'll find whatever else you're hiding. But that drive was in Olivia's computer. All of her messages were stored on it. Kids these days do that a lot. Physical security to protect against prying parental eyes. How did it end up in your desk drawer?"

"I have no idea."

"Really? But you knew about the drive, didn't you? Knew what was on it. When you installed that spying software on her machine, you spotted it. Probably searched through it. You didn't take it then, Gregg, but you took it this morning, didn't you?"

"Of course I didn't!"

"Are you telling me Olivia gave it to you?"

"No!"

"So, maybe it was last night after you met Ray. Either way, you went back to the house to retrieve it. Gregg, Marissa was drugged, and Olivia was missing."

"I didn't know."

"Bullshit!" Carter thumped the desk. "Of course you knew! You were covering your tracks! What kind of man does that? It's ice-cold."

Gregg's cool exterior was a memory now. He sat there, eyes wide, mouth hanging open.

"Gregg, start with telling me everything you know about Josh."

"I don't—"

"You do, Gregg. Of course you do." Carter clutched the messages in his hand. "Olivia and Josh have been exchanging messages for almost a year now. We found this on that drive. One message she sent to him. The rest have been deleted. Convenient for you, maybe. But I suspect you've read them, wondering if Olivia was aware of what you were up to. Maybe she suspected, maybe she even knew, but you needed to get inside her head, find out what she thought. And she seemed to talk to this Josh a lot. This kind of thing happens all the time, you know. Girls meeting guys on the internet, falling in love with them. Messages are so intimate, gets right into their skulls. It's like telepathy if you think about it. And I suspect you're the sort of man who *has* thought about it. It's how you engineered Jen, Shania, Olivia, and countless others. You were grooming her. Building up a picture of her life to use against her."

"It's not what I was doing."

"So you're just a voyeur?"

Gregg shrugged.

"Now, I've done a bit of analysis on these messages from Josh. Funny thing, when guys our age were taught to type, we'd use a double space."

"What?"

"Kids these days barely use any punctuation, right? But a single space, all the time. Thing is, your school reports are full of double spaces. Admit it, Gregg, you are Josh."

"No!"

"Talk to me, Gregg. Help me pull you out of this deep hole you've sunk into."

"I read those messages, but that's it. Liv's just a kid. They were full of teen drama. I mean, she shared a lot of messages with this Josh. I read the first twenty or so, but I stopped and just deleted them when they arrived."

"Did you read the messages from her to Josh about running away?"

"What? Running away?"

"Where is she?"

"That's news to me."

"I don't believe you."

"What?"

"If you are Josh, then that makes a lot more sense to me. More cover for you. And it means Olivia's running away to you, isn't she?"

"Why would I do that?"

"Because you've been grooming her. I don't know. Maybe she's pregnant with your kid. Maybe she's threatening to tell her mother about you. Maybe she found out she was being snooped on. I don't know. You do."

"This isn't me. I'm not Josh."

"I need you to give us access to your server in the Netherlands."

"No way. I'm never giving you access."

And that made it even worse. An innocent girl's life was at risk here, and still he was keeping secrets. "What else do you have in there?"

"You don't want to know." Gregg swallowed hard. "You must think I'm a lowlife, but I did think of her as my own daughter. It's sick, I know, what I've been doing, that I can't stop. But it's a watching thing. It's not a doing thing. I would never do anything to her. You need to believe me here, I am not Josh."

"Just give us access to that server."

"No!"

"She ran away from home and the only lead I've got is this kid. I need to investigate. If we're going to recover her, this girl you think of as your daughter, then you need to talk to me. Okay?"

"I can't!"

"Gregg, right now we are going to prosecute you for manufacturing child pornography. I can offer you immunity for prosecution against Jen and Shania, or any other victims on that server, in exchange for access to the server."

Gregg looked tempted. His eyes and lips twitching.

"But you've got to be completely honest with me, and I need to know that none of the girls on there have been killed or abducted, or are even missing."

"Okay." Tyler sat back and nibbled at his thumbnail. "Well, given that he won't give you login credentials to that server, I've done the next best thing." He tapped the nail off the laptop's screen. "I've backed up the evidence trail on Olivia's laptop and tied it up with Gregg's."

"Bottom line, Peterson?"

"Bottom line is I think I know what he's been doing."

"You think you know?"

"This is more like faith than science. The messages went from her machine to a local directory. He went in and manually copied these videos and messages to the server in the Netherlands. None of it is saved locally, so each time he did it, he didn't leave an audit trail. I know where the server is, but I can't get in."

"Why do that?"

"To hide things. We've got our own snooping operations for stuff like this. Putting a man in the middle like this blocks that. Gregg is a smart guy. Probably not his own work, probably connected to some kind of network."

Carter felt that sting in the pit of his stomach. Organized crime always targeted the vulnerable, exploited their weaknesses and used it all against them. And if he was in some kind of network, there was no chance they would ever be able to unpick it. Those guys were always too smart, unless someone was dumb enough to leave a door open, which was more faith and prayers than active detective work. "How long has he been doing it?"

"Looks like a year."

"He's got a year's worth of videos of her?"

"He only keeps nudes of her. And all these messages, they've been deleted at his end. Once I've got access to this server in the Netherlands, then I can try to recover them."

"That won't happen, Tyler."

"Supposed to just believe that?"

"Is Josh real?"

"You think it's Gregg, don't you?"

"All this social engineering, reading these messages, stands to reason, doesn't it?"

"Sure. I mean, I've got some messages back. She sent him photos of her breasts."

"Christ."

"After getting a dick pic or two."

Carter would never know why people would do that. "Is it worth searching Gregg's computers?"

"He won't give us the hard drives, so we can't. I mean, it's unlikely to be his johnson, sir. Most likely he got it off the net somewhere. I could try a reverse image search, but it might be from a private part of the internet."

"Do it."

"Okay, but here's the thing. I've found video chat records from Olivia with Josh. Josh is real."

"Have you got any of them recorded?"

"One. It's weird. Those messages? They were all back and forth, right? Well, in this he just gives her statements."

"Show me."

"Sure. This was three weeks ago."

The screen filled with a two-up video call. Olivia was on the left, and on the right of the screen was a teenaged boy.

His eyes were almost blocked out by his long bangs. Braces like rail tracks across his teeth. "Hey Libby, good to finally speak to you in person." Local enough accent. And he had his own pet name for her. He laughed. "I mean, it's not in person, but—"

"I know what you mean." Olivia wasn't looking at the camera, just off to the side. And she wasn't staying still at all. She was clearly nervous as hell.

Tyler's laptop chimed and he switched screens, but the audio kept going. "Aha."

"Aha, what?"

"Messages." Tyler tapped the screen. "I figured the local copies would be deleted, but his school laptop was keeping them."

Three messages sat in a folder.

"That's it?"

"That's it." Tyler nodded, but he was working away with some arcane magic. "All the rest have been cleared. No coming back." He opened the first message, the most recent one. "This is what Olivia is replying to."

From Josh:

> *Hey Libby. Yeah, my dad got tickets for the ball game on Saturday. I'm super pumped about it.*
>
> *So, I know you're unsure about this, but you have to* need *to do this, okay? No pressure from me, Libby. It's all good, but you have to commit to running away.*
>
> *I've sent the stuff, it should turn up. Watch your mail. It's addressed to your dad, so she'll hopefully toss it in the trash, then you can grab it.*
>
> *And you know where to meet. You just have to say when.*
>
> *And if there's heat there, any heat at all, I'll meet you at the other place we talked about on the video call. It's special to me.*
>
> *Here's a screenshot of where to meet.*
>
> *And Never Forget.*

Tyler double-clicked the thumbnail and opened it.

Carter recognized the place immediately.

Carter stood in the middle of a wide clearing in the woods, maybe a hundred paces from the parking lot.

Up ahead, an old building was close to getting lost in the evening gloom. Huge and built of brick, though it was crumbling in the corners. Very few windows, just a couple by the front door, and some up high. Must be pretty dark in there. Carter figured it must have been something for the war.

Elisha clapped his back. "Just googled it, Max. This was a building used in the Second World War. It's been shut forty years and left to go to ruin."

"It's far enough away from Seattle that no enterprising realtor has snapped it up and tried to flip it."

"Or some hipster turned it into a microbrewery."

"Then the woods took over."

"Perfect place to hide out."

Out here in the wild, it was like the frontier was thriving.

"Come on." Carter set off, his shoes soaked through for the second time that day, taking it real slow.

Elisha was matching his pace. Behind her, four banks of agents fanned out to surround the building at strategic points. "Think she'll be here?"

"If she's not, then I don't know what the hell I'm going to do next." Carter tried the door, a big lump of old wood. The handle twisted and he got inside.

Whatever Olivia had been doing here, the building was empty now. A large hall, empty. Two doors at either end.

"I'll check in there." Elisha set off away from him.

Carter stood in the middle of the giant room. Back in the day, it would have housed hundreds of operators, each manually connecting customers to other parts of the country. Then it had gradually been automated, and those jobs were moved elsewhere, never to return.

He knew Olivia was not here, but he needed to find out if she had been.

Carter walked over to the door, still signposted CANTEEN.

Locked.

Well, there you go. A fresh mystery.

Footsteps behind him, clicking off the marble floor. Elisha, shaking her head. "Checked that door. Same as this one. A whole heap of nothing."

"No sign of anybody?"

"Nope."

Carter felt his shoulders sag. "Great."

"Well, there's something. It looks like someone's jury-rigged the electricity supply. Messy job, but it seemed to work."

"So people have been here?"

"No idea when, though."

Carter tried playing it through. He got out his cellphone and found the snapshot of Josh and Olivia's video call. Josh's background was blurry, but it could have been in this place. He tried the canteen door again. Sounded like a mortice. Could be broken with a shoulder and a bit of precision. He pressed his ear against the cold wood. The paint was peeling and sharp against his skin. "I think I can hear something. Someone might be in there. We've got to get in." He stepped back three paces. Then took a deep breath. He flew at the door like he was back on the football field, spearing a wide receiver with the ball. His shoulder cracked into the wood and it never stood a chance.

The door flew off its hinges and tore the lock out of the wall with it.

Carter rolled over the marble tiles and pulled himself up to standing.

Cardboard boxes filled the space, floor-to-ceiling. Plain, unmarked. There must have been thousands of them in there.

A boy stood there, panic filling his blue eyes. Long bangs, swept back with sweat. Carter recognized him right away.

Josh.

CHAPTER THIRTY-THREE

Lori

The basement was like a teenage boy's room even though Steven Blackhurst was thirty-nine. Posters of female film and pop stars in bikinis, mouths open for him. Female wrestlers in bikinis. Others of fantasy worlds with over-muscled barbarians, sinister wizards, and women in bikinis. Bit of a theme running there.

The room was the size of the house, but divided up into smaller sections. A sleeping area with a single bed. Display cases filled with books, DVDs, and old video games consoles, with walls and walls of games—he must have owned everything Nintendo ever made.

And in the middle, a huge TV with a reclining chair in front that looked like it belonged in a sports car. Dane Rodgers was in the corner, crouching by a big black box full of flashing blue and green lights, with cables running to the TV. A fan blew hard and sounded like a hairdryer.

Lori knew the sort of machine—her ex-husband had one, used to call it his gaming rig, and this was Steven's. And as much as the components cost when they were put in, they soon got out of date and needed upgrading.

If Albert Blackhurst was telling the truth, Steven's machine hadn't been used in two years. While Lori wished she had Tyler Peterson to do this, Dane was good enough. She hoped.

Lori joined him by the machine, leaving King with Blackhurst.

"This is a tall order." Dane reached over to the back of the machine and wiggled a cord. "I'm way out of my comfort zone here. I can smash people's heads against walls to get them to admit to child abduction." He smiled at her, but he wasn't enjoying himself. "I'm man enough that I can admit defeat. You need to get a specialist in. Or Tyler Peterson, if possible."

"Tyler's tied up with the Olivia Davis case. Anyone else you can think of?"

"The problem is there's nobody I know. I've seen Tyler tear one of these machines apart. He builds them in his spare time. He made me mine. I know how to use it, just..."

"Dane, call him up and ask for his help. Whatever he can give you. Tell him I approved it. Max can't have him twenty-four seven."

"Okay." Dane stood up and got out his cell. "Okay." It looked like this was the biggest challenge of his life. Asking an agent ten years his junior for some help.

Lori took her time walking back over. She had read somewhere that the old gaming consoles were now collectors' items, worth almost as much as paintings if they were in the right condition. A sealed *Mario Brothers* game from the eighties had sold for a good six-figure sum recently. The only difference was that Steven's collection was filled with slightly battered boxes, not still-sealed ones. So he loved the games for playing, rather than some monied douchebag reliving his childhood.

Not that Steven's childhood seemed to be worth living the first time through.

But that was what a lot of that sort of hoarding came down to. Nostalgia, reliving, call it what you want, it was all about reclaiming that youth, a time when things were okay, or at least seemed that way.

Blackhurst sat on the bed, sorting through a pile of paperwork. "There's nothing here that I haven't been through a million times before in the last two years."

"Did your son have any savings?"

"I don't know." Blackhurst shrugged. "I mean, he had money from his job, but he lived quite simply. Just spent some cash on his games. And he didn't take any of them, did he?"

"Okay." But it didn't feel okay to Lori. She had to remind herself why she was here. This was King's case, not hers. Bill Carter had finally admitted what he'd been responsible for, and it had led them here, to another man in the same situation as Max. But Steven Blackhurst was trapped in amber, stuck in his teenage years, reliving that.

Max's coping mechanism was entirely different, spending his adult life hunting down missing children.

King was yawning into his fists, the long travel catching up with him and biting his ass. Or "arse," as he would say. "Strange how he'd just leave a machine like that behind."

"You're a gamer?"

"God no, but one of my colleagues is."

Lori nodded. "Then again, Steven has left his whole life behind."

King cast his gaze around the dim room. "There's a lot of time and money wrapped up in this collection. Surely he would've taken that?"

"I'm struggling to see what else we can get out of this, Chris. Maybe you should stop now. Take the night to catch up on some sleep. Get some dinner, watch a movie. You've made good progress on day one."

"This will just eat away at me, I'm afraid. I came to this country with a mystery, and it's only getting deeper. I didn't know anything about Steven Blackhurst this morning, but now, standing here? Well, I can see the impact his childhood trauma had on his adult life. He drove a truck long-distance, which is a very manly and adult vocation, but when he comes home, he plays video games all day, every day. Look at these posters. He's losing himself in something, hiding from the trauma. All those days on the road, he must be reliving it, then when he comes back, all he can do to escape it is sit down here, play video games, and eat ramen."

"Ramen?"

"Noodles." King pointed to the corner. "I found boxes of the stuff. Don't know if that's what he's been transporting."

"Lori?" Dane was over by the gaming machine, clutching his cellphone. "Just spoke to Tyler. Kid's stressing out, got hassle at some school. Carter won't let him help me out here."

Max.

"Okay." Lori stomped over to the stairs and hit dial.

Answered right away. "Carter." Sounded like he was driving.

"Max, it's Lori. I need Tyler Peterson."

Carter sighed down the line. "Lori, I've got him on a priority-one activity. No can do."

She looked over at Dane, clueless in front of the gaming computer. "I just need him to help guide Rodgers through accessing a PC."

"Lori, I'm close to recovering Olivia Davis."

"Seriously?"

"Well, Tyler's effort is critical to that."

"I just need like a ten-second phone call. That's it."

"Why, Lori?"

"I can't tell you that, Max."

"This is Bill stuff?"

"Afraid so."

"So, I can't know, but I'm stuck in a bind, Lori. I can't release Tyler's time without good reason. And if we lose Olivia's trail, then Karen will toast my balls."

Lori had no choice here. Her need was less than Carter's, but still, they had a trail. And if King's fears were real? "We're searching for a Steven Blackhurst."

"Steven?"

Something tickled at the back of Lori's neck. The way he said it, it meant something to him. "Can't say any more to you than that, Max."

"I know you want to, but this is tied in with what Bill did."

"Can't say, Max."

"Steven Blackhurst."

"That name mean something to you?"

"What if it does?"

"Max, can I get access to Tyler?"

"Okay." And he was gone.

By the time Lori had walked back over, Dane's cell was ringing. King was frowning at her. "Everything okay?"

"Just hate having to leverage people, that's all."

"Part of the pain of this job, isn't it?"

"Most of the pain."

Dane gave her the thumbs up. "Tyler's given me something that might work." He pulled out a cord and plugged it into his laptop. "Sneaky."

Lori followed King over.

Dane collapsed into the gaming chair and the screen lit up, but it showed the standard FBI desktop. "Got my machine to take over his. Tyler... He's some kid. Knows a ton of tricks." He jabbed at the keyboard and the screen filled with a long list of what looked like websites. "Well, Steven Blackhurst's internet search history stopped almost two years ago to the day."

"Back to when he went missing." Lori looked over at Albert Blackhurst, but he was lost in his son's physical mail history. "What about before that?"

Dane was scrolling back through pages and pages of links. "Well, it looks like it matches his pattern of being on the road for a week, then four or five days off."

"What's he been looking at?"

"Not that different from mine, to be honest. Some sporadic searches for where to go next in a game, some looking into detailed strategies for an MMO."

"A what?"

"A massively multiplayer online role-playing game. *World of Warcraft* is the big one. It's like virtual reality, without the helmets and shit. It's full of real people doing stuff, and I mean a ton of people. It's a huge business. People lose themselves to it." Dane sat back, still scrolling down the list. "But most of the time, it looks like he was researching the people who had brought him here."

Lori walked closer to the screen. Dane was right—Steven had been doing deep research into historic flight manifests from England, among many other things. "This is... Well. Has he been in touch with anyone regarding it?"

"Pages and pages of history, but I can't see any messages, Lori." Dane was grimacing. "His email app is empty. Thing is..." He scratched at his chin. "He's got Tor installed."

Lori wished for a time when law enforcement was about people and not technology, with its secret three-letter acronyms and arcane mythology. "Which is?"

"It means he's been on the dark web. I can't access that history. It's not stored."

So it was looking like a dead end, then. Especially to King. Every minute that passed, he looked that much more tired. "Any clues as to where he's gone?"

"Just a sec." Dane tapped at the keyboard. "Okay, so there is a secure chat app here. If this was a smartphone, it'd be asking for biometric information. Fingerprints, face scans, you name it. But it's not, so I'm in. His machine thinks I'm him, which is good." He pursed his lips as he read. "Okay, there are a ton of messages to go through, but I'm checking the latest one."

It flashed up on the screen.

Lori checked the date. "This is the day before he went, isn't it?"
Blackhurst was now leaning against the gaming chair.
The message was short:

> *I think you can help me. We can do this, Steven. We can win. Just come up to the door and ask for me. We can change this around. Here's the address of where we are.*

Dane clicked on the hyperlink and the screen opened into a maps app.
Lori knew exactly where it was.

This airport isn't like the one we boarded at. It's nowhere near as fancy. In fact, it's not fancy at all. And it's so much busier. Smelly men in dirty shirts are walking around, talking. Smell of cigars like Uncle Steve.

Alice is standing by a door, talking into a phone handset.

"Why didn't you play my Nintendo?"

"I didn't want to."

"Don't you like Mario?"

"I don't care." But the boy's eyes are searching around for something, then he looks over at me. *"This isn't London, you know."*

"I know."

"I think it's America."

"America?" I frown at him. *"But my daddy lives in America."*

"Mine does too."

"I'm supposed to meet my mummy here. Do you know where she is?" He sniffs. *"That what they told you?"*

"What's that mean?" Now we're standing, I can see that the boy is older than me. Three years maybe. I feel like I need to pee again. *"I'm scared."*

"Me too."

"What's going on?"

"I don't know."

"You're older than me, aren't you?"

The boy nods at me. *"I'm eight."*

"I'm six."

Alice waves at us. "Come on, boys. We're here!"

I feel even more scared now. Definitely will pee myself. I take the boy's hand. "What's your name?"

A big man comes running towards us and wraps up the other boy in a hug. "My boy!"

I can't keep a hold of the boy's hand, and I have to let go. There's no sign of Mummy.

The older boy looks back at me. "My name is Max. Never forget it."

"I'm Steven. Steven Blackhurst."

CHAPTER THIRTY-FOUR

Carter

Carter opened the door and thumped across the floor. He sat, gazing deep into Josh's eyes. "So, Josh. You want to give me your surname?"

"Nope."

"That's how you want to play it? Cool." Carter eased his suit jacket off and slipped it over the back of his chair. "You want to explain to us what you were doing in a storage room crammed full of drugs?"

Josh just stared at the table.

"You were caught red-handed in there. That was a *lot* of drugs. I mean, the DEA will be weeks just *cataloguing* it. Must be in the tens or hundreds of millions. Right?"

Josh shrugged.

"You know you're in deep, don't you?"

"I'm only sixteen."

"You won't be sweet sixteen forever, kid. With that amount of contraband, you'll be doing a lot of time. Twenty-five years' time, you'll be forty-one. Same age I am now. No such thing as good behavior with what you're going down for." He let it sink in, but the kid was super-delusional. "Only hope you've got is to give up your superiors. They were trying to kill you, weren't they?"

Another shrug. "I'm cool."

"Josh, I'm pretty sure you're not the boss of this whole thing. So who is?"

"That's Vic's place."

"Vic, huh?"

"Vic Jordan."

"You want to talk to me about him?"

"You wouldn't understand."

"Try me."

"Not worth the effort." Josh blew air up his face. His bangs barely moved. "Someone locked me in there."

"Sure."

"It's the truth."

That was how he was going to play it. But Carter had other cards to play. "You spoke to Olivia, right?"

"Olivia?"

"You might call her Libby."

"No idea who you mean."

"Josh, I think you need to tell me the truth here." Carter reached into his jacket pocket for a still, then slid it across the desk. "This is you and her. You spoke to her on a video call."

"Ah, her. Yeah. Nice girl. Cute, nerdy. Hated her mom."

"You hate your mom too?"

"She hates me. Big diff."

"That why you left home?"

"Why do you think I left home?"

"Well, you won't give us your full name. Most runaways do, but some are pretty streetwise. People like you. So, was that why you left home?"

"Partly."

"But there were other reasons?"

"Man…"

"You want to tell me why you were there?"

"Look, man, you haven't lived my life. You don't know what it's been like for me. You're some fancy-ass FBI agent. Harvard, Yale, Princeton. Ivy League bitch. That life's so *vanilla*."

"That's what you think?"

"Tell me it's any different."

"You want me to tell you about my life?"

"Only if it's true."

"Josh, I went to Washington State after two years at community college. Paid my own way by joining the United States Army. Served two tours overseas." Carter started rolling up his left shirt sleeve. Slowly, focusing on the scar halfway up. "This is a shrapnel wound from a live round I caught in Basra. So don't think I've had it easy."

"Vanilla."

"And I was born in London, England."

"What?"

"My dad, Bill, he got a job over here, but my mom didn't want to come. So what did my dad do? He moved, divorced her. I was young, much younger than you. Thing is, he missed me. Or he thought he did." Carter could think of a hundred reasons why he was saying all this, stuff from the training manuals and operational procedures. But unburdening himself like this, maybe it was because of everything Lori was doing, investigating Bill and how far his talons dug. "My father paid these guys to abduct me and fly me over to this country. Then my mom started trying to get me back, but these same guys, they had her killed." He started on his right sleeve now, but there were no scars on that side. "I've lived with this all my life. I try to do good in the world, but it just feels like everything is getting worse."

"Sorry, man." It looked like he meant it. He sat there, taking his time thinking it through.

Carter saw only two options. Josh would give him the truth, or he would try and play him. "Josh, you don't owe those people anything."

"My name's not Josh. It's Kelvin." He shut his eyes. "Kelvin Jamieson Munro. I grew up in South Seattle. My dad left before I was born, and Mom wasn't a strong woman. Tried her hardest, but raising me and my brother was difficult. Ended up with so many uncles."

Boy, had Carter seen that play out so many times. Still, now that he had Josh/Kelvin talking, he let him keep going.

"These uncles, man. Temporary dads who'd move in, bang my mom for a few months, then move on. Some used to beat me. Got much harder when my brother died."

"What happened to him?"

"Kyle was six years older than me. Different dad." Kelvin swallowed hard. "Kyle got involved with these kids who had cars. One time he was driving out in the boonies and smashed into a tree. Dick wasn't wearing a seatbelt. None of them were. Died on the way to the ER, but he never stood a chance. He was eighteen."

"I'm sorry to hear that."

"Made Mom worse. She let this one guy move in. Theodore. Big dude, and stacked. He used to beat on me. I mean, what is it about a dude that big that he needs to beat up a kid?"

"Makes him feel like a man. Maybe his father beat him and it's the only thing he could think to do."

"Well, whatever, man. He must've had a tiny pecker. But he stayed around, and Mom couldn't stop him kicking the shit out of me."

"Couldn't or wouldn't?"

"Both. She was drinking all the time." Kelvin ran his hand through his hair and swept it back. "One day, I got high with some buddies, then came home. Mom and Theodore were out, and I was completely wasted, so I split."

Carter sat back, arms folded. "You ran?"

"Right."

"What happened?"

Kelvin swallowed hard. "That place you found me? I broke in there, stayed a night. Had some food, but then these dudes turned up. I tried to run, but they caught me."

"When was this?"

"Couple of weeks ago. This dude was going to kill me, but then this other one, he had a use for me."

"Grooming Olivia?"

"That wasn't me."

And there it was, that same psychopathic refusal to acknowledge blame. The poor kid had endured a tough life, one he probably coped with by compartmentalizing the beatings and the abuse. But the denials were stopping Carter from finding Olivia.

"Kelvin, you're on the video call with her, talking about running away. Olivia Davis. The girl you spoke to. You were supposed to meet her at that building. That was you, Kelvin. You sent her all those messages."

"Not me, man."

"We recovered it from her laptop, Kelvin. You're facing human-trafficking charges for your part in her abduction."

"Man…"

"Where is she?"

"I don't know. Listen, Olivia seems like a good kid, so I want to help you. I just can't."

"Did you meet her there?"

"No."

"Sure?"

"Sure."

"If you talk, there may be a deal on the table."

"That's not what I meant. I'd love to talk, love to get that deal. Walk out a free man. But I can't. Because they didn't tell me anything."

"Who is they?"

"Man, I just did that video call. I spoke to this girl on a video call. He fed me lines to say on script and…"

"Who did?"

"Can't say, man. Cos I don't know. These guys, they abduct kids. Okay? They do it for money. Either they reunite them with paying parents for money, or they go to the highest bidder for human trafficking. Either way, they don't care if the kid is loved or used or killed, they just facilitate the delivery."

Carter pieced it all together now, and it stung his gut deep. "So Josh is a scam?"

"Could be Josh, Chad, Travis, or Kim, Beth, Dani. Whatever. The names aren't important. They find disaffected kids. And they're really not hard to find. Facebook, Instagram, Twitter, Schoolbook, you name it. They spill their guts all the time."

"Who is 'they,' Kelvin? Who is doing this?"

"I don't know. Look, they gave me a script for the video calls. Okay? Trained me and fed me lines if she went off script. Did some role play. I was prepared."

This was not what Carter expected. It was much wider and deeper. "Who did this?"

"Look, all I can say is there's this dude who works the scam, except for this one time. For Olivia. And I was told not to talk to him."

"You know why?"

"I heard someone say it's because Olivia is Deacon's daughter."

CHAPTER THIRTY-FIVE

Carter

Deacon was still in the interrogation room. Sweating so much his hair was soaked. He was rocking slightly, his lips moving but his voice silent.

Carter sat down. He needed to break this wide open. He needed to find Olivia. She had run away, sure, but she had been lied to. As good as an abduction. "Deacon, you want to talk to me about the 'Josh' scam?"

"Josh?"

"Could be any teen name. Jayden, Micah, Oliver. Same with girls too. You know about it?"

"I'm not going to talk about it."

"Why not? You going to give me some line about how you're helping kids in difficult situations? That there's nothing wrong with what you are doing?"

"You wouldn't understand."

"Deacon, I know that you take these troubled kids, then you ransom them to disturbed parents. Or you sell them to human traffickers. Some like Kelvin, you'll keep on, though I suspect you'll kill him soon enough."

"They live with terrible parents, then we help them."

"You *help* them? How do the drugs help people?"

"You wouldn't understand."

"You've played it well, Deacon. Getting Kelvin to do your work for you."

"Kelvin?"

"He snared a girl in the scam. Name of Olivia."

"What?"

"Deacon, you got Kelvin to encourage Olivia to run away, didn't you?"

"What?"

"Do you have a hearing problem? Are you struggling to understand what I'm saying?"

"No, it's just… What?"

"You honestly don't know?"

"They've taken Olivia?"

"Who is 'they,' Deacon?"

But he was gone, lost to his inner madness.

Carter needed to get him back, needed him talking.

The door opened and Elisha walked through. She leaned in close to Carter and whispered, "Missing person's report. Mother's name is Wanda Jane Munro."

"Thanks." He gestured for her to sit. "Kelvin's story checks out, Deacon."

Deacon was staring at the desk, shaking his head.

"Kind of ironic that he is pulling the same trick on your own kid."

"This is such bullshit."

"It's not, Deacon." Carter opened the evidence pack in front of him. "Here are the messages Olivia exchanged with Josh. The ones we've recovered, anyway." He passed the sheets over the table. "And these are stills from a video call with Josh. His real name is Kelvin Munro, as you know, and he claims he was only pretending to be Josh on the video, but he won't tell us who was sending the messages."

Deacon was clenching and unclenching his fists.

"Was it you, Deacon?"

"No."

"Sure? She seems to fit the pattern of what's go—"

"It wasn't me!" Deacon was finally seething now. Acting like a parent of a missing child.

Carter was getting somewhere. "Olivia sent him this message." He passed the page across the table.

Deacon took his time reading it, mouthing the words his daughter had typed, but he barely got halfway down the page before he broke down. "All your fault, Deacon. All your goddamn fault!" He pounded the desk. "STUPID ASSHOLE!"

Carter had to grab his wrists to stop him. "Hey, hey, hey."

Deacon shook free, but it looked like something had broken inside him. Whatever it was, he had calmed down.

"Why are you surprised, Deacon? She seems to fit your racket perfectly. Troubled kid in a difficult situation."

"After our divorce, after what I did, I thought leaving Olivia alone was the best thing for her. Letting Marissa bring her up." Deacon picked up the pages and kept reading. "I didn't know about this."

Carter got out the message with the map. "Deacon, she went to this location to meet Josh."

"No, no, no."

"It's where we found him. He was locked in a room filled with a ton of drugs. Probably a hundred tons. I don't think he was guarding it, was he?"

Deacon tugged at his long beard. "Look, when my world fell apart, I was on so many drugs. I had this huge debt. You know all this, but he gave me another chance to work off the debt. Working for him."

"Vic Jordan?"

"He had this tented village in the Jungle. They were running drugs and illegal gambling rings. All at Vic Jordan's orders."

"What about trafficking people?"

"That too."

"Are you telling me that body we've found isn't Vic Jordan?"

"No, it's him. He's dead."

"So what happened?"

"A man stepped up and took over. Called himself The Savior."

Elisha scraped back her chair and dashed off, cellphone to her ear.

Deacon leaned forward, eyes wide, eyebrows high. "Those drugs were Vic Jordan's, but they're all of ours now. We share the profit."

"That sounds like a lie to me, Deacon."

"No! The Savior cleared my debt."

The door clattered open and Elisha stormed in, her face twisted. "He's not in custody."

"Is he still in the Jungle?"

"Sending agents over."

"Thanks." Carter sat back. "Deacon, it looks like Olivia's been groomed by The Savior. Encouraged to run away from home. I need you to help me find her."

"Look, I have no idea why he's taken her. I never thought he'd go after my daughter. I'm clearly out of the loop now."

"Who is The Savior, Deacon?"

"If I tell you, what'll happen to Olivia?"

"Come on, Deacon. This is your own daughter. This is your one chance to save her life. You know his name?"

"I can't!"

"Why?"

"I just…"

"Talk to me about him, Deacon. Why is The Savior doing this?"

"He's guarded about his past. I think he had a shit life and suffered as a kid. He joined Vic's gang a while back, then he took it over."

"Deacon, I need to know anything you can tell me about him. Olivia's life is at stake here."

"Well, I know his name."

CHAPTER THIRTY-SIX

Lori

Smelled like roasting meat, but there was no sign of anyone. Must be oppressive inside that pavilion tent.

King was leaning against a tree. Even though they were out in the wild, this one had been pruned back, meaning someone had cared for it, and many people could have leaned against it. "You want a Waco on your hands?"

Lori looked at the place again and felt that shiver of fear tingling her spine. Yeah, he was right about the prospect of that. But she didn't want to give him any satisfaction. "When me and your boss worked down in Florida, one of the supervisors there had been in on the Waco raid."

"Seriously?"

"Deadly. Way she told us, it was absolute hell. She's retired to her ranch in Wyoming. Last I heard, anyway."

"So, what's the plan then? We need to get inside, don't we?"

"Assuming Steven is real, yeah. Weird how a guy in his forties just disappears like that."

"Not so much, Lori. Think of the trauma he's been through. It explains a lot to me."

"Maybe."

The tent flaps opened and two men walked out, then stood on either side of the door, shooting the shit like they were working the door at a downtown nightclub. Big bulges in their coats and pants pockets, so they were packing heat and a lot of it. Whoever they were, they wanted anyone approaching to know they were armed to the teeth. Looked to Lori like they were professionals, ex-marines maybe. And hard to tell them apart, square jaws and shaven heads.

But Lori didn't have a play here. No SWAT team hovering in the background, ready to strike. And no justification for one. This was deep background stuff, escorting a British cop on her territory to investigate historic crimes, with the outside possibility that they were still operating.

King believed they were, but Lori wondered how much of that was true. Would not be the first time someone had over-reached in an investigation or overstated their case just to get more leeway.

Now that Steven was missing, all they had was his gaming PC in the basement of his dad's beat-up old home. And some messages indicating he was heading here, to this place.

Full of god knows what. Deep in the New Jungle, it was probably drug dealers.

Lori checked the messages again:

> *I think you can help me. We can do this, Steven. We can win. Just come up to the door and ask for me. We can change this around. Here's the address of where we are.*

She had to take it back to first principles. They were here because some kid had been abducted back in the eighties, possibly on the same flight as Max. It sent shivers up her arms, that deep connection with a close friend's history.

No, she needed to help King figure out if there was anything going on here. If this was connected with his recent abductions.

"Okay, let's do this." She left King by his tree and walked over to the guards, armed with a gun in her holster and the flirtiest smile she could muster. "Hey, fellas. Looking for Steven."

The two dudes stood up tall at pretty much the same time. The one on the left was a couple of inches taller than his buddy, but they were both stacked and armed.

The other one had an eagle tattoo climbing his neck. "Who's Steven?"

"Steven Blackhurst. Heard he's here."

"Who told you that?"

"A guy."

"A guy, huh?" Eagle grinned at his bigger buddy. "Hear this, Donnie? A guy."

"A guy. Heard that so many times. This *guy* has a lot to answer for."

Eagle stared at Lori, but his grin was gone. Eyes narrowed, lips pursed. "You cops, huh?"

Lori had no option but to give them the truth. "FBI."

"Feds, huh?" Eagle was grinning again. "What brings the EFF BEE EYE here?" Each letter was almost shouted, like he wanted someone to hear it. Someone inside.

"Just need to speak to Steven Blackhurst."

"Nobody of that name here."

"Sure about that?"

"Sure about that. Nobody of no name here, sweet cheeks. Sure you got the right place?"

"Sure." Lori swung her head around. "Unless there's another underground militia in this neck of the woods?"

"Underground militia." He stared down at the ground, then back up at her, then at King, each time with birdlike movement, his neck snapping into place. "That ain't what we are, you hear me?"

"So what are you?"

"I ain't going to let you in without a warrant and a ton of dudes playing at being ninjas."

Lori examined him. Every inch of him. At least two guns. Big muscles, strong and functional rather than for showing off in a T-shirt. Thick neck, with a bald eagle covering football-player muscles. She and King were outnumbered and outgunned. "Maybe I will come back with that warrant."

"You do that, sugar."

Sugar. Sweet cheeks.

Lori almost smacked a fist into his throat, in the exact spot where she would catch his Adam's apple, then choke him out. But she didn't. She nodded slowly. "See you around." She tipped her imaginary cap at his buddy. "Donnie." Then she walked off, head low.

King jogged to catch up. "What are they hiding in there?"

"More than Steven Blackhurst, that's for sure." Lori kept on the path that led back to her Suburban. But what they were hiding, she couldn't figure out. "Those guys were heavy duty security, right?"

"Way above my pay grade. And yours too." King passed by the tree he had leaned against before back into the wide-open meadow that led back to the Suburban. "I've seen stuff on the news about militias here. Do you really think that's what this is?"

"That's more an Oregon thing. They call it Ore*gun* for a reason. Same rules for Montana too, and bits of this state, but that's way east of here. Anywhere with a low population density that hasn't had the benefit of the tech boom in the last thirty years."

"You almost sound sympathetic."

"I grew up in Oregon. Wouldn't say sympathetic, so much as... I've just seen what they go through."

"Sounds a lot like empathy."

Lori stopped in the middle of the meadow and looked back at the path worn into the long grass. "Doesn't look like any vehicles have come here, just foot tracks."

"That a hunter's instinct?"

"Hate to admit it, but yeah. You grow up in Twin Mountain, Oregon, you're going to hunt a few deer, whether you like it or not."

"Must be strange having that wilderness all around—"

Her cellphone rang.

Max Carter.

She answered it. "Hey, what's up?"

"I need to talk to you about Steven Blackhurst."

The gangbangers were slouching against the wall, thumbs in belt loops, showing off pieces tucked into their jockey shorts.

Lori clutched her cellphone tight. "Max, do you really think Olivia's here?"

"I need you to search for him."

"And you?"

"Trying to get Deacon to open up to me."

"Okay, Max. I'll let you know how this goes." Lori killed the call and put her cell away.

King frowned at her. "Bad news?"

"Always." Lori peered over at the tent again. Two goons on the door meant they were hiding things. And now she knew. "Seems like Steven Blackhurst has renamed himself and become The Savior. And he has Olivia Davis."

"That's who Max Carter is looking for?"

"It is. Is this your present-day abduction ring, Chris?"

He looked flustered. "I, I don't know."

No. He was out of his league.

Lori set her jaw tight. "Let's do this." She walked back over to the entrance and got in the eagle tattoo guy's face. "Where is Olivia?"

"Who?"

"Olivia Davis. Deacon Hill's kid."

"You're dumber than you look."

King stood there, arms folded. "Sure that's how you want to play this?"

Eagle shrugged.

"What's your job here, son? Stand there, make sure nobody comes in?"

"Pretty much."

"Why?"

"Not my place to ask, man."

Lori got in his face again. "Listen to me, I need inside. Now. There are a ton of cops and FBI agents on their way here. I'm sure a guy like you doesn't need that kind of heat."

Eagle looked at Donnie, then nodded away from the place. "Let's split, yo." He shuffled off with that gangster waddle.

And Lori just let him. Those two assholes were not the goal here. She reached over and tugged the flap open wide.

Inside, the place was empty. It smelled of Indian food, with some empty cooking trays. Sleeping bags were all rolled up.

And only one person. A thin woman sat in the middle, meditating. Eyes closed, thumbs touching middle fingertips, breathing so slow Lori thought she was dead. But her eyes opened, and she pushed up to standing like she was made of liquid and someone was pouring her out. "Can I help you guys?" She was smiling, at least.

Lori stayed over by the entrance. "Looking for Steven Blackhurst."

"He's not here."

"But you know him?"

"That's correct."

"Why are you here on your own?"

Her smile widened. "We're moving. It's really exciting."

"Oh?"

"The Savior has a new place for us. Our people are moving there now, but I'm here to make sure nobody steals our things."

"That why you had two armed guards outside?"

"They left?"

"They left." Lori walked over to her. "Listen, we believe that Steven might have taken Olivia Davis. She's Deacon Hill's daughter."

"Oh my." Her hand covered her mouth. "That's... Oh my."

"You know Kelvin?"

"Sure."

"He was speaking to her, backing up Steven's messages. They arranged to meet. She was supposed to meet him at the old war building, but she didn't show. Do you know where else they could go?"

"Sorry."

"Where *could* they take her?"

"I'm sorry, I just don't know."

"Anything? A bus stop, train station, airport. Anywhere."

"Look, there's one other pick-up place I know of. But you may be too late. From what I've heard, they left already."

CHAPTER THIRTY-SEVEN

Carter

The battered old diner sat behind a row of eighteen-wheelers, with other trucks hissing through the rain on the freeway. The diner was a beat-up old place, with blinking neon reading ROSIE'S DINER. Steam wafted out of an outlet near the back, but it was probably burger grease. Place had that kind of look about it.

A black Suburban rolled across the darkening parking lot toward them.

"Here we go." Carter got out of his and walked over to meet Lori. "This is where Bill took you?"

Lori nodded. "Said he had to wait a few hours here before they took him to meet you."

Carter looked around the place, but he couldn't remember being there as a kid. "I can recall being at an airstrip in England, then one over here. But not this place."

"He told us he got driven somewhere to pick you up."

"Okay." Still nothing though. Carter shook his head. "So, she's meeting him here?"

"Or she's already met him."

Carter felt it right in the pit of his stomach. One child echoing his trauma all those years ago, just in reverse. The same place, the same operation. Maybe the people were different, but there would always be those people. They would always traffic human beings across the world. Where there was money, or sex, or power.

"Right, let's see, then." Carter waved to Elisha and Dane to follow, then set off across the cracked asphalt, surprised it was still in as few pieces as it was, given the hulking trailers being hauled around. "Let's see if this gives us anything."

Lori fixed him with a hard stare, the kind he'd only seen when she interrogated a perp. "You know that if anything comes up relating to Bill's case, then you have to back off."

"I know." Carter opened the door with a ringing bell and stepped inside.

A long bar ran up the middle, with a few truckers sitting on stools a few apart, minding their own business. An older guy stood behind, scribbling on a notepad. "Be with you in a few seconds, guys. Take a seat."

"Sir, I need a word."

The guy looked up at them with a slight frown. "Come again?"

Carter walked up to the counter. "You the manager here?"

"Uh, yeah. Dwight."

"You got a surname, Dwight?"

"Mitchell. You got a badge?"

"FBI." Those three letters got a lot of attention from the truckers at the tables. "Special Agent Max Carter. This is Special Agent Lori Alves."

"What business do you have here?"

Carter casually slipped a headshot of Olivia along the white tiles of the counter. "You seen this woman, sir?"

"Looks more like a girl to me."

"Either way, has she been here?"

"Not that I've seen."

"You been on shift long?"

"Couple hours." Dwight pointed at Lori. "This one was just leaving when I came on. Enjoy your meal?"

"Had worse." Lori flashed a smile. "You mind if we take a look around here, Dwight?"

"Sure do mind, but I can't stop you, can I?"

"Sir." Carter nodded at Lori and she went into the ladies' restroom. He took the men's room, leaving Elisha and Dane with Dwight the manager. The bathroom was empty, with that funky smell you got from nobody ever cleaning the place. The soap dispenser had been hauled off the wall and not replaced. Two stalls, both empty. Carter went back into the restaurant and stood there, scanning the faces. Nobody who looked anything like Olivia or Steven Blackhurst.

Lori reappeared from the ladies' room with a curt shake of the head. Olivia was not here.

Carter took a longer look at Dwight. Handlebar mustache, thickened with surrounding stubble. Long hair, long since faded to white. Plaid shirt over a white vest. Probably early sixties. "How long you been working here, Dwight?"

"Thirty-five years."

"You own this place?"

"Bought it off of my old man."

"Huh." Carter felt the anger flash inside him. "So, you would've recognized my dad when he was in here?"

"Max…"

"Who's your dad, son?"

"Name's Bill." Carter tried to bulk himself up, like that old pop video where the singer wore a massive suit. "Big guy, mostly bald, glasses."

Dwight nodded at Lori. "He was with her, right?"

"So I'm told."

"Max, I told you…"

"Lori, it's cool." Carter stepped between two truckers and rested on the counter. He took another long look at Dwight, and it all came back. "This guy is one of the guys who took me from England."

"Son, I don't know what you're talking about."

Carter stood up tall. "This place, the people who ran it, they're to blame for my mom's death. Directly or indirectly."

"You shouldn't have stopped taking your meds." Dwight looked over at Lori. "Ma'am, I need you to get this guy out of here."

But Carter was going nowhere. "See, these people arranged a hit over in London, killed my mom in a car crash."

"Not on me, son. I just run a diner."

"Listen to me, we are here to track down a girl who is under the impression that she's meeting this teenage boy, but in reality, she's meeting someone a lot older. The guy who's running this whole operation. The Savior."

"Son, I don't know what you think's going on here, but it ain't."

"Is The Savior here?" It sounded ridiculous even to Carter.

"Son, have you lost your mind?"

"You know him as Steven Blackhurst."

"Means nothing to me."

"Albert's kid, right? Albert Blackhurst." Lori thumbed behind him. "Lives about six miles up that track. Sells you eggs. That name means the world to you, doesn't it?"

"I need you to leave."

Carter got between them. "See, Albert's son, Steven Blackhurst, he calls himself The Savior now. Like me, he grew up in England until the age of six, when some men brought him over here to his dad. Talk to me about this whole thing."

Dwight sighed and suddenly looked very, very old. "Look, my old man was under the heel of this gang. Bikers. They started with a protection racket, okay? Had him over a barrel. Forced him to run this whole thing from here."

"Human trafficking."

"This is my old man we're talking about. Not me."

"No, Dwight. You were there. In England. You told him you were his uncle."

"Bullshit."

"Uncle John, wasn't it?"

Dwight leaned back against his counter. Burgers sizzled behind him.

"Those same men brought me here. There's a federal investigation into them. An international one."

"Well, son, you better get away from here, because—" The door tinkled open. "Shit."

Carter swung around.

Olivia Davis stood in the doorway, her mouth open wide. She stood there, inches away from Elisha and Dane. "Help me." She was bleeding, a cut running down her arm, her open flesh blending with torn plaid.

Carter raced over and held her tight, his fingers biting into her shoulders. She wasn't getting away. "What happened?"

"He— He—"

The door clattered open this time and a man stood there. Same age as Carter and something in his eyes clawed him back to the distant past. Bulky, but lean. Shaved head. The Savior. His eyes bulged and he spun around.

The door swung shut again.

Carter passed Olivia to Elisha and burst through the door. He chased after The Savior, hopping down the steps and splashing across the sodden asphalt through oily puddles.

But he was fast and he could sure run.

Lori was faster than Carter, outpacing him already, but she was still no match for The Savior's long legs.

A van's lights flashed and The Savior got in the driver door. The engine was still pluming in the air.

Carter rushed toward the van, but the angle gave Lori the advantage. She tore at the passenger door. The van slid back around, and she lost her grip.

Carter aimed his handgun at the driver-side tire and fired, then into the other tire.

The tires deflated, but Steven Blackhurst was out of the van now. He caught sight of Carter rushing over, then grabbed hold of Lori, wrapping an arm around her throat, knife to her head.

Where the hell had that come from?

Carter stopped ten feet away from them, his pistol trained on The Savior's left eye. No time or space for a takedown shot, he had to go in for the kill. "Steven, it's okay."

"Don't call me that!" The buddha-like serenity from earlier was gone, replaced with some sort of mania.

"Just let her go, Steven, it'll—"

"Stop calling me that!"

"Just let her go."

"I can't. I *can't.*" Steven was scanning around, clearly looking for options. And seeing how few he had. The parking lot was swarming with cops, and the main road was thick with traffic. "What the hell…"

"Just let her go."

"No! I can't! This is all… This is all… It's…"

"It's over, Steven. Let her go. She's a federal agent. Please."

Steven took the knife away from her head and let her go.

Lori stepped away.

But Steven still had the knife, hanging from his side, dripping with blood. Olivia's blood.

Carter needed to get it off him, arrest him and stick him in an interrogation suite, get him telling the truth. "You want to give me the knife, Steven?"

He pointed it at Carter. "You can't know what it's like."

"I do. Steven, I was on the plane with you over from England."

"You? You're Max?"

"I am, Steven. Never forget."

"Shit."

"I've been through the same stuff as you."

"We're mirror images though. You're an FBI agent, I'm… I was a nobody. I was trying to help these kids. Nobody else was. But it's all ruined. I tried to take someone I shouldn't have. Olivia. Such a mistake." Steven raised the knife, holding the blade out to Carter.

But instead of passing it, he dropped the knife and ran off into the road. Brakes squealed and a horn droned out.

Carter braced himself for a bloody collision.

CHAPTER THIRTY-EIGHT

Lori

Steven Blackhurst sat in the interrogation room. Lori could see none of his father in his face. His shoulders slouched, full of defeat. "I've been trying to do the right thing. All my life has been a mess."

Lori glanced over at King, who had the wired energy of the hyper-caffeinated, then back at Steven. "Go on?"

"I was driving trucks. Interstate. Over to Chicago, Detroit, down to Arkansas. Every day, all day long. I was away for weeks at a time. Then back home for a week off. Sitting in my dad's basement, playing video games. I paid my dad good money, made sure he could look after our house, but I'd have to go back out on the road. And I was alone with my thoughts. I mean, I had audiobooks and my iPod, and I had satellite radio, but I kept thinking through everything that had happened to me. How my dad had paid them to take me away from my life. Brought me here. I didn't get a choice. So I wanted to undo it all."

"How, Steven?"

"This operation, these assholes who brought me to this country, the ones who got my mom killed, I found them. It was hard, I could only do it in motel rooms or when I was back home. I found a man who had just joined."

"Deacon Hill?"

"He told me what happened to him. How Vic Jordan helped ruin his life. Hooked him on drugs, broke his legs, forced him to work for him, breaking other people's legs. All for money. To pay this debt that was just getting bigger. So I joined up, then I took over the operation."

"You killed Vic?"

"Didn't have to. Deacon knew some people who didn't like the guy. I just had to leak his whereabouts. One night, they came in, took him away. Me and Deac followed, watched him get killed. And then the hard part."

"Becoming The Savior?"

"I took over a group of a hundred people. Men and women. All living in terror of Vic Jordan, whether they admitted it or not. I acted like I killed Vic, but I made them change."

"How? You helped them deal drugs and kidnap kids."

"I wanted to help kids like me. The lost, the lonely, the ones without hope. The ones living in terrible situations, give them the tools to live good lives. Fulfilled lives."

"You abducted them, then extorted their poor parents."

"I…"

"You were doing that with Olivia, weren't you?"

Steven shut his eyes.

"She's Deacon's kid. You can't tell me you didn't know."

Steven looked right at her with The Savior's eyes. Deep, intense. "Deacon used to talk to me. He asked for help, to get over the black hole that was his life. I was helping him come to terms with everything. He told me how his drug-taking had ruined Olivia's life. How Deacon and her mom divorced, about how he had left her with deep trust issues that he couldn't help her resolve."

"What did you do with that?"

"I tried to reassure him how children can be very robust. But he didn't believe me. So I wanted proof. I found her on social media, and… Well, she fit the profile of other children we were helping. Olivia… She posted once about how troubled she was. All the details of her life, how her mother had ruined her life. The truth was that her father had done that, but… Anyway, the message was quickly deleted, but I saw it. And I got in touch."

"As Josh?"

"Correct. The rest… It was painfully easy. She fell into the trap."

"And Kelvin did the video call with her?"

"He did. He was perfect. Had that Justin Bieber thing about him. Girls swooned."

"But the words were yours?"

"They were."

"Usually you got other kids to contact them, didn't you?"

"I did, but I didn't want Deacon to know. So I did it myself."

"You knew that Deacon's family's rich, didn't you? Knew that his dad's desperate too. Plenty of cash to extort. Olivia was just another commodity to exploit."

Lori sat back and folded her arms. "Why did you attack her with a knife?"

"I didn't."

"You did. Of course you did. Your prints are on the knife. Only yours. And so is her blood."

But The Savior was gone again, leaving poor Steven Blackhurst in the room with them.

King looked over at Lori, eyebrows raised. He tilted his head toward the door.

"Back in a second."

Steven nodded at her, like he was giving his approval.

Lori held the door for King, then followed him out. "This getting you what you need?"

"Not so sure." King's chin was dotted with stubble. "I came over here expecting to tear apart a child-abduction operation. People trafficking, the whole thing."

"But Steven Blackhurst got there first?"

King folded his arms and leaned back against the door. "Indeed. I mean, he just took over, didn't he? Didn't stop anything, but he took out the people who can help with my case."

"Not all of them. Dwight's still in custody."

CHAPTER THIRTY-NINE

Carter

Carter opened his office door with his hip and carried the two cups into the room. His with coffee, hers with tea sweetened with sugar. Just how Bill took it, always with that joke about how people say he is sweet enough. He set the cups down on the desk and took his chair. "Your mom's on her way in."

Olivia was wrapped in a foil blanket but was still shivering, her teeth chattering. "*Great*."

"How you doing, Olivia?"

"How do you *think* I'm doing?"

Carter sat back and blew on his coffee, but it was too hot to hold for much longer. "What has happened to you today, it's going to be hard to process. Okay?"

"I can't believe it. Why would he do it? Any of it?"

Carter thought back to watching Lori and King interview Steven Blackhurst. "That man had been through a tough ordeal. He's had a very difficult life. But he was doing some very bad things."

"He attacked me." She looked down at her knife wound, covered in gauze and tape. It had looked bad back at the diner, but it was only a flesh wound. It'd heal in weeks. "Why was he there? What happened to Josh?"

"Olivia, Josh doesn't exist."

"But I spoke to him on Zoom."

"No, you spoke to a kid called Kelvin. Kelvin was the kid you spoke to, sure, but his words and those messages, Olivia, they were Steven's. Steven, the man you met, he worked this system where they rescued children like yourself from difficult situations. They'd extort parents or sell to traffickers."

"God. What was he going to do with me?"

"Extort your mom, I think. Your grandfather has money, so…"

She picked up the tea and sipped at it. "I take it you read our messages?"

"We only got hold of some of them."

"I'm such a sap."

"Olivia, you've been through a lot for a kid your age. I'm sure it wasn't easy. And this is a confidence trick, Olivia. They prey on kids like you, kids who have suffered traumas. Your parents' divorce was your trauma. You're not alone, very far from it, so don't feel bad."

Snot was bubbling in her nose. She looked like she was the age of Carter's daughter, not a teenager. Still a child, fighting against all those hormonal changes. "I miss my dad."

"We found him."

"What?"

"He's alive."

"Oh my god." But she was frowning, some emotional ice chilling her. "Why did he leave?"

"That's something your mom should tell you."

"Please."

Carter looked at the door. No sign of Elisha with Marissa. "It's a long story, but your dad made a lot of mistakes. They cost you and your mother your home. Your college fund. Savings. Your father isn't a well man."

"Was it drugs?"

Carter nodded.

"My god." Olivia covered her mouth and nose with her hands. "And Mom knew?"

"She did."

"Oh my god. She kept it from me."

"She thought she was protecting you."

"I know. All that time, I'd been blaming her, but... Man." And Carter could see it sinking in, the realization that all the teenage angst aimed at her mother had been misdirected. Her father had been responsible for so much, and maybe she would start to appreciate the sacrifices her mother made for her.

Olivia looked up at him. "What did she think had happened to me?"

"You did really well, making it look like an abduction. We were all fooled. The message in the mirror was the clincher."

"That was Josh's work." Olivia wiped tears away. "God, I can't... I can't... Who did she say took me?"

"I had a very long list to work from. Your father made a lot of enemies, Olivia."

"Is my grampa okay?"

"He's fine. Fit as a fiddle."

"Can I see Frankie?"

"You'll need to check with your mom."

"Why?"

Carter knew he had overstepped the mark. He hated being the one to break other people's news. So he took a drink of coffee. Still melting hot, but it excused him from speaking for a few seconds.

"What's wrong with her?"

"That's something you need to—"

"Tell me now."

"Olivia, it's not my place."

"Is she sick?"

Carter had backed himself into a corner. "She is. Blood cancer."

Olivia's face twisted up tight. "God." She jerked into a flood of tears.

Carter reached into his desk drawer for another Kleenex and held it out for her.

Olivia snatched the tissue out of his hands. "Is that what the blood test was about?"

"It was."

"God."

The door opened and Elisha stuck her head around the side.

Carter beckoned her in.

Marissa burst past, pushing Elisha out of the way. "Liv!" She raced over and wrapped her daughter up in a tight hug.

"MOM!" Olivia was pushing away.

But Marissa wouldn't let her go. "I never... My god. I thought someone had taken you, Liv."

"I'm here, Mom."

"Why did you run?"

Olivia couldn't look at her mother. "I'm sorry."

"It's all my fault, Liv. I should've told you the truth. But I didn't and... It left you vulnerable, left both of us vulnerable." Marissa locked eyes with Carter.

He knew she meant Olivia was vulnerable to the psychological manipulations of Steven Blackhurst, but it could equally apply to the predations of Gregg Ingram. At least both men were out of their lives now, for good.

She hugged her daughter tight. "I forgive you, Liv. Will you forgive me?"

"I will, Mom. I'm so, so sorry." Olivia met her in the hug. "Is there anything I can do to help Frankie?"

CHAPTER FORTY

Lori

King was leaning against the wall in the field office, arms folded, head bowed. Looked very much like he was sleeping standing up. He jerked awake. "Lori?" Then he blinked hard a few times. "Almost dozed off there."

"Looked like you were on a Business Class flight to the land of nod." Lori handed King his coffee. "Sure you need another coffee?"

"I need my bed." King blinked again. A few more lines around his eyes. And another yawn, one that stretched his neck out wide. "God." He slurped the coffee. "This is good stuff."

"And it's decaf."

"Sneaky."

"Just looking out for you, Chris. You'll be awake at five tomorrow either way; just want to make sure you've actually had some sleep before."

"Wise." King grimaced. "Spoke to my travel agent and it's going to cost me too much to change my flight, even with how much my Airbnb costs, so I'll be here a while longer."

"Well, it's a good part of the world to spend some time in. Happy to show you around town."

"I'd like that." King took a deep breath. "So, shall we get this finished?"

"Let's." Lori opened the door for King to go first, then followed him in.

Bill Carter stood in the corner, hands in pockets, a fierce look on his face. "Listen, I need to get out of here. I'm supposed to be looking after my granddaughter."

"I understand, sir." Lori waved a hand at the chair opposite. "Please, have a seat."

"Rather stand. Why am I here?"

King rested his coffee on the table, but the smoky smell was already filling the room. "Bill, your help has gone a long way towards finding the men responsible for... Well, what happened back in the dim and distant past."

"Thank you, son." But Bill didn't seem to be feeling any relief. No, he knew.

That message King had just given was a phone call at best, a curt thank you from Carter to his dad. Not a trip in from two FBI agents.

King smiled. "The trouble is, Bill, you are up to your armpits in this. You didn't just arrange for these men to do this. We've spoken to one Dwight Mitchell."

"What? Who the hell is he?"

"Bill, he worked for the men who took your son. He was in England himself, for a while. He abducted Steven Blackhurst. And he's sitting in the room over the corridor just now, spilling his guts."

"I ain't done nothing."

"No, Bill. His story tallies with evidence I've obtained back in London. You called a known hitman several times. I'm afraid that you're going to be extradited for the murder of your ex-wife."

"What?"

"I've got you booked on a flight next week. I advise you to get your affairs in order..."

EPILOGUE

Carter

Carter drove across the Fremont Bridge, the taillights blurring in his vision. Another case down, another kid reunited with their parents. Strange to have a happy ending for once, to not have something drag on for so long.

He wouldn't believe it until it was all over though.

Steven Blackhurst was right. He was a mirror image of Carter. They had both been on that plane, two boys taken from parents to selfish assholes in the New World. Against their will.

Something caught in his throat, and he tried to cough it clear. Nothing seemed to shift it.

Bill.

It always came back to that. Why Carter did this. And that was all before he had learned that Bill had paid some London hitman to murder his mother.

He had been through all the options. Prosecute him. Kick him out. Forgive him. Settled on sticking with it, showing him the love he had never received from him.

But what Lori was working on with DI King. What would that do to him? Would he deserve it?

That lump was back in his throat as he drove through his neighborhood, that homing instinct guiding him back automatically. He drove into his space outside their house, pulled the parking brake, and let the engine die.

Could he ever forgive Bill?

For killing his mother?

Bill had done what he thought was right, back then, to raise his son thousands of miles away. And Carter had done well out of it too. He wasn't too emotionally damaged by his upbringing, unlike Steven.

He had served his new country in two careers, had a loving wife and a child they were both determined not to screw up, no matter how hard that was proving to be.

But the knowledge that Bill had paid someone to kill his mother—it stung the pit of his stomach.

Carter took out his cell and called Lori.

But she bounced his call.

Huh.

He pocketed his phone and stepped out of his car—a heavy step rather than a sprightly hop—then walked up the short path to their front door. The place seemed quiet, just as it should be at this time of night. All the Halloween decorations were out. Meaning Bill had a use after all. He had done a good job too. Saved Carter a world of hassle over the weekend.

It hit Carter in the gut again. That realization of what his father had done. The twisted logic that had driven him to think that was okay. The gnawing fear that he had gotten away with it.

Carter walked inside. He rested his briefcase on the floor and kicked his shoes off. Everything ached. His head, his shoulders, his neck. But most of all his brain, from all the thinking. The usual bedlam was replaced with eerie silence.

He took off his jacket, hanging it over his beaten leather coat. First, he'd check on Kirsty, watch her sleeping for a few seconds, tuck her in again, then go get something to eat from the fridge.

The light burst on, almost blinding him. "Max?" Emma was standing in the doorway, wearing her coat and holding Kirsty's hand. "What are you doing here?"

"Coming home to see you. What's Kirsty doing up at—"

"Max, Bill had a heart attack."

*

Carter ran through the hospital corridor, his feet heavy on the floor as he swerved a corner and dodged a man in a wheelchair. Into the ER and he spotted Lori immediately, standing with DI King. He raced over to her. "Where is he?"

"Max, I'm so sorry."

"Lori, where is he?"

She nodded off to the side. "In there, but the doctor is with him right now."

King patted Carter's arm. "I'll check if you can see him."

"Thanks." Carter looked over at the room, a small alcove really, but filled with a doctor and three nurses checking on Bill Carter. He focused on Lori. "What happened?"

"It's a long story, Max. We found a chain of evidence. That guy at the diner, he's talking and... King... He's taking Bill back to England. He's going to stand trial for what he did to your mother."

Carter shut his eyes.

"Max, I'm sorry. I didn't know King had this other stuff."

"Okay. How did he...?"

"When King told him, he just... Stood there, uncertain, then angry, then he collapsed. King was golden. He knew all about heart attacks. He carried Bill down to my car, and we drove him here. He saved his life. I called you, but your cell was off. Emma picked up and..."

Carter looked over at the room, wondering if that was the best outcome. A recovery might take months, but Bill would still be extradited in the end, and face trial. Was that any better? He just didn't know.

King walked over, eyes narrowed. "Max, you can see your father, if you want."

"Thanks." Carter felt no malice for the man who had caused the heart attack. Who was he kidding? Bill had been the cause; King had just been the inciting incident. Just doing his job. He stared deep into his eyes. "Is it true?"

"It's all true. Your father paid them to kill your mother. Not whatever he's told you."

"Okay." Carter took a deep breath, tasting of cleaning chemicals and stale coffee. "Back soon." He walked over to the room and knocked on the door.

The doctor took one look at him, then smiled. "I'll give you a few minutes."

"Thanks." Carter took his seat and unclipped his tie. He could barely breathe. "How are you feeling?"

Bill lay on the bed, all tubed up. His heart rate pounded on a machine, strong, steady, and slow enough. "I feel horrible. Like I died."

"Good."

"What?"

"Bill, I know that you paid someone to kill my mother."

Bill sighed. "Son, how could you—"

"Don't. This is the least you deserve."

Bill sat there, huffing and groaning. "I paid the guy, but he was just supposed to send your mother a message."

Carter barked out a laugh. "A message."

"Son, she was suing me, and she was going to clear me out. Both of us. It was a full-on scorched-earth attack. Your mother was a nihilist when it came down to it."

"And you only ever wanted what was best for me, huh?"

"Max... I only paid that geezer to frighten her."

"And what happened, Bill? The guy killed her."

"Accidentally. I received her life-insurance payment, put it into a trust fund for you, which you haven't touched."

"You wonder why?"

Bill had nothing for that.

"Dad, he covered it up, made it seem like an accident. Stop lying to me, okay? Tell me the truth."

"Son, I've been worried about this for years, all the guilt. That's why I tried to kill myself last year. The sheer guilt, it eats away at you. When I drank, I didn't think about it. Pretty quickly, it's all I was doing."

Carter had heard that before. Not just his dad, but other people in other cases. Deacon Hill sought it in heroin, that same thrill numbing the agony for a few brief minutes. All these broken men were peas in a pod.

But it gave them no reason to do what they did.

"Son, I wish I could suffer enough for it. But that's just not possible. What I did was unforgivable. But that King geezer, he thinks that prosecuting me can change the past."

"But it's not going to, is it? I hate you for what you did. I let you stay in our home, let you get close to Kirsty, put you on my insurance to pay for your treatment."

"Son, I'm selling my house. That and your trust fund will pay for Kirsty's college."

"Don't."

"I mean it. Son, let me help her at least. She doesn't deserve this."

"You've got nerve."

"Son, please"

"Bill. You have no right to ask anything of me. You're lucky that I've let you even see Kirsty, let alone live with us for this long."

"Please."

Carter had tried to be the good guy, and he had put his faith in Bill. But Bill had dropped the ball. He had lied, covered up what he had done. And he had taken no ownership for his failings.

All Carter had left was the bitter taste of disappointment. "I'll never forgive you for what you did. And I'll never forget."

Bill stared at him, hard, for a few seconds. Then the beeping raced, getting faster and faster. "Son!" Bill's face racked up in pain, and Carter was pushed aside. Doctors and nurses elbowed him back, calling orders Carter hadn't heard since his days as an army medic.

But he could see Bill wasn't going to pull through. All the self-torment at what he had done, this big mistake he had made, it was all over.

Carter stood there, watching the medical staff work away, but the light behind Bill's eyes had gone out.

The paddles on his chest were just electrocuting a corpse.

Bill Carter had left the building.

Carter would have to pick up the pieces of a broken life.

He had time to grieve finally, to grieve his lost mother and now his father, who always should've been dead to him.

And he could walk into the future, unburdened by the bad decisions—his, his father's—of the past.

Max Carter was finally free.

A LETTER FROM ED

First, thanks for reading *Before She Wakes*. If you enjoyed it, and want to keep up to date with all my latest releases, just sign up at the following link. Your email address will never be shared and you can unsubscribe at any time.

www.bookouture.com/ed-james

Aside from the terrifying subject matter, this novel was the most enjoyable for me to write. I've written almost countless British police procedurals from a single point of view, and I needed to try something new, to develop new muscles and to experience a new location. I hope you enjoyed meeting Max Carter and his team as much as I did. They'll be back soon enough.

While the military operations in *Before She Wakes* were fictional, they were based on real events in the USA. Operation Jade Helm 15 in the southwestern states carried as many conspiracy theories as column inches in the news, and something in the Pacific Northwest seemed like the perfect place to hide a clandestine operation on American soil. I also don't want to diminish in any way the sacrifices of the heroes and heroines who protect their country, with Max and Tyler among their number before they became federal agents.

The FBI CARD unit sadly have to exist, but they provide a great service in the most trying of times. I wanted to thank the FBI for reading and commenting on the novel for procedural accuracy.

And I hope you loved it. If you did, I'd be grateful if you'd be able to write a review. I read every one—good, bad and ugly—and I love hearing what you think. It can also help new readers discovering my books.

Finally, I'd love to hear from you. However you want: Twitter, Instagram, Goodreads or an email through my website. And if you want to subscribe to the mailing list for my British police procedural series (Cullen, Hunter, Fenchurch, Dodds): http://bit.ly/EJMail

Thanks,
Ed James
Summer 2019
Scottish Borders

🐦 @EdJamesAuthor

📷 @edJamesauthor

Ⓖ 6552489.Ed_James

🖥 www.edjamesauthor.com